Dear Reader,

Money has never been very important to me. I can do without fame, and I can do without high-level career success. What I can't do without—what I *won't* do without—is family.

Unfortunately, I haven't been lucky enough to find that special woman…just yet. But that hasn't stopped me from being "Daddy" to my boys.

At my foster ranch I "parent" kids who, unlike me, weren't lucky enough to come from loving homes. But I'm stepping in as "Dad" and teaching them that there *are* people you can count on in this life. All you have to do is open your heart, take the hand offered and then turn around and help someone else. Because the surest way to make yourself happy is to make someone else happy…. And the surest way to get more out of life is to give more of yourself….

Unfortunately, local judge Diana Tomlinson doesn't see it my way. But I'm working on her….

Mike Harrigan

Ranch Rogues

1. Betrayed by Love
   Diana Palmer
2. Blue Sage
   Anne Stuart
3. Chase the Clouds
   Lindsay McKenna
4. Mustang Man
   Lee Magner
5. Painted Sunsets
   Rebecca Flanders
6. Carved in Stone
   Kathleen Eagle

Hitched in Haste

7. A Marriage of Convenience
   Doreen Owens Malek
8. Where Angels Fear
   Ginna Gray
9. Mountain Man
   Joyce Thies
10. The Hawk and the Honey
    Dixie Browning
11. Wild Horse Canyon
    Elizabeth August
12. Someone Waiting
    Joan Hohl

Ranchin' Dads

13. Ramblin' Man
    Barbara Kaye
14. His and Hers
    Pamela Bauer
15. The Best Things in Life
    Rita Clay Estrada
16. All That Matters
    Judith Duncan
17. One Man's Folly
    Cathy Gillen Thacker
18. Sagebrush and Sunshine
    Margot Dalton

Denim & Diamonds

19. Moonbeams Aplenty
    Mary Lynn Baxter
20. In a Class by Himself
    JoAnn Ross
21. The Fairy Tale Girl
    Ann Major
22. Snow Bird
    Lass Small
23. Soul of the West
    Suzanne Ellison
24. Heart of Ice
    Diana Palmer

Kids & Kin

25. Fools Rush In
    Ginna Gray
26. Wellspring
    Curtiss Ann Matlock
27. Hunter's Prey
    Annette Broadrick
28. Laughter in the Rain
    Shirley Larson
29. A Distant Promise
    Debbie Bedford
30. Family Affair
    Cathy Gillen Thacker

Reunited Hearts

31. Yesterday's Lies
    Lisa Jackson
32. Tracings on a Window
    Georgia Bockoven
33. Wild Lady
    Ann Major
34. Cody Daniels' Return
    Marilyn Pappano
35. All Things Considered
    Debbie Macomber
36. Return to Yesterday
    Annette Broadrick

Reckless Renegades

37. Ambushed
    Patricia Rosemoor
38. West of the Sun
    Lynn Erickson
39. A Wild Wind
    Evelyn A. Crowe
40. The Deadly Breed
    Caroline Burnes
41. Desperado
    Helen Conrad
42. Heart of the Eagle
    Lindsay McKenna

Once A Cowboy...

43. Rancho Diablo
    Anne Stuart
44. Big Sky Country
    Jackie Merritt
45. A Family to Cherish
    Cathy Gillen Thacker
46. Texas Wildcat
    Lindsay McKenna
47. Not Part of the Bargain
    Susan Fox
48. Destiny's Child
    Ann Major

Please address questions and book requests to: Harlequin Reader Service
U.S.: 3010 Walden Ave., P.O. Box 1325, Buffalo, NY 14269
Canadian: P.O. Box 609, Fort Erie, Ont. L2A 5X3

RANCHIN' DADS

WESTERN *Lovers*

CATHY GILLEN THACKER
ONE MAN'S FOLLY

Harlequin Books

TORONTO • NEW YORK • LONDON
AMSTERDAM • PARIS • SYDNEY • HAMBURG
STOCKHOLM • ATHENS • TOKYO • MILAN
MADRID • WARSAW • BUDAPEST • AUCKLAND

For David,
the family philosopher/comedian
who sees every angle
and is a genius at figuring out
what the people/players will do next.

HARLEQUIN BOOKS
225 Duncan Mill Road, Don Mills,
Ontario, Canada M3B 3K9

ISBN 0-373-88517-2

ONE MAN'S FOLLY

Preface

Having grown up in a large midwestern family, I've come to notice how birth order influences your character, life choices and profession. It's always been a personal fascination of mine, and it's also winning new converts interested in family dynamics. In fact, the study of birth order is becoming an important new field, helping to provide keys that'll unlock our understanding of ourselves and ultimately improve our relationships.

One Man's Folly deals with birth order and how it has affected the adult children of the Harrigan clan—a prominent Texas family—all in their thirties, who've reached crucial stages in their lives. It starts with middle child Mike Harrigan: social worker, dreamer, a man on the brink of personal transformation, and his burgeoning relationship with a woman—the local judge—who seems intent on stifling his dreams.

What is a middle child? Well, the consensus seems to be that they're great negotiators, excellent managers, people who enter the "helping professions"—teaching, social work, medicine and law. Caught in the middle, they grow up feeling "squeezed out" because their parents focused on the firstborn and the lastborn. They resolve the dilemma—this sense of neglect—by reaching outward to others, cultivating extensive social networks.

To distinguish himself or herself from the firstborn, the true "star" of the family, the middle child will deliberately cultivate contrasting, even rebellious, qualities, and may as a result be a riddle to others. But a beneficial side effect of getting caught in the middle is that the middle child learns how to mediate different viewpoints and will go to great lengths to avoid conflict wherever possible—lengths that even Mike Harrigan would find extraordinary....

Chapter One

"Diana, you have to help us. We can't let that Harrigan fella turn Libertyville into a haven for criminals!" Myrtle Sims said, her plump face suffused with color.

It was Monday morning and the town had been in an uproar for three days. Billy Reaves had heard from a realtor in Marble Falls of newcomer Mike Harrigan's plans to establish a foster home. Word had spread through the small central-Texas town like wildfire, upsetting everyone, including Diana. Harrigan hadn't breathed a word of his intentions when he'd bought the property through his Houston attorney and an outside real-estate agent weeks before. People had just assumed, as he'd apparently figured they would, that he'd bought the place for investment purposes, since he came from a wealthy well-known Texas family and probably had money to burn. No one had ever dreamed he planned to start a foster home for teenage boys! Boys who might be so old, they were beyond help, Diana thought nervously.

Even worse, this was bringing back all sorts of unwanted memories from her youth. Diana's father had been the same type of crusading do-gooder, content to live in near-poverty while he pursued his hopelessly quixotic ideals. A social worker, he had worked tirelessly for the poor people in the rural community surrounding theirs, to the exclusion of his wife and two young children. He had worked himself to death—and for the greater good of whom?—dying of a heart attack when he was thirty-four. She had been eleven, her brother seven.

There'd been no insurance, no savings in the wake of his death; nothing but bills and despair. Diana had been left to raise her younger brother while her mother, who had no other marketable job skills, worked as a housekeeper to support them. Later, when her brother had been old enough to stay home alone, Diana had also worked, using her small salary to buy essential items like groceries, clothing, shoes—most of which came from garage sales or Goodwill.

Diana had never forgotten those early years of deprivation and pain, and it angered her to think that someone was bringing that to Libertyville. Charity was all well and good, but there were limits.

Despite her personal aversion to Harrigan's plans, Diana knew she had a job to perform. She held both hands in front of her in calming fashion. It was hotter than blazes in her tiny office, and she felt she would suffocate in her black silk judge's robe. "Look, I know you're upset—" she told the crowd soothingly. At age thirty-two, she felt more than able to cope with whatever came her way in the courtroom, including the lynch mob in front of her.

"You're absolutely right we're upset," Agnes McCarthy said, coming to the front of the crowded chambers. As editor and owner of the local paper, *Libertyville Press*, she took her position in the community very seriously. "And we have every reason to be! Why with those young hoodlums around, none of us will be safe!"

Privately Diana shared their concerns. After all, what guarantee did they have that the kids Harrigan brought in would be even remotely governable or well-behaved?

They might disdain the upper middle-class values embraced by the town. Or they might try to test them openly and create all kinds of chaos and trouble, and ultimately heartbreak—not just for Mike Harrigan, but for all who came in contact with them.

Yet as the chief peacekeeper of the town, Diana also knew that professionally she couldn't jump to such conclusions. Not without at least giving Harrigan and crew a chance.

"Now hold on a minute." Diana held up a hand, admonishing everyone to be silent. She trained her serious golden brown gaze on the crowd around her, willing them to silence. Slowly the uproar died down enough for her to speak. "These kids haven't even arrived yet," she said. "Maybe...maybe we're all overreacting."

"I notice you included yourself in that tally, Diana. Does that mean you're scared, too?" Hardware-store owner Hal Sims moved out of the throng of local business people to stand beside his wife.

"Are you forgetting what happened to my sister?" Billy Reaves spoke up, anguish in his voice.

"No, of course not," Diana replied quietly. Jenny's death would weigh on all of them for years to come. She'd been run down by a drunken teenager who'd been driving through Libertyville after a party in a neighboring town. He wasn't a local resident and hadn't obeyed the Libertyville speed limits. Jenny, returning home from baby-sitting, was in the wrong place at the wrong time. It took a while, but the town finally captured the youth, after scrapes on his car and statewide news broadcasts alerting citizens to the crime, identified him. That'd been only two years ago, and the wounds were still fresh.

"All we need is more thrill-seeking hoodlums who don't care about the local laws," Iris Lansky shouted. She shook her head disapprovingly, hating the picture created.

"I agree with Billy. I don't like the idea at all," Kay Reaves, the court stenographer and Diana's secretary said emotionally, moving to stand next to her husband. As she spoke, her lower lip quivered.

"All right, all right. I admit..." Diana's voice wavered anxiously before she could steady it again. "I admit that the idea of having boys that age around who haven't had the right kind of adult guidance in the past does make me uneasy." It brought back images of her youth, of the rough undisciplined boys she'd encountered in her own neighborhood on the wrong side of the tracks, but she was determined to do her job, no matter what it cost her personally. "But I'm also the justice of the peace in this community. I've sworn to uphold the law, and under the law, we have to give those kids a chance."

Agnes McCarthy drew herself up to her full height—an imposing six feet. Placing her hands on her hips, she stomped up to Diana until they stood nose to nose, with Agnes towering over Diana by a good six inches. "You can't seriously mean you're equating the rights of those...those thugs with the rights of your friends and neighbors."

"Agnes," Diana said tiredly, backing up until she could sit on the edge of her desk. She knew this was one battle the fifty-year-old spinster would never give up without a ruckus, and the townspeople would back the emotional woman completely.

Their backing would be fine if Agnes was always civic-minded and fair; unfortunately she was all too humanly flawed. And her flaw was that, when riled, she displayed a mean streak so strong that, if not acted upon, could make her carry her grudge to the grave.

Wearily Diana ran a hand through her cloud of golden brown hair, pushing the errant chin-length strands away from her face. "Those boys would never have been sent to Harrigan's ranch if they belonged in a juvenile detention center. We may not like it—'' she sure as hell didn't ''—but as sure as I'm standing here, we have no right to prevent those boys from coming to the foster ranch Harrigan has set up.''

She could only hope against prior experience and common sense that the boys would give her no cause to reverse her decision.

Silence fell in her chambers. All eyes were on Diana's flushed, delicate countenance. It was clear the citizens were unhappy with her. If an election were held today, she thought grimly, she'd be soundly defeated, out of a job— and scraping for pennies.

''Meaning you won't help us get rid of Harrigan and his crew?'' Myrtle Sims asked in a disgruntled voice. She wrung her hands together and cast a worried look at her husband.

Again, Diana had to take a deep calming breath. ''Not if he and his boys behave themselves,'' Diana replied evenly, already thinking, on the other hand...

''And if they don't?'' Hal Sims asked.

''Then that's another matter entirely,'' Diana said with equanimity, her expression serious, determined. She wanted the citizens to know she would put up with no nonsense. She'd give the boys a chance—but it was going to be a very limited one. ''If they pull one prank or steal as much as one hubcap, I'll have them doing appropriate penance faster than they can say spit. And that's something you can all count on!''

''WELL, HERE WE ARE, guys. Your new home. The Harrigan ranch.'' Mike made his voice cheerful as he pulled the Suburban into the gravel lane leading to the Harrigan ranch house. Although he was greeted with silence from the three teenagers lounging in the back seat, Mike didn't let their expected lack of excitement dampen his own enthusiasm.

Starting this ranch for homeless boys was his life dream; counseling and guiding disadvantaged youths was the work he knew he had been born for. He had figured the start-up of the flagship program would be rocky—the boys' continuing wariness bore his hunch out. But with lots of time, love and patience, their collective mistrust of him—a person they didn't know yet—would evaporate.

It wouldn't take long he reasoned, for them to learn firsthand that his commitment to social causes was both genuine and lasting. And once that happened, Mike felt everything else would fall into place.

Mike parked the truck next to the house and shut off the engine. One by one, they climbed down from the dusty truck. Mike hopped out and circled around to the back, where he unlocked the rear doors and pulled out the three duffel bags, handing one to each boy.

Carlos was already traipsing on ahead. At fourteen, he was the youngest of the three. "Not bad," he remarked, sizing up the large rambling ranch house, made of white stucco and a red-tile roof. Several red barns and white-fenced corrals were within easy walking distance of the house. The rolling front lawn was peppered with cedar and oak trees. The land to the rear and sides, had been left wild, with meadows and trees and brush. "Not bad at all." He cast Mike a sly sidelong glance, looking suddenly a lot more worldly than his physical years would dictate. Mentally Mike reviewed what he knew about the boy. Orphaned at an early age when his parents were killed in a car accident, Carlos had six brothers and sisters, but no relatives able to take them all in. Subsequently the children had been split up. A survivor and a middle child, Carlos had quickly learned to adapt to whatever environment he was in. He was also a very high-spirited kid. He loved high jinks and pranks of all kinds, and in school had the reputation of class clown. Spending a lot of time socializing, he'd devoted very little to studying, and as a result had been held back twice. Mike felt, from looking over the records, that Carlos could do better, given motivation and guidance. And Mike planned to provide them in spades.

"Don't suppose you got any girls out here, do you?" Carlos asked.

Mike was all too aware that the primary reason Carlos had been moved from his last foster home was because he'd encouraged some of the local teenage girls to sneak out at night. "Not any your age," Mike said dryly.

"Any neighbors, then? Maybe an all-girl school nearby?" Carlos asked hopefully.

Mike shook his head slowly. "You're out of luck, bud."

"Well, I'm sure we'll find some close by somewhere," Carlos said, undaunted. "There's gotta be something to do!"

The caseworkers hadn't been kidding when they said he had a teenage lothario on his hands, Mike thought, smiling.

Ignoring Carlos, Kevin strode slowly toward the front of the ranch house. At sixteen, Kevin was the oldest of the three, and right now he looked anything but happy.

Mike was all too aware that of the three kids Kevin had suffered the most. An only child of upscale, career-oriented parents, he'd lost his mother to cancer three years ago. Up to that point, there'd been no history of abuse, and despite the turmoil in his life Kevin had maintained an A average. But he hadn't cultivated any close friendships since then, as far as the caseworker could tell. Simultaneously, over a nine-month period, there'd been three suspicious household "accidents" that had landed him in the emergency room. That, coupled with his father's arrest and conviction on embezzlement charges from his brokerage firm, had landed Kevin in the state's foster-care system. In the year and a half since his father's imprisonment, Kevin had retreated into a shell his foster family had been unable to penetrate. Feeling his stony presence was detrimental to the well-being of other children in their family, they had finally given up. Mike wasn't sure he could get through Kevin's shell, either, but he would put as much muscle into the effort as possible. It wasn't right for anyone to be so alone.

"Do we have to share rooms?" Kevin asked tightly as they headed inside.

"No, you'll each have your own private quarters," Mike reassured him, feeling that it was very important for each boy to have his own personal space. "You share a bath, though." Kevin frowned, but said nothing in response.

Ernie brought up the rear.

He was the last to enter the house, the last to choose a room. Looking at the raw fear on the lanky fifteen-year-old's face, Mike felt his heart go out to him. The oldest of two kids who'd been abandoned, Ernie was dyslexic and at fifteen still couldn't read past the second-grade level. His baby sister had been adopted several years earlier, when she was still a toddler, but Ernie's problems in school coupled with his age had prohibited a similar happy placement. Mike didn't know how much improvement to expect; the reports he'd read weren't encouraging, but what he could work on was Ernie's obvious lack of self-esteem. Fortunately Ernie wasn't much of a discipline problem—his former foster parents had stressed how much the teen had wanted to please those around him. Mike did worry that Ernie wouldn't be able to stand on his own if a conflict erupted between the boys. However, he knew Ernie wasn't the type to go looking for a fight, and that in itself was encouraging. As for the other boys, Mike would just have to see. In the meantime there were chores to do, and the sooner they all got started the better.

"ENOUGH'S ENOUGH," Kevin swore heatedly several days later as he stalked into the stables; taking one whiff of the strong smell made him whirl and stride right back out. "You think I'm shoveling up horse manure again, you got another think coming."

Mike turned, surprised at the display of emotion from his quietest boy. He'd known at the outset that Kevin, with his sophisticated background, would have the hardest time coping with ranch work. And yet it had to be done for a variety of reasons. The aging saddle horses Mike boarded for a small, privately owned rodeo generated income that helped finance the operating expenses of the ranch. The boys also needed to be kept busy, and their daily chores were a good way for them to learn responsibility, earn an allowance, and pick up a part-time job skill that might later help them earn their way through college or vocational school.

Calmly he handed out shovels to the other two boys. "If you don't want to do your chores today, Kevin, it's okay. Just be aware there's a penalty for avoiding work. Come Saturday, when everyone else has earned enough points to entitle them to a liberty day to be spent in town, you'll have to stay here at the house with the other two counselors." Mike was referring to Melanie and Jim, a young married couple from Houston, who not only were trained in handling kids, but were happy to take on the cooking.

"I hate the scut work, too, but I'm going on liberty, man," Ernie said. Dark skinned, tall and lanky, his black hair combed neatly into place, he walked into the first empty stall and began shoveling. "No offense, Mike, your ranch is nice and all, but I can't stand much more of this ranchin' business.''

''Me, neither,'' Carlos muttered. Taking the bandanna from around his neck, he fashioned it bandit style over his nose and mouth. His ebony hair sticking up at strange points around his head—he'd shagged and spiked it himself with a pair of scissors shortly after arriving at the ranch—Carlos got straight to work, making jokes as he did so.

Only Kevin stood motionless at the barn entrance, scowling angrily as he watched, his arms rigid and held away from his sides, his hands balled into fists. ''Some trade-off.''

Mike continued to watch Kevin. He'd half expected him to blow up at some point during their adjustment period. The poor kid had been holding so much inside for so long that an eruption was inevitable. Mike was prepared for the situation when it came. In fact, he'd almost prefer a blowup to watching Kevin remain locked in his shell, miserable and unreachable.

''I know what you mean.'' Sensing trouble, Carlos commiserated, giving his housemate a compassionate glance. ''Shovelin' this smelly crud just to go to some two-bit town where there ain't nothing to do hardly seems worth it. Did you see what was on the theater marquee? Some stupid movie that's already been out for two years. Of course—'' he winked slyly at the other two ''—the three of us could get lucky. There might be some girls around there, too.''

Mike stifled an inward groan.

''So what if the movie's old?'' Ernie said, ever cooperative. ''We'll see it again.''

Carlos laughed and did an imitation of John Wayne that soon had them all laughing—except Kevin. Smiling at the glee his antics had evoked, Carlos continued,

"Anything's got to be better than those old Westerns and war movies Mike is always watching."

"Yeah, you know, you need to get one of them satellite dishes," Ernie said conversationally, pausing to wipe a grimy streak of sweat from his forehead. "Then we could watch all kinds of stuff."

"And have you three sitting in front of the TV vegging out all day?" Mike said, disappointed to see Kevin still wasn't joining in despite the efforts of the other kids to include him—efforts that had been going on all week. The boy was a loner, through and through. He had to be reached somehow. "No way," Mike said to the others' continued plea for a dish. "This world already has enough couch potatoes."

"That why you don't have cable?" Ernie asked, curious.

"A town like this doesn't get cable," Kevin said under his breath. He opened the buttons on a faded, well worn polo shirt. Like all his clothes, it was expensive designer-labeled apparel, obviously several years old.

"You're right." Mike stopped shoveling and regarded Kevin curiously. He was a tough one all right. He was about to suggest Kevin go on back and help Melanie and Jim fix dinner, when Kevin came to life and picked up a shovel.

He glared at Mike and began to work, his motions violent and aggressive. "I hate everything about this place."

Ignoring the boy's behavior, Mike silently congratulated himself. He'd gotten a reaction from Kevin, and an emotional one at that. It was far from the major breakthrough Mike had been hoping for, but at least it was something.

"FREE AT LAST," Ernie grumbled as Mike gave them each four dollars and turned them loose on the streets of

Libertyville. "You've got three hours—plenty of time to get a soda or an ice cream and take in a movie."

"We're all thrilled, aren't we guys?" Kevin muttered, just loud enough for Mike to hear. Ernie and Carlos guffawed.

"We'll meet here in front of the courthouse," Mike continued, making eye contact with each of the three. They'd already been over the rules of the game at home. He was certain, despite their bad talk, he could trust them to behave. Call it instinct. He knew that beneath the occasionally gruff and casually disreputable-looking exteriors they were good kids, caring and decent human beings.

Satisfied, Mike watched as the boys ambled off in the direction of the movie theater. Turning and walking into the supermarket to join Melanie and Jim, who'd taken the opportunity to come in for groceries, he sighed his relief to have a short reprieve from his parental duties. In retrospect, he realized that taking in the boys was proving to be every bit as stressful and emotionally draining as he'd feared. Perhaps even more demanding than his colleagues and family had predicted. And yet it was a challenge he relished and felt good about. True, it hadn't been the easiest week of his life, but in some ways it had been the most gratifying. There was still much to do, but he felt they'd made a fine start. The boys were doing their chores, and although none of them wanted to be in a group home, they were achingly aware there was nowhere else to go.

Up the street, Kevin watched until Mike disappeared from sight. Turning to his pals, he said, "I don't want to see that dumb movie. I've already seen it, anyway. How about you guys?"

Carlos shrugged. "Nah, I don't like Westerns much, either."

Kevin grinned. "So what do you say we go check out this town?"

Ernie slapped palms with Kevin and Carlos. "Guys, I am with you!"

DIANA WAS AT HOME cutting the grass when the sheriff's car pulled up at the curb.

"Trouble?" All too aware of her sloppy pink T-shirt and grubby khaki shorts, Diana wiped the sweat from her eyes. Apprehension ran through her. It seemed as if she had been expecting this visit for days.

The deputy sheriff got out, hitched up his pants with both hands. "Yeah, there's trouble," he confirmed grimly, his eyes bleak, "like you wouldn't believe. Those three foster kids have been picked up on a misdemeanor. They're holding them at the jail. I know you don't usually come in on Saturday, but..."

So the showdown was about to begin, Diana thought. Maybe it wouldn't be as hard to get rid of the crusading, impractical Harrigan and his crew of ill-adjusted foster kids as she'd thought.

"Sound like an emergency," Diana said, already cutting off her mower. Now that the crisis was upon them, she felt stronger, more in control than she had in years. "Just let me go in and get my keys and lock up, and I'll be right there."

It took less than two minutes for them to drive to the ancient limestone building that served as a courthouse, city hall, and a police and fire station all in one. Once there, Diana leaped out of the squad car and dashed up the back steps. She'd barely gotten into her chambers and reached for her black robe when the outer door swung open with a bang. She turned toward the sound, furious at the intrusion. A tall, angry-looking man strode toward her, his glance sliding dismissively down her slender body before returning to her face. At his boldly assessing look, she felt her face color. She knew the betraying flush accurately telegraphed her low opinion of him and she regarded him in icy hauteur.

"Justice of the Peace Diana Tomlinson, I presume?" he spat.

Her eyes on his scornful, penetrating gaze, Diana lifted her chin and finished drawing on her robe. Deliberately she made her voice as gritty and unpleasant as his. "Yes."

"I want those kids back and now!" He took a threatening step closer, and the frown lines on either side of his mouth deepened. "The sheriff had no right to arrest them!"

That wasn't what the deputy had told her en route to the courthouse. She tilted her head back and met his arrogant stare inch for inch. "Don't tell me," she said dryly, her words ringing in the charged air between them. "You must be Mr. Mike Harrigan. The quixotic do-gooder in person."

"Dr. Mike Harrigan," he corrected through gritted teeth, a muscle working angrily in his jaw. "I'm the psychologist out at the Harrigan Ranch."

Before Diana could respond Agnes McCarthy barreled into her office, her sun hat perched jauntily on her gray curls. "Diana! There you are! I thought you'd never get here!" She paused to catch her breath and glare at Mike before turning back to Diana triumphantly. "Well, they've done it. They've given you the excuse you need to ride them out of town on a rail!"

Not taking his eyes from hers, Mike looked explosive, his face slowly turning a very angry red.

"Agnes—" Diana began, but the sudden pandemonium outside stopped her.

"And I'm telling you we didn't do nothing wrong!" a boy could be heard shouting in the hallways. Then with a great deal of commotion three boys and a deputy stumbled into Diana's chambers.

Everyone talked at once. The noise was deafening.

Diana's peacekeeping talent went into overdrive. She stood on a chair, put two fingers between her teeth and let out a shrill whistle. The commotion stopped. An eerie atmosphere of expectation took hold of the room.

Diana stepped down off the chair, furious at the discord Mike and his boys had instigated, and pointed toward the door of her chambers. "Everyone into the courtroom! Now! And, bailiff, the first person who speaks out of turn is going to be cited for contempt of court." She paused, giving her words time to sink in. "Got it?"

The bailiff nodded. So did the rest of the people in the room. "Now go," Diana said, and watched as everyone silently filed out of her chambers and entered the courtroom.

When everyone was finally settled Diana took the bench and began to address the group. "All right, we're going to start with the deputy," she said sternly, her warning glance signaling the crowd to behave. She glanced back at the deputy. "You tell me what happened."

"I had a call from Miss McCarthy. She said three delinquents were making mincemeat out of her lawn and for me to get right over there. When I got there, those three kids—" he turned and pointed accusingly to the three seated next to Mike Harrigan "—were standing on her lawn. She was yelling at them to get off the grass and leave the vicinity, but they wouldn't budge." When he finished, his words were heavy with indictment.

"Did you ask them to get off?"

"Yes, ma'am, I did."

"And?"

"They said they didn't like being treated like garbage, and refused to move until Miss McCarthy apologized to them."

Which Agnes certainly hadn't been about to do, Diana noted. Not that she could blame Agnes for feeling outrage at the boys' trespassing on her front yard. Diana had flower beds, too. To keep them well maintained was a tremendous amount of work. And Agnes's flowers, like Diana's, were her pride and joy.

Struggling to be fair and not jump to any false conclusions, Diana looked at the deputy. "Was her yard damaged?"

To Diana's surprise, the deputy suddenly looked sheepish. "Well, no, 'cept the grass was a little trampled, and so was part of her flower beds. But they wouldn't get off her property, and you know as well as I that's trespassing."

"We weren't anywhere near her flower beds!" Carlos shouted, incensed.

Diana turned her glance to Mike, who also looked about to revolt. "Mr. Harrigan, keep your charge quiet!"

Mike glared back at her wordlessly, letting her know that he was the type of man who gave back every bit as good as he got. He was no simpering wimp who would allow others to push him around.

Diana felt a stab of uneasiness and, despite herself, admiration for his unabashed show of strength and masculinity and the ease with which he was able to comfort the teen.

When things had quieted down enough for her to proceed, she continued, "Boys, what do you have to say for yourselves?" She looked at the tall youth, who throughout the proceedings had looked as if he were about to burst into tears.

His lower lip trembling, he introduced himself as Ernie and said, "What Carlos said about the flower beds is true. We weren't anywhere near them. But we did walk through her yard. We were cutting through some yards, instead of walking down the rest of the block. See, we were out just walking around, having a good time, and then before we knew it, it was late and we were supposed to meet Mike. And we figured he'd be mad or worried or somethin' if we didn't show up. So we were running, and then Carlos tripped and I fell on top of him. We were horsing around a little, but we didn't mean no harm. And she didn't have to yell at us like she did.'' He pointed an accusing finger at Agnes McCarthy. His lower lip trembled again. ''She scared us to death, screaming and carrying on like that. And we woulda left, too, only she told us not to go nowheres 'cause she was going to have us arrested anyways, that the sheriff was already on his way.''

''Agnes, is this true?'' Diana asked, troubled that an injustice might have been done by her calling the sheriff prematurely, yet understanding full well why Agnes reacted as she did. Often, just knowing a kid came from a bad environment was enough to make a woman who lived alone fearful. ''Did you call the sheriff before you asked them to get off your property?''

At Diana's careful probing, Agnes's face turned various colors. ''Of course I called the sheriff first! You don't think I was going out to face those three hoodlums alone without any backup, do you? Besides, the damage was already done. I'm not a bleeding-heart liberal, Diana.'' Agnes glowered at Mike, intimating that he was. ''I wasn't about to let them get off scot-free. I told them to stop wrestling on my grass and get onto the sidewalk— which they refused to do.'' She shot another accusing glance at the boys. ''And if they didn't damage my flower beds, I'd like to know who did.''

Good question, Diana thought wryly. Certainly the town hadn't had any trouble with property damage before Mike Harrigan and his crew had shown up in Libertyville.

The Mexican American youth raised his hand, as if he was in a classroom. "May I say something, judge?"

Willing to hear the boy out, Diana nodded to him. Carlos was bolder than Ernie, but no less frightened. "Ernie's telling the truth. We didn't go anywhere near her flower beds. And we didn't mean her grass no harm, either. We don't want to cause no trouble."

He looked so sincere, so upset by all the unrest, that Diana wanted to believe he was telling the truth, and yet— "Oh, come off it, you guys! Stop accepting all the blame!" Without warning, the tall preppy-looking youth who'd been silent throughout stood up and pointed at Agnes McCarthy. "The truth of the matter is she's a mean old witch who's out to get us just like everybody else in this town." He turned to Diana. "Do you think we don't notice everybody looking at us like we were dirt? Do you think it doesn't hurt us to be treated like that?"

Diana swallowed at the raw pain she heard vibrating in his voice. Agnes merely raised her brows at the blond-haired youth's outburst, as if to say I told you they were no good. See, they don't have any manners. They speak rudely, and out of turn—

"Kevin, sit down!" Mike Harrigan said and pointed to the bench. He gave Kevin a stern glance. "I know tempers are flaring, but you're out of line, son. Now apologize to both the judge and Miss McCarthy."

Kevin's jaw jutted out truculently. He clamped his arms defiantly over his chest and stared back at Mike. "I'm not going to lie and say I'm sorry when I'm not. Everything I said was true. She does have it out for us, and so does everyone else in this one-horse town, and you know it!"

The truth in Kevin's words rang out, but Mike knew that the chip on the boy's shoulder stemmed from problems that went back much farther. Mike worried about times like this, when Kevin viewed everyone as an enemy. He wondered if he'd ever be able to reach Kevin, achieve the emotional breakthrough Kevin so desperately needed. Would there be more trouble with local citizens in the meantime? Would Kevin get worse instead of better? And what would happen to him if, God forbid, Mike couldn't give Kevin the help he needed?

With effort, Mike pushed the disparaging thoughts away. Pessimism wouldn't help solve the problems each boy presented. Right now, Mike needed to get them out of this mess. The worrying could come later.

Mike turned to Diana politely. "If I may have a moment alone with my charges . . . ?"

Diana nodded. She'd heard enough to know everyone had overreacted—mostly out of fear—and she didn't want this scene to set a precedent. She still hadn't figured out what had happened to Agnes's flower beds, but since there were no eyewitnesses to the crime, they would probably never know for sure. She suspected, however, that the boys had had something to do with the vandalism, and perhaps they were too ashamed or afraid to admit it.

"Afterward, I'll see you in my chambers," she said to Mike. "Bailiff, keep an eye on the boys. Agnes, Hal, Myrtle, everyone else here can go home." For now, Diana thought, the show was over.

Haughtily Agnes stood. She walked out, her head and posture regal. Diana headed for her chambers.

"I'm sorry about Kevin," Mike said when he joined her minutes later. "Agnes's attitude toward him pushed all the wrong buttons. He's normally a lot cooler."

"This wasn't a good beginning for you in this town." She looked up into his midnight-blue eyes, resentful because he hadn't kept a better handle on things.

He frowned, thinking. "The boys were right about one thing, though. It seems the townspeople have been expecting the worst." Diana opened her mouth to protest, but he cut her off suddenly. "I saw for myself just now how ready they are to organize against us." His bluntly stated observation seemed an indictment of the town. She bristled, for she was among those he disdained. How dared he be so quick to judge? Maybe the people here—including herself—had reason to be concerned about a foster home in their community. After all, when she was growing up, she'd seen firsthand what happened to people who didn't look out for themselves, or their families. They ended up turning into victims, a status she'd vowed never to fall to again.

She sent Mike a deliberately self-possessed glance. There was a silence as he evaluated her, and then without warning, his mood changed. He suddenly became more amenable.

"Their behavior will be extremely commendable—eventually," Mike Harrigan was saying as he moved closer. His voice dropped another persuasive notch and a warm glint appeared in his eyes. "But right now the kids are still settling in and—"

She didn't want to hear platitudes and empty promises; she'd heard enough of them in her time, and from men like this Mike Harrigan. "Not good enough, Dr. Harrigan."

At her reprimanding tone, his brows lowered like twin thunderclouds over his eyes. The seconds drew out uncomfortably, and he let her feel the full impact of his anger. "Is that a threat?" he questioned caustically.

"I prefer to think of it as a fact," she retorted, just as bitingly. "If you want to stay here, you had better be sure this sort of thing doesn't happen again."

He was silent, fuming. He turned his back and walked over to the window, to stare out on the square below.

Since it seemed a time-out was not only in order, but very much needed if the two of them were to avoid a fracas, Diana gave him a chance to compose himself. Whether she wanted to admit it or not, she realized he was a handsome man in a rough-hewn way. Tall with an athletic build, he had remarkable dark blue eyes and dark slashing expressive brows. He was strong and fit, all healthy virile male, but he was capable of gentleness, too, as she'd seen when he'd comforted his boys earlier.

But as he turned back to her, there was no gentleness in his eyes, only worry and anger, and contempt as he tried to decide how to proceed.

"Look," he began reluctantly, tersely, after a moment, running a hand through his dark brown hair. He sighed heavily, his unhappiness with both Diana and the general situation obvious in the stubborn set of his jaw. "I realize this hasn't been a good start." He frowned again, looking as if he were mentally counting to ten. "But there's a lot you don't know about us. Maybe...maybe if the two of us could just talk, one to one. I don't know. Have dinner together or something...." His voice trailed off, and he gave her a hopeful look, one full of charm, one that said he would be more than willing to meet her halfway.

Diana stared at him, unable to believe his gall. Oh, she knew there was nothing remotely romantic or personal in his request for an off-site tête-à-tête, but still! Did he really think he could weasel his way out of this predicament that easily? Did he think she could be won over with a few persuasive words, regardless of the behavior of his charges? He must think her a naive fool. Either that, or he assumed she was a soft touch simply because she was a female justice of the peace. "I can't be bought off, Mr. Harrigan," she reprimanded icily. "Nor can anyone else in this town." As far as she was concerned, the matter was closed, the invitation to dinner rejected. "So you can forget the charm, and your connections will get you nowhere, either."

His frown deepened. "What are you talking about?"

Diana sighed. She hadn't wanted to get into the subject, but now she had no choice. "I'm talking about permits from the state. Generally, for this sort of program, they're submitted from the local level up. Your request came from the top down. That means you must have some powerful friends."

Besides, it was no secret he had a wealthy, privileged background—another reason she found his stab at do-gooding so intolerable. When he tired of playing Father Flanagan to those boys on his ranch, no doubt he would leave and expect the rest of them to pick up the pieces.

His jaw hardened mutinously at what she'd revealed. She noted he didn't deny his "connections" or the fact he'd made flagrant use of them.

He sent her a challenging smile. Both his eyes and his tone were frosty. "So what if I do have connections?"

Her eyes glittered right back at him, an indication she refused to give any ground to him. "Then you do, but they won't help you here."

He watched her sagely. For a moment she thought he would bite his tongue and let the meeting end then and there, but eventually his temper got the better of him, and he retorted with silky contempt, "How well I know that. You see I overheard some talk as I came to the courthouse today. The word on the street is you'd be tough on juvenile offenders—ridiculously tough—because the citizenry expects it."

He was right, Diana thought without remorse. She did feel the need to side with the townspeople. Did feel the need to take up their cause—preserve the peace. She lived here, too. Was that selfish? Or was she just fulfilling her role as preserver of the peace? Shaking off her introspection, she stared at him. "Dr. Harrigan, you would be advised to keep your opinions to yourself."

He nodded curtly, his demeanor as icy and formidable as hers.

"As for your charges," Diana continued tightly, "you are responsible for them. Any more trouble and I'll see that you all land in jail, yourself included. Am I making myself clear?"

He returned her steady gaze. "Quite clear."

She nodded stiffly, feeling the beginnings of a tension headache. "Fine, then you may go pick them up. I'll let them off with a warning this time—" an act she knew she'd pay for later when Agnes heard about it "—and I suggest they make some sort of apology to Miss McCarthy. Written would probably be better."

"Done," he said. Without warning, Mike stared at her with exaggerated reasonableness.

As the moment drew out, she felt uncomfortable, as if she'd just stepped into a mine field. She longed for a brush to restore her tousled golden brown hair, longed to feel more in control of the situation and of him. The woman in her sensed this was only the beginning, that before it was over she and Mike Harrigan would really have it out. "Anything else?" she asked, noting the sardonic expression on his face.

He nodded slowly and approached her until he was leaning across her desk, his palms flat on either side of her. "Just one more thing," he said softly, in a silk-over-sand voice. "I don't know how you got on the bench—maybe your good looks got you elected—or how you've managed to stay on it when you're so obviously prejudiced against the less fortunate, but let me tell you this. Not everybody who comes into this world has a peachy-keen background. Not everybody has parents who love and nurture them and keep them out of trouble. Some kids—like the three in my charge—have had it worse than you could imagine. And yet they've survived. They still keep right on fighting. And you know what? I find that admirable, a hell of a lot more admirable than the selfish whining I'm hearing from you and everybody else in this one-horse town! Grow up, would you? Try to find it in your heart to have some compassion for someone other than the town biddy."

So he thought she'd had it easy.

Diana stood abruptly, banging into her desk. She leaned forward over the desk, so that they stood chin to chin, only inches apart. Because she had no intention of sharing any details of her personal life with him, she let his erroneous assumption pass. "You are the one who doesn't know what he's dealing with, Dr. Harrigan! As it happens, this town is a wonderful place to live in. It's full of ordinary people, raising healthy, loving families. The people here are kind and generous to a fault, but I don't want them taken advantage of." As Diana had been in the past. "I don't want something to happen we would all regret."

Not until this moment had she realized how strong her desire to protect the town was.

He stared at her incredulously, shock draining the color from his face. "What could my boys possibly do to any of you?"

"They've already done it, by disrupting the peaceful climate of this town!"

His expression became even more contemptuous, and his eyes narrowed and became supremely critical. "You mean stagnant," he corrected curtly. "Self-involved."

His portrayal stung. She went pale. "That's no description of our town!"

He thought it was, and the reality of it didn't please him any more than it did her. His glance was so searing, so probing, she had to turn away.

She wasn't selfish! She was practical. Whereas he...he was naive, hopelessly so!

"Don't like hearing the truth, huh?" he baited, leaning so close she could smell the tantalizing scent of his woodsy after-shave.

"Mr. Harrigan, you are trying my patience."

At his proximity, Diana's face flamed with more than the afternoon sun. She drew back, refusing to let him know how much his nearness affected her. Her expression closed, and she folded her arms at her waist.

"All right." He straightened slowly, his jaw hardening subtly as he moved. "Maybe you're right, but remember—you're not the only person with a stake in this."

Giving her no chance to reply, he turned and stalked out, slamming the door behind him. Diana stared after him, her chest heaving with indignation beneath the hot black robe. *Well, Mr. Harrigan,* she thought, *let's hope your stake in this keeps you out of trouble and out of my courtroom.*

Chapter Two

When she did see him again, it was none too soon.

"I figured you'd be here," Mike Harrigan said early Monday morning as Diana started down the sidewalk, briefcase in hand, her lunch in the other. "I wanted to apologize for the other night."

Diana glanced at him, taking in the abject apology confirmed on his face. "I accept." Still, remembering the way he had stormed out of her office, she decided the previous evening that Mike Harrigan didn't belong in Libertyville, nor did those three kids. The town's interests would remain foremost in her mind.

Noticing her reticence, he continued, "You look like the type who walks to work," he said, as charmingly as possible.

"Not a very hard task, since I live only five blocks from the courthouse," Diana said crisply, keeping her eyes trained away from his unsettling gaze. Nonetheless, she could see his profile in her peripheral vision. He'd had a haircut since she'd last seen him, Diana noticed reluctantly, wondering if that was supposed to impress her. Regardless of the fact that she would've much preferred not to notice anything about him at all, she had; and she had to admit he looked good this morning—too good for her comfort. He also clearly wanted something from her. That would become apparent soon enough, she supposed.

"Still, many people would elect to drive." He went on falling into step beside her.

"Not me." She liked to stay fit. She also liked the peace and quiet of Libertyville at seven-thirty in the morning. It gave her time to think and collect her thoughts as she walked to work—usually alone. Now, unfortunately, all she could think of was Mike. She would've liked to find fault with him, his attire. Something. Anything. She couldn't. He was dressed unpretentiously in jeans and a neatly pressed navy-burgundy-and-white plaid shirt that brought out the dark blue of his eyes. His grooming was impeccable, his attitude friendly and approachable. Maybe even a bit penitent.

He wanted to make peace with her, she thought.

But was that what she wanted? There was bound to be more trouble in the future. She felt she could handle her role as judge better if her guard was up. Whereas he obviously figured he could handle the situation better if they were on more affable terms.

"Is that why you're wearing the tennis shoes with the suit?" Mike asked, bringing her attention back to her attire. His glance dropped down the sophisticated lines of her pale rose linen suit and tailored white blouse, then down her stocking-clad legs to the neat white shoes and pristine cotton sport socks.

He looked quite at ease, she thought a bit exasperatedly. And insouciantly, arrogantly attractive.

She knew her legs were good, but it was disconcerting to have him obviously think so, too. Ignoring the darkening of his irises, she tossed him an indifferent look and said, "I have heels in my office, but they're not very comfortable for walking."

Surprisingly he let her crisp tone pass. "I stand corrected," he said kindly. His determined good manners made her feel guilty, as if she were being unnecessarily rude to him. She pushed the remorse away, recalling he had provoked her plenty the last time they'd met. However, she also knew she wasn't going to get rid of him until he'd had his say. Making no effort to hide her impatience, Diana shifted the weight of her briefcase to her other hand. "What brings you out on this fine morning, Mr. Harrigan?" she asked wearily. And then unable to help herself she added, almost as an afterthought, a tad too anxiously for her own comfort, "And where are your charges?" She feared to think about what they might be up to.

He gave her a steady survey. "The boys are back at the ranch with Melanie and Jim, the two counselors I employ." He paused, letting his reassuring words sink in. "The reason I'm here is I need to talk to you—about Saturday. I realize I owe you an apology. In retrospect I see I never should have let the boys go off on their own, not until the townspeople had gotten used to their presence."

"Then why did you?" Diana asked irritably, skidding to a temporary halt in mid-stride. She hated irresponsibility of any kind. Life was too short and often too hard for people to go around making excuses that did little to correct the damage already done.

At her harsh tone, his face clouded with anger. "Because I trusted them, and because they had earned a little time off."

Diana found his lack of judgment intolerable. The truth was that by Saturday he'd probably already tired of playing nursemaid to those boys and had jumped at the chance to free himself from the role of chaperone for a few hours, and for that they had all paid. "Time to harass the townspeople by stomping on their lawns?"

His eyes narrowed, but only for a moment. "Oh, come off it! You saw Agnes McCarthy!" he said angrily. "She enjoyed causing that big scene. Besides which, I had the distinct impression that you, Justice Tomlinson, were just waiting for the boys to do something so you could throw them out of town!"

Diana felt her face heat up. "I don't deny I expected something like this to happen," she commented archly, when he seemed to be daring her to try to deny it. "Self-discipline and respect for others are not easy concepts for foster children to grasp."

They stood as they were for a moment, assessing each other angrily. She sensed the fight in him and knew there was contention in herself as well. Never before had she met a man who rather than step aside at the first sign of conflict, preferred to stay for the duration, countering blow for blow until some mutually satisfactory arrangement had been worked out. She respected his courage, even as she railed against the headaches the coming weeks were bound to give her.

The silence continued. For a moment, she had the feeling he wanted to argue back, really read her the riot act. But abruptly, realizing nothing would be gained, he changed his approach.

"That's why I'm here, Diana," he said soothingly. He shoved his hands into the pockets of his snug-fitting jeans. "I want you and the other people in this town to learn more about kids with problems."

She had to stifle the impulse to laugh as they started walking again. The man really was a lunatic if he thought his kids would ever be accepted on those terms.

"We'll learn all right," she murmured dryly, more to herself than to him. She decided to appeal to whatever common sense he possessed. "Wasn't the fiasco on Saturday enough? What are you trying to do? Give us all a crash course on foster care?" *How it shouldn't be done!*

He shrugged nonchalantly. "In a manner of speaking." He reached into his pocket and handed her a folded piece of paper. "I've designed a program that could be implemented in the community—with your help, of course."

Stunned, Diana stopped walking and set her briefcase down on the sidewalk. Mike took the brown paper bag containing her lunch. She read the boldly lettered script: "Neighbors Helping Neighbors—a volunteer program designed to pair adults with teens. First project: house-painting for the elderly. Needed: donations of supplies, and your time! Contact Mike Harrigan, Harrigan Ranch..."

"You see the idea is to get people here in town working with Kevin and Ernie and Carlos on a one-to-one basis. But it wouldn't only be for my boys, it would be for all the kids here. And the good thing about it is you don't have to be sixteen to work. The kids could get work experience, and positive recommendations, which would look good on resumes when they apply for paying jobs later."

He was thinking about other kids in the community, not just his own. Despite her determination not to let him charm her, she was impressed. Still, there were considerations—plenty of them. "Whoa!" She put up a hand to stave off further details. "You're really serious about this, aren't you?" Realistically she thought it ludicrous for him to even hope the idea might ever really work, especially after what had happened on Saturday.

"Of course I'm serious." He studied her bluntly, looking aggrieved. "Why? Don't you think it will work?"

Diana rubbed the back of her neck, to no avail; it was as tense as a stretched-out rubber band. "In a word, no," she said tersely, then sighed.

He looked put off by her lack of enthusiasm. "Why not?

Wearily she dropped her hand. Damn, but the man was persistent. "Because no one will ever go for it, that's why."

He smiled at her. "You're telling me the people in Libertyville are that hard-hearted?" Hands hooked loosely around his waist, he stood before her invincibly, his expression one of disbelief.

Diana's spine stiffened. She knew an insult, even when it was cloaked in velvet tones. "No, of course not."

He shrugged his broad shoulders carelessly, appearing almost indifferent to whatever concerns she might harbor. "Then what's the problem?"

The problem was, Diana thought, that the town was small and needed to be proved wrong. But she held her tongue.

He glanced impatiently across the street at the Country Kitchen, a family-style restaurant renowned for its sumptuous luncheon buffet. "Listen, we can't continue this out on the street. Breakfast—on me."

Before she could stop him, he had her arm and was hustling her across the street. Diana felt herself flushing as she tried unsuccessfully to rescue her arm from his determined grasp. "This isn't necessary...." She didn't need a man barging into her life, deciding what was best for her.

When they reached the entrance to the restaurant, he stopped and turned to her. His face went still and he regarded her silently for a moment. Then he said, "Sure it is—if you're really as interested in preserving the peace in this town as you say you are."

She stared at him, the sizzling retort on the tip of her tongue vanishing as she realized she agreed with the motivation behind his mission, if not with the way he wanted to carry it out. Wasn't peace in Libertyville her ultimate goal?

He opened the door with a flourish and ushered her inside. There were five people in the spacious one-room restaurant. Diana knew all of them, including the owner, Iris Lansky, another ambitious yuppie who, like herself, had fled the stress and impersonality of the city.

"Hi, Diana," Iris said. She gave Mike a visual once-over, not necessarily liking what she saw, then immediately lowered her glance.

"Hi, Iris," Diana said casually, resigning herself to the situation.

Iris smiled at Diana. "Have a seat. I'll be with you in a minute." She looked at Mike, her eyes convicting him without trial. "The menus are on the table."

Mike ignored Iris's behavior and scanned the menu. When she returned he ordered apple oatmeal for Diana, bacon and eggs for himself.

All the while Diana couldn't block out the stares they were receiving. By nine, Diana figured it would be all over town she'd had breakfast with that lunatic Mike Harrigan. Great, just what the local justice of the peace needed, she chided herself silently. She could hardly wait for the next election. Nonetheless, since they were here, she might as well brazen it out. There'd only be more talk if she didn't.

Mike waited until Iris left before continuing in a less-combative tone. "Look, just think about helping me out, would you? I wouldn't ask if it weren't important. These kids deserve a chance at a normal life, and I'm trying to give it to them."

His compassionate tone struck a chord in her. Diana sighed. When put that way, his actions sounded noble. But Diana refused to let herself be swayed by fairy tales. The world wasn't perfect, much as she might wish it to be, and neither were his kids. Not by a long shot. She remembered how often her father had pinned his hopes on the education of people who were bound to frustrate his tireless rehabilitative efforts. "It's been my experience that the older the foster child, the less chance there is for he or she to make adjustment." A troubling thought indeed.

"I know the odds are against me," he said roughly, "but I'm no less determined."

Diana leaned back in her seat, regarding him steadily. Perhaps neither of them wanted to admit it, but they were both too stubborn to back down. "I don't want trouble here in Libertyville while you experiment." Diana was adamant about that. The citizens didn't deserve the turmoil and pain. She was sorry Mike's boys had had it tough in the past, but that didn't mean others had to suffer for it now.

Mike's gaze narrowed angrily. He leaned toward her fervently, his voice dropping to an emotional whisper that betrayed more than anything just how much he had at stake in this—personally and professionally. She realized then just how much he cared about his kids. This wasn't a walk-in-the-park type project for him, but his whole life.

"You talk as if this was a game," he said, "and it's not. These are their lives we're talking about, Justice." The only chance they would ever have, his rough tone implied. "And as for trouble, I'll keep it to a minimum."

Diana raised her brows and regarded him warily. Although he'd leaned back again, she found herself incredibly aware of his presence, could still smell the woodsy scent of his cologne. Her feelings irked her. She worked with men all the time. None of them had ever had this effect on her. "Not promising perfection, I see," she commented, pretending insouciance.

"Saturday taught me something," he said quietly, his gaze serious and penitent. "All I'm asking is for a second chance with you and Agnes and everyone else."

His words were vaguely familiar. Diana shifted uncomfortably in her seat, remembering how her father had always asked for quarter after neglecting her for weeks. He would do better, he used to promise, be home at night before she went to sleep, be there to read her a bedtime story or take her to the park. Only he'd rarely if ever kept his promises. There'd always been some street kid in need of his attention. He'd always let her down.

Her marriage had been much the same story. Her husband had never been there when she needed him, and finally she'd had enough. After her divorce, she resolved to stay away from driven men—and she had, in her personal life. But perhaps her professional life was another story.

"No, scratch that," Mike continued, frowning in aggravation. "I'm asking for a first chance. The boys were right when they said so far we haven't been given much of one."

Diana hesitated, wavering indecisively.

Mike Harrigan was like her ex-husband in terms of ambition, of needing to achieve his every goal over obstacles that would defeat most people. But there the resemblance ended, because like herself, her ex had been concerned with building financial security, for living an easier life.

When Diana married him, she thought that would be enough to build a life together. She hadn't counted on their never seeing one another because of the demands of their jobs. She hadn't known that all the wrong buttons would be pushed, about her youth, her father's neglect. Now, she knew it took more than shared goals or similar ideals to make a marriage.

"Diana?" Mike's voice brought her out of her fog. "Are you going to give us a chance?"

His impassioned plea, so reasonably asked, struck a chord in Diana. Realistically, the J.P. in her said his plan would never work; what Mike was offering those boys was probably too loose a unit for a troubled kid with low self-esteem. But she also knew that society had a responsibility to place the boys somewhere. Libertyville, with its quiet streets and solid citizenry, would probably be deemed ideal by a social worker. And as much as she wanted to, she couldn't ignore the hurt looks she'd seen fixed on those boys' faces the other day in her courtroom. She knew they needed love and understanding, and that Mike would do all he could to give it. Try as she might, she wasn't immune to someone who wanted to provide a warm and loving home.

But another side of her was skeptical, feeling too little was being offered too late. It would all come to a bad end no matter how much they tried to make it work. However, Harrigan and crew were here. And thus far, she had no valid legal reason for evicting the kids from Libertyville. A compromise would have to be reached if they were to live together in the same community.

"All right, you've convinced me that we at least need to give this a shot," she said finally, not bothering to hide her reluctance. "But it'll be up to you to keep those boys in line. You understand me? Trouble again, especially on something like this, and the town residents won't give them another chance. Nor will I blame them if they don't." In fact, Diana would be the first to urge them to go.

His shoulders relaxed, and relief tinged his smile. He leaned back as Iris, still watching them both carefully, put his breakfast down in front of him. "Thanks, Diana. You won't regret this."

She hoped not, she thought, as Iris set down her bowl of oatmeal, regarding Diana skeptically.

"ARE YOU CRAZY? Diana, you cannot really mean to support such folly!" Agnes McCarthy shouted, late on Wednesday afternoon.

"I think we have to," Diana countered with as much patience as she could muster. "Tensions are already running very high. Unless we do something to diffuse them—"

"I'll tell you what you can do! You can run that Mike Harrigan out of town, that's what you can do!" Agnes shouted, waving both her arms.

Hal Sims, the owner of Hal's Hardware, intervened. "Diana is right, Agnes. We've got to try and work with these boys, get to know them, not start fighting them right away. It's the only decent thing to do."

"What do those boys know about decent?" Agnes scoffed.

"Maybe it's time they learned," Myrtle Sims said quietly, moving to stand next to her husband behind the counter. A solicitous expression on her plump face, she continued, "Look, Hal and I have the same fears you do. We don't want any more trouble here in Libertyville—"

"Then help us get rid of them," Billy Reaves cut in gruffly. "Unless you want to see a repeat of what happened to my sister?"

They were all grimly silent, remembering Jenny's death in the drunk-driving incident, which took a year to resolve.

Myrtle's eyes filled with tears. "Do you think a day goes by when I don't think about that?" she whispered hoarsely.

Disturbed they'd upset his wife, Hal said, "One bad apple doesn't spoil the whole bunch."

Diana agreed, at least in principle; reality was a lot harder. She sighed, wishing Mike had never moved to the area. "Like it or not, we have to give these kids a fair chance," she said.

"Fools!" Agnes shook her head. "All of you! And you'll live to regret it. Mark my words."

"Agnes, please! " Hal remonstrated. "I know we had a bad experience before, but this is all going to work out. You'll see."

Diana was unable to share Hal's Utopian vision of the future. She regarded him skeptically, thinking Hal and Mike Harrigan had a lot in common. An impractical, romantic streak a mile wide, the need to nurture—at any cost; a penchant for rooting for the underdog, which was something Diana, having learned harsh realities early on in life never did.

Agnes glared at Hal and his wife, unable to believe they could be so willing to try, after what they'd all been through. "It's true, then? You're donating the supplies for this folly at cost?"

They nodded, and Diana felt amazed by what Mike Harrigan had been able to accomplish in the space of two days. "Most of the businesses in town have contributed something, as have many of the residents," she told them. "Mike Harrigan has compiled a list of over fifty volunteers, and an equal number of houses of senior citizens that need special attention. I admit I was skeptical at first, too, but now I believe this project will be good for the whole town."

Agnes glared at them all. "Well, I want no part of it, and if you're smart, you'll take the same stand."

Hal picked up on the menace in Agnes's words. He glared at her, their difference of opinion on this matter all too apparent. "Is that a threat?" he asked pointedly.

Agnes shrugged, looking at him with feigned indifference. "I own the newspaper here in town. I can print advertising or not, depending on space."

Diana sucked in her breath at the threat. Hal reddened and shook his head in disapproval.

"Oh, Agnes, you don't want to bar advertising," Myrtle said, frowning. With determination she tried to talk some sense into her friend. "That would hurt you, and your business."

Agnes shrugged uncaringly. "I'll do anything I have to to save this town. And I expect you, Diana, to do the same."

"And if I don't?" Diana questioned coolly, her heart racing.

"Then you'll all pay, including you, Justice Tomlinson," Agnes retorted. "You're only an elected official, you know. You can be replaced." On that derisive note, she stomped out of the store. Billy and Kay Reaves followed.

Iris Lansky remained. Though she'd been silent earlier, her skepticism of the Neighbors program was evident. "You are going to keep tabs on this pilot program of Harrigan's, aren't you, Diana?" she pressed, her concern evident.

"Yes, I will. And if any of you experience problems, or hear about any, bring them to me," she said.

"Great," Iris said, relieved. The matter settled, she departed.

The three of them that were left gave a collective sigh of relief. Diana in particular was glad the latest commotion over Mike and his boys was more or less settled.

Hal couldn't quite contain the worry in his eyes, but his face was set in determination. "I really want this to work, so despite Agnes's threats, I'm not backing out," he said. Myrtle agreed with her husband.

"Neither am I," Diana said slowly, seeing the way the situation was dividing the town even as it drew them together. She couldn't help regretting what Mike Harrigan had gotten her into.

"THANKS FOR COMING," Mike told Diana early Saturday morning as he passed out work gloves and paint scrapers to both Kevin and her. "I have a good feeling about this project."

If only she did! For the sake of the town, Diana wanted to be hopeful. She wanted the division between the residents and Harrigan's crew to end. And this was as good a way as any for the boys to prove their worth. If only they would behave themselves throughout the project! But even as she hoped for success, she knew Mike's gamble was a long shot, with little chance of real or lasting success.

Nonetheless, she was here and she might as well give it a try. "Where do you want us to start?" she asked, pulling on an old baseball cap over her ponytail. As long as she had to be there, she'd decided to work right along with the rest of the volunteers rather than just stand around and police the boys.

"Why don't you two start at the front, and I'll tackle the second story," Mike suggested genially, watching her face. She refused to show any reaction whatsoever and kept her expression inscrutable.

But he would leave her alone with Kevin right off. "Okay." She tried her best to disguise her unease. Kevin didn't react either way.

As they worked, Diana couldn't help but sneak some glances at Kevin. At fourteen, he looked at least a decade older than his physical years would suggest. As the time passed it was clear he wasn't overjoyed about the work or the situation but he wasn't openly combative, either. She found herself wondering about his background, wondering what could have made him so sad, so... devoid of hope. But Kevin gave her no clue, and as time passed, Diana found herself wishing that Mike had told her more about the individual backgrounds of his charges, or that she had asked.

Half an hour passed, and then another, and—to Diana's increasing frustration but somewhat relieved acceptance—Kevin remained uncommunicative. By midmorning, when they stopped for a break of lemon Gatorade and sandwiches made by the local ladies' club, she had resigned herself to spending hours with more of the same.

Beside her Kevin picked at his food, eating as if he had no appetite. He also looked tired, as if he hadn't been sleeping much.

Disturbed, Diana pushed from her mind any sympathetic thoughts she might have formed and got back to work, again concentrating on her scraping. Kevin wasn't her problem; he was Mike's. If she was to be an effective mediator, she had to remain impartial and objective, as Mike so obviously couldn't. She couldn't allow herself to start feeling sorry for the boys, and thus, not hold them accountable for their actions.

They were nearly finished when the accident occurred. One minute Kevin was scraping away, the next he was crying out in pain. When she looked over, she saw Kevin doubled up and clutching his hands at his waist.

"Mike!" Diana yelled, dropping her own tools and rushing to help.

Mike rounded the corner at a run, took one look at the blood dripping from the gash across Kevin's palm, and sprinted for his truck. His own face white, he muttered an oath. "I'll get the first-aid kit."

Knowing from the way Kevin was swaying that he was about to faint, Diana half pushed, half guided the boy to a sitting position on the porch. Quickly she yanked off his torn work glove. Using the antiseptic cloth Mike pulled out of the first-aid kit, she applied direct pressure to the wound. "Looks like he's going to need some stitches," she said, very much aware that Kevin was trembling. Although obviously in terrible pain, he wasn't making a sound, but white beads of sweat had broken out on his upper lip and brow.

"I'll call the doctor, let him know we're on our way." Mike headed into the house.

"You're going to be just fine," Diana murmured bluntly, wishing she could do more for the silent, stoic kid than just utter words of consolation.

It wasn't until she'd stopped the bleeding that she noticed the scars on Kevin's hands. They were raw, ugly and semicircular in shape. Seeing her glance, her horror, Kevin flinched and pulled his hands away.

Mike came back, his voice brisk as he snapped out orders. "Doc said he'll meet us at the clinic. Let's go."

They reached the clinic in minutes.

Diana stayed while the doc stitched up Kevin. When they came out into the waiting room several minutes later, Kevin's face was even whiter than before.

"He's going to be fine," the doctor said. "His hand is numb right now because of the local anesthetic, but when that wears off his palm is going to hurt like the dickens. I can prescribe something for pain." He sent a questioning look at Mike. "Or you can start with acetominophen if you prefer."

"Yes, we'll start with the Tylenol. Thanks."

The doctor nodded agreeably, adding, "Take care of him. And have him take it easy for a couple of days. No getting those stitches wet or getting his hand dirty around the barnyard, you hear me?"

Mike nodded. He patted Kevin on the back, withdrawing his hand when Kevin moved away, obviously feeling uncomfortable. "I better get you back to the ranch," Mike continued calmly, as if his gesture had not been rejected.

"I'll go on back and finish the scraping," Diana said awkwardly, still wishing, despite her earlier resolve not to get emotionally involved with any of the kids, that she could do more for the stoic child. Of course, she consoled herself briefly, she would do as much for anyone who'd been hurt in her presence. Even so, the sensation of caring about one of Harrigan's kids was disquieting. Very disquieting. She didn't want to fall into the same trap Mike had set himself up for—caring for someone who couldn't return the affection or esteem. The way she saw it, Mike Harrigan was bound to get hurt.

Three hours later, she had almost finished the front porch and was taking a break. She was sitting in the shade, drinking lemonade, when Mike parked his truck at the curb and vaulted out. She watched him move effortlessly toward her, aware his spirits had picked up immeasurably since she'd last seen him. "Sorry I couldn't get here sooner," he said easily, his eyes serious, "but I wanted to wait until Melanie and Jim got back with the other two before taking off."

Immediately, she conjured up a picture of Kevin as she'd last seen him—washed out, emotionally drained, frightened. "How's Kevin?" Diana asked quickly, forgetting for a moment her decision to stay aloof from both Harrigan and his foster kids.

Picking up on the compassion in her voice, Mike smiled slowly. He leaned closer, peering at her with highly exaggerated fascination. "Why, Diana, I do believe you have a heart in there after all," he teased.

"Very funny, Harrigan. You know I care." At least to a point, she amended silently.

"Yeah, I do." He was silent a moment before sobering and continuing bluntly, "Kevin's fine. In obvious pain, which he won't admit, but I made him swallow some Tylenol anyway."

"He didn't want to?" Diana wasn't sure Mike should've forced medication on Kevin.

Mike caught the direction of her thoughts. "All I had to do was look at him to know his shot of Novocaine had worn off. He was white as a ghost, cradling his hand next to him, grimacing at the slightest movement. I know how he feels, too. I had stitches three different times when I was a kid."

Diana could well imagine. She bet that as a kid he'd been even more foolhardy and recklessly adventurous than he was now. The thought of his unpredictability both disturbed and excited her. She'd never met anyone quite like him. She doubted she ever would.

Annoyed at her rambling, fanciful thoughts, she pushed them away and concentrated on the present. Mike was sighing and sat back to catch his breath. Diana felt the same need. The porch was cool and shady in direct contrast to the heat of the day. All afternoon Diana had told herself she wouldn't get any more involved with Mike or his kids, but as the seconds drew out, she couldn't let this opportunity to learn the truth go by. She had to ask, "Mike, how did Kevin get those scars on his hands?"

Mike's mouth turned grim, and he averted his gaze, as if his own pain were something he didn't want anyone else to see. "I don't know," Mike answered curtly after a moment. "He won't talk about it. Never has. I'm hoping he will someday, because I think it would be cathartic for him. But it has to be his choice."

Suddenly restless, she stood. "Well, it's about time we got back to work."

He took the paint scraper from her hand before she could begin again. "You've done enough today," he remonstrated gently, his gaze gentle but firm. "I'll finish the back of the house."

Diana hesitated. She was bone tired, but she didn't want him to think she was running out on him, or the others in the project. "You're sure?"

"I'm sure," Mike said firmly, anticipating her argument. "And, Diana, thanks again. It meant a lot to me today, having you work with Kevin. In some respects he's the toughest of the bunch."

Diana had sensed that, too. Wanting to find out more about what was going on at the Harrigan Ranch without appearing to pry, she observed casually, "You seem to be handling him okay."

His eyes were steady but evasive as he met her glance. Although he knew it would earn him Brownie points if he agreed with her he wasn't about to lie. "Don't let appearances fool you," Mike said. "Things aren't much better now than they were the day Kevin arrived." Mike sighed, for a moment looking very depressed. "The difference now is that he knows the rules and he's learned that I mean what I say. He's stopped challenging me on chores and stuff, but only because he thinks he's just marking time. He doesn't want to be here, doesn't really want to be anywhere right now, and he makes sure I know it every time I turn around." Mike finished on a note of genuine frustration.

Perplexed, Diana studied him. She was glad Mike had confided in her—it eased her curiosity a little—but now her worry had risen a notch. "What do you mean, Kevin's just marking time?"

Mike shrugged, his face becoming impassive again. Diana sensed he regretted opening up to her at all. He enjoyed discussing his foster-care plans, but he clammed up on more private matters. He seemed to need to keep everyone at arm's length.

"He's a real loner," Mike said finally, his voice calm and accepting. His eyes met Diana's, before he continued softly with conviction, "I know I could help him if he'd just give me a chance, really talk to me and tell me what's on his mind." Mike sighed again, frowning. "But he won't."

"That really bothers you doesn't it?" More than he wanted to admit, she thought.

After a moment, Mike nodded, his eyes serious. "I'm not interested in surface intimacy," Mike said softly, his frustration evident. "I want the real thing."

A shiver went down her spine at the tenaciousness in Mike's voice. He was definitely not a man to be taken lightly. She wondered briefly what it would be like to be in his arms then pushed the thought away. Of all the people she could possibly date, he would be the absolute worst, most disastrous, choice.

His eyes softened unexpectedly and he changed the subject. "By the way, you were great today, and I really mean that. You handled the emergency like a pro."

"Thanks." She felt proud of what she'd done, how calm she'd stayed in the medical emergency. She'd never been needed in quite that way before; it was reassuring to know she could cope.

He leaned against the post, and watched her with growing satisfaction—as if he, too, had seen a whole new side of her the last few hours. "In return," he continued easily, a new purposefulness in every line of his body, his blue eyes both guileless and intent, "I'd like to do something for you. How about dinner?"

This isn't an invitation for a date, she told herself firmly. More like the return of a favor from someone who would rather die than feel beholden to someone else. Still, the color rose in her cheeks, and she could tell from his smile that it pleased him in some perverse way to know that she was wary of him. She swallowed hard around the sudden tightness in her throat, aware of the gathering tension in her limbs. "Thank you, but that's really not necessary," she said politely. Damn him for making her feel like a woman—Jane to his Tarzan.

His brows rose and fell in mocking fashion as he disagreed. "I think it is." He smiled again, and she had a glimpse of what a devil he must've been as a kid.

Never tell Mike Harrigan he can't do something, she thought, because then he'll have to go out and prove that he can.

"Why not let me take you out to dinner?" His invitation was casual, but behind the lazy, I'm-harmless tone was a dare she'd have had to have been blind to miss. He seemed to be taunting her, asking her to prove she wasn't afraid to spend time alone with him, afraid of the sure but subtle chemistry beginning to flare between them. He continued amiably, "I'm off tomorrow night."

Despite the challenge, she'd sooner have a date with a wrestler who raised turkeys on the side. "Thank you, no." Her voice was firm. A ceaseless do-gooder like Mike was not the kind of man she wanted to get involved with on any level.

He cocked his head slightly to the side. "That's not just a no—it's a *no*." He was both curious and miffed.

Diana successfully fought back a blush; at this rate she was only hanging on to her composure by her fingernails. If he kept pushing, she didn't know what she'd be goaded into saying. Probably something revealing. And she didn't want the psychologist in Mike analyzing her. "I don't think it's a good idea, that's all," she responded with finality. They'd already had breakfast; the town was still talking about that tête-à-tête. He might not care what people said or thought about him, but she was an elected official and had to care.

He was motionless, watching her. "There's no one else?"

She stared at him coolly, realizing that although he was curious about her, he was also provoking her for the sheer sport of watching her squirm. Considering the way she had laid down the law to him perhaps that wasn't surprising. He wanted to fence with her, to find a way to win their silent but still raging battle of wills. Her chin lifted defiantly. "I date, if that's what you're asking."

Half his mouth lifted in a thin semblance of a smile; he was amused by her emotional reaction to his prodding. "But no one seriously."

Diana sighed loudly, tempted not to answer. He lifted his brows again and wordlessly transmitted his desire to uncover the truth, no matter how hard it was, or how she resisted. Diana sighed again, all too aware that information would be easy enough for him to obtain. All he'd have to do is ask. Probably at least half the people in town would be all too glad to tell him whatever it was he felt he needed to know, especially if they felt they were helping her out romantically. "No, no one seriously," Diana said at last, telling herself wearily it was easier just to tell him what he wanted to know than have him ask around about her.

"So, why not dinner?" He moved slightly closer, until he was so near she could feel his body heat.

She shifted away from him, all too aware of his faintly predatory air, the smug satisfaction in his eyes. "Because I need to keep my professional perspective where you're concerned, just on the off chance there's more trouble later on." She lifted her challenging gaze to his steady blue one.

"I see." He didn't appreciate her assumption, although, she noticed wryly, he seemed to half expect it.

Not liking his sardonic assessment of her, and all that it seemed to imply—that she couldn't be impartial in this situation if she tried—she hastily bid him adieu. He continued to watch her carefully, as she scrambled out the door.

Alone, Diana thought how she hadn't seen the last of him, not by a long shot. Mike Harrigan wasn't the kind of man to give up easily on anything. She sighed again, even more wearily, knowing this was one battle—for her own sake—she would just have to win. She couldn't let herself get any more involved with an impractical dreamer like him.

Chapter Three

"Dad, I need a favor," Mike began steadfastly, several days later. "The Neighbors project was approved, and we've been planting trees in the park across from the Libertyville courthouse—"

"Let me guess. You need donations."

"A few trees or shrubs would be nice, yes."

"Consider it done."

Tom, Sr., motioned for Mike to take a seat opposite him in the broadcasting booth of the Astrodome. Although the game wasn't due to start for four more hours, his father, a sports announcer for the Houston Astros games, had already arrived and was preparing his notes for the day in the otherwise empty booth.

Although Tom, Sr., had always tried to be supportive of his children in whatever they chose to pursue, he had more than once expressed his qualms about Mike's involvement in the foster ranch project, and for a variety of reasons. He hadn't liked the fact Mike had used his entire trust fund to buy the ranch, although admittedly the money was there for Mike to use as he pleased. Nor had he liked the idea of Mike's having to rely chiefly on donations to keep the program going. Nonetheless, Mike could count on both his parents to help raise money for his flagship program whenever he asked it of them. He was hoping, however, that it wouldn't be often once he got his program going, that donations would pour in without solicitation after he had some proven success. Even if donations never poured in, Mike had no intention of quitting something of such value.

"How's everything else going?" his father asked.

Mike sighed and, at his father's probing look, admitted "There are a few adjustment problems, but nothing that can't be worked out. The main problem at the moment is the justice of the peace in Libertyville, Diana Tomlinson. She's been kind of a thorn in my side." Was that ever an understatement!

Mike had known the first moment he saw Diana in her chambers that she was going to be trouble. She'd given him a disdainful glare, and everything had gone downhill from there. He'd ended up losing his temper, something he rarely did. He'd let the situation turn personal.

Of course he'd tried to make up for that later, by going back to see her when he was calm. He'd known she was irked at the way he'd approached her on her way to work, but he'd had no choice. If he'd called her and asked her to meet with him casually, she would've refused.

So he'd had to wing it.

And he'd sensed her thawing out a little too—until their breakfast had created such a gossipy stir in town. She hadn't liked that, not one bit. And he didn't like the fact that appearances were so important to her.

Tom, Sr., made a thoughtful sound in the back of his throat. "Have you tried to get to know her better?"

"Yes, without much success."

"Well, keep trying. I'm sure if you two get to know and appreciate one another as individuals, you'll eventually work things out."

Mike wished it could be that easy. But even if he and Diana weren't fighting about his foster boys, he knew there was little chance they'd get along.

Not that he didn't want them to. She was slender and very good-looking and obviously kept herself in great shape. She was also very into an upscale life-style; her clothes were top quality, current, yuppie in the extreme. Sexy and smart, she would prove to be one hell of a challenge for any man foolish enough to pursue her.

Tom, Sr., cleared his throat. Aware he'd drifted off, Mike turned his attention back to his dad. He realized suddenly, not having seen his parents for a few weeks, he was anxious for news. "So, how's Mom?"

Tom, Sr., shrugged. "The usual. She's worried—about you being out there alone with those boys."

Having people worry about him, and agonize over his decisions—decisions that were his to make—was nothing new to Mike. It had gone on since he was a boy and had carried on into adulthood, happening first with his parents and then with the women he'd dated. They all seemed to expect that because he came from a well-to-do family that he would naturally pursue the trappings of success rather than social causes.

Sensing his dad was also apprehensive about his physical safety, Mike said, "Mom needn't worry, Dad. The boys are good kids—even if occasionally they look a little, uh, rough around the edges. They just need stability and guidance." All of which Mike had been giving with slow but steady result. He was pleased with the progress that had been made—at least on his ranch. The town of Libertyville was another matter.

His father was silent, debating, then finally decided to speak his mind. Even if they didn't agree, they'd always been able to be honest with one another. "I wish I could believe that a little tender loving care is all it would take, Mike," his father said gently. "But those kids are pretty

old now, almost men. Big enough to take you on if one
of them got angry."

"Physically I can hold my own against them, Dad."

"One on one, yes. But if it comes to three on one..."

The two men stared at one another, locked in silent
conflict. "Melanie and Jim are there, too," said Mike.
"Besides, it won't happen."

"I hope not, son, I really do." But Tom, Sr., still had
his doubts.

Mike felt himself getting defensive. Irritated with
himself for letting his dad get to him, Mike reiterated
firmly and calmly, "They are good kids. And I already
care about them, a lot, and I think you and Mom would,
too, if you'd just give yourselves a chance."

Tom, Sr., exhaled slowly and for a moment didn't respond. What his dad didn't say spoke volumes about
what he felt. A truculent silence fell between them as the
two men continued to size one another up. Mike knew his
father was irritated at his "reckless" refusal to conform
to his parents' concept of what was right for him—which
was his own private practice in the suburbs or a position
in a prestigious hospital or clinic, a home and a family on
the side. But to date, Mike had pursued other goals; he'd
always wanted something different, something more demanding. Like most middle children, he was a bit of a
free spirit. Dammit, when would his parents ever see him
as he was, instead of how they wanted him to be?

Mike swore impatiently, as hundreds of earlier argu-
ments came rushing back to him. "When are we going to
stop playing the same old song, Dad?" he asked quietly.
"The truth is, hell, sometimes I wish you'd just tell me
to get lost instead of giving me one of those long-
suffering glances! You're never going to approve of me,
are you?" The angry words rushed out before Mike could
stop them, and he rose to pace restlessly in front of his
father, his hands jammed into his pockets.

"Mike—"

"Can the speech, Dad. The simple truth is no matter what I do or how much I try, I'll never please you. I'll always be the second son, the one that came after Tom, the one that never quite measured up to the golden path blazed by my big brother."

Tom, Sr., pushed back his chair and walked over to his son's side, his expression grave. "It isn't a question of me approving or disapproving of you, Mike." Tom, Sr., stood, one shoulder against the glass.

Wasn't it? "Dad, the main reason I became a psychologist was to help troubled kids. And I knew, for a variety of reasons—the least of which being the fact I was in and out of so many scrapes myself as a youth—that I could help others, given half a chance."

"Your mother and I don't dispute that you have a great capacity for understanding and helping others. But must you put your own life on hold to do that? And what about your personal life? Don't you want a family of your own?"

"Of course I do." Mike sighed his exasperation, realizing he'd never get through to his father.

The bottom line was they thought his latest gambit was just another in a long series of rebellions, Mike's habit of doing everything except what was logically expected of him. Right now Mike just wanted the argument, and the unpleasantness, to be over.

Apparently his father did, too. Sheepishly, he forced a smile. "I'll see what I can do about getting you those trees. Maybe some of my friends would like to make a donation, too."

Mike grinned and offered his hand, glad the storm of moments before was to be tactfully forgotten. "Thanks, Dad."

"You're welcome." Tom, Sr., shook hands with his son and then embraced him briefly. "If you have time today, you might drop in on your mother at work."

"I'm on my way over there now, just as soon as I finish meeting with the child-welfare department." Which was yet another reason he'd come to Houston that day. He had to give a report on how the boys were progressing.

Mike was halfway out the door before his father called him back, a hint of laughter in his voice. "One more thing, Mike. This Diana Tomlinson, the one who's a thorn in your side. Is she pretty?"

Mike grinned, amused at his father's query, so typically him. Pretty didn't begin to describe the impossibly strong-willed woman with the cloud of golden hair and the sparkling golden brown eyes. "Very," he said dryly.

His father broke out in a grin and said, Mandarin-like, "Interesting."

MIKE WAS ALONE in his study when the phone jangled late the following evening. It was his father.

"Mike, I'm glad I caught you. I got the trees you wanted. They'll be delivered in a few days."

"Thanks."

"You're welcome. Listen, about that J.P. you mentioned—Diana Tomlinson. I, uh, I did some checking—"

Mike swore. This kind of interference hadn't been invited. With effort, he kept his tone level. "Dad, when I told you I was having trouble with her, I was just letting off steam. I didn't want you to do anything."

"I know that," Tom, Sr., said gently, sounding not the least bit apologetic. "Still, it bothered me to find out you were having trouble with the local J.P., especially when you're just getting started out there."

People meddling in his life infuriated Mike. Nonetheless, he was also conscious of how much he owed his dad. Without his parents' help, he never could've started the ranch. In an effort to hold on to his soaring temper, Mike mentally counted to ten. "What'd you do?"

"I called a friend of mine at the Texas Bar Association who did a little checking. It's quite a story, Mike. She used to be a defense attorney here in Houston for one of the big firms, pulling in quite a hefty salary."

A defense attorney? Diana? Yes, now that he thought about it, he could imagine her in the fast lane, pursuing a high-powered career. Still, he felt he was prying, learning even this much, especially in such an underhand way. He started to tell his father to cool it, but his dad was already going on matter-of-factly.

"Then a few years ago she quit and moved to Libertyville. No one knows why exactly, although there's all sorts of speculation." When Mike didn't respond, he said in a perplexed tone of voice, a little piqued his detective work wasn't more appreciated, "You don't sound thrilled by any of this, Mike."

Mike sighed. "I'm not. Dad, you know I always try to respect others' privacy." That was why he never told his parents anything, because they always felt they had to act on it.

"I respect others' privacy, too, Mike, but if someone's giving you a hard time I think we owe it to you to try and find out why..."

Reluctantly Mike admitted to himself his dad had a point. Maybe he should follow his initial gut instinct, which had told him it would be politic to try to get closer to Diana, to let her see firsthand he was no threat to either her or the community. Neither were his boys.

With everything that had happened, with his workload and his increasing responsibilities regarding the

Neighbors project, he had all but abandoned that tact. Maybe now it was time he went back to it.

DIANA HELPED HERSELF to some punch and looked around the crowded fire station. It certainly wasn't the usual place for a fund-raising dance, but under the circumstances, it was perhaps the most appropriate. She only had to look around the century-old brick building to see how out-of-date it had become, how cramped. There was no room to store the latest fire truck inside, so it sat outside on the concrete drive. The sleeping and eating quarters for volunteers were small and not air-conditioned, a situation never more apparent than now, for the weather had taken a hot, humid turn. She was burning up in her white, vivid rose and mint-green floral sundress. Fanning herself, Diana sipped her lemonade and listened to the country-and-western band play its rendition of the latest George Strait hit.

"Hi."

Diana looked up to see Mike Harrigan approaching her. He, too, had dressed up for the occasion, wearing a dazzling white Western dress shirt, and black string tie. His soft, dark blue jeans clung to his muscular thighs and calves. His leather boots were shined. Her senses spun as she inhaled the rich woodsy scent of his cologne.

She hadn't seen Mike in days, and although she'd been avoiding him deliberately, she realized that, on some remote level of her subconscious, she had missed dealing with him. Perhaps he made her utilize her every intellectual and emotional strength, that sort of engrossing mental challenge was something she had never before experienced. At least not to the point where, on sight of him, her every nerve ending came alive with sensation.

"Hi." Finally she managed to return his greeting with an air of normality, although her pulse was racing wildly.

"Quite a gathering here tonight," Mike murmured approvingly, looking around.

"I think everyone wants a new fire station." Trying to quell her reaction to his nearness, she lifted her cup to her lips.

He watched her take a drink, his absolute concentration on the movement, and on her, unsettling her even more. "Do you think they'll have enough to build one after tonight?" he asked. She could swear his mind was still on her, even as he attempted to make small talk.

Despite the drink, Diana's throat felt parched, and she hastily took another swallow. "No. I'm sure it'll take years to raise the funds, but there'll be good reason for lots of parties in the meantime."

Nodding thoughtfully, Mike helped himself to more lemonade.

Although she would have liked to walk away and distance herself from Mike Harrigan for the rest of the evening—a smart, safe move on her part—Diana felt a tug of responsibility as justice of the peace. "How are the boys?"

Mike's eyes lit up at her inquiry, as if he read more into it than warranted. "They're doing great, actually. We're finished with the major portion of planting on the south side of the courthouse lawn."

She nodded, looking around, still wishing she'd been able to avoid Mike Harrigan altogether, aware her pulse was still racing. "And yourself?" This was just small talk, Diana told herself. No more and no less. Besides, she'd be departing for the night at any minute.

"I'm fine, too," he said curtly. Silence. He shifted beside her, looking slightly uncomfortable. "Of course I've been busy. I went to Houston earlier this week."

Houston held few happy memories for her and unconsciously Diana stiffened. To her dismay Mike noticed her unease, and changed his demeanor to that of a psychologist listening to a patient. In fact, he seemed to see everything she would have rather kept hidden. She felt tense. "You've lived there, too, haven't you?" he added casually.

Diana's chin lifted and she put her cup aside. So he wanted to fence again, did he? "Yes, right after I graduated from law school." She paused, unable to help asking, "How did you know that?" With a great deal of effort, she kept her voice cordial.

Mike shrugged nonchalantly. "My dad mentioned it to me when he called the other night. He has a friend who's vice president of the Texas Bar Association. They were talking about me, my ranch, Libertyville in general. I guess your name came up." Mike hesitated, clearly wanting to understand her. He was silent for several moments, as if trying to decide whether or not he should ask more questions. In the end, his inherent curiosity got the better of him. "He told my dad you could have had quite a career as a criminal lawyer if you'd stuck with it."

"I suppose that's true," Diana admitted distractedly. She wasn't pleased to be forced to remember a time when she'd been so burned out and disillusioned, both in career and personal life, she could barely get through the day. Suddenly she felt suffocated in the flower-scented room. "If you'll excuse me, I need some air."

Diana left her cup on the table and started for the door, not daring to look back for fear he would see the new tension on her face.

To her unchecked annoyance, Mike followed her amiably into the dusky light. He let her walk on her own for maybe half a block and then caught up with her, not willing to let her go without an apology. "Look, I'm sorry if I upset you—"

She stopped walking and turned angrily to face him, wishing it were as easy for her to stop remembering as it was for him to apologize. Because even now those memories nagged at her, reminding her of how naive she had been then. Fortunately that unenlightened period in her life had passed. "Are you?"

There was an uncomfortable silence. Mike looked at her curiously, still trying to understand what was disturbing her. "You're sure you're okay?" he murmured, concerned.

"Yes. I just don't want to talk about Houston."

He could see that. "Again, I'm sorry I brought it up."

Diana sighed. Was he really? It was hard to tell, especially since she had just given him an unexpected insight into her character, however. involuntarily. He had to wonder...

"My life there is over," she insisted, "so there's really no need to go into it." No need to dwell on her greenness then, the ingenuous way she had seen the world. Which was not so different from the way Mike saw it now—simply. Too simply.

"I agree, So—" his voice softened "—let's just drop it."

"Fine," she snapped then, flushed, realizing how rude she sounded.

To her relief, Mike let her tone pass without comment. "I'm heading back to the dance." He started in the other direction, his attitude cordial, forgiving. "You want to walk with me, or stay here for a while?" Either option was okay, he was more than willing to give her the space she needed.

She was behaving foolishly, letting her pent-up emotions govern her behavior, taking her unhappiness with the past out on him. "Wait, Mike, I..." She hesitated, running a hand through her hair. "I know I'm acting crazy." Irrational. It was just that he'd caught her off guard, made her feel vulnerable, when she didn't want to feel vulnerable. Especially not when she was with him.

"Not crazy—upset," he corrected, coming toward her. "Not to worry," he soothed. "That's everyone's right. I understand. I do—"

"I know you do," she interjected softly. It was rare, she thought, for someone, especially a man, to know so intuitively just what she needed. And then to give it to her at his own expense. "And maybe that's why—" she took a deep bolstering breath, so she wouldn't lose her nerve at what she was about to say "—we should, well, talk about this a little more." She really didn't want him to think she was demented. Bad enough he thought her a grinch.

"Okay." He shrugged, letting her know he was there for her. "If you want to." He regarded her patiently, without judgment. And suddenly she knew that not only could she trust him to keep this conversation in confidence, but that she'd been holding too many roiling emotions inside for too long, telling absolutely no one the truth about her life in Houston. She still wasn't ready to divulge much of it—the intimate details of her marriage, for instance—but she sensed she needed to unload some of her emotional baggage. Besides, she reasoned further, most of what she was about to tell him was already speculated about in Houston legal circles.

The only problem was, she didn't know where to begin.

She lowered her glance, embarrassed, suddenly shy. "I wasn't very happy living in Houston."

"That much I gathered." His appreciation of her confidence was reflected in his gentle regard.

Ignoring his steady assessment, she tried valiantly to keep up the insouciant facade. "Part of it was my work." Remembering, she sighed heavily and moved away, finally settling against a nearby storefront. "You see, I came out of law school believing that every person in this country was entitled to a defense, no matter what, and as a competent, uninvolved professional I was going to give them that. Because I was new at the firm, I got the criminal cases. Oh, they were petty offenses, but they turned up in criminal court nonetheless."

Mike's eyes narrowed briefly. She could see the wheels turning.

Clearing her throat, she continued, "Some of the men and women I represented were innocent, others were not." Mike seemed ready to interrupt. She cut him off. "I admit that bothered me at first, the thought of my defending—perhaps even successfully—someone who had committed a crime. But I persevered."

"Did you ever get anyone off you knew was guilty?" he asked gruffly.

"Yes." She stopped short. She remembered all too well the contradictions she'd felt then. In fact those people were similar to the types she had grown up with—from the same class and background she'd vowed to escape.

"Why?"

Diana wouldn't apologize for the path she'd taken. Her five years in Houston, the long hours, the exorbitant salary, were largely responsible for her financial security today. She lifted her shoulders carelessly, but found she wasn't quite able to meet his direct, analytical gaze.

"One, because I fancied myself some sort of female Racehorse Haines in the making, and two, because that was their right, to have an attorney." She sighed again, feeling unutterably weary. He seemed to guess instinctively how much her conscience had sometimes weighed on her and how much she'd eventually come to hate her work.

"And in among the guilty ones there were innocent victims," she continued, "people and kids I kept from being erroneously sent to jail or j.d. And I did get satisfaction out of that." Quite a lot, as a matter of fact.

Mike closed the distance between them and leaned one shoulder against the glass. "But then there were the others. Exactly how many did you get off scot-free?" he asked quietly.

Diana shrugged. "None, without some sort of penance. Mostly it involved a lot of plea-bargaining. Vandals, traffic violators, some robbery cases."

She turned to him, wanting him to understand that she had tried to live a moral life while doing the best job she could do in her profession as well. "Basically, I did all I could to keep the good guys out of jail while simultaneously not letting anyone who was guilty get off scot-free, even when I plea-bargained."

She'd expected to win his praise for efforts. She didn't.

He raised an eyebrow, indicating he was frankly disappointed in her, and shifted his weight restlessly. "Sounds like you were doing your share of judging even then."

At the direct hit, Diana reddened slightly. "Exactly why I had to get out of it," she said lightly, knowing his assessment was on target. "So that's when I quit criminal law."

Not long after that, her marriage had fallen apart, adding to her misery. "Anyway, since I didn't want to practice corporate law, I decided to come to Libertyville and open a general practice." Back then it had been simply a place on the map to her; now it was her home. She hadn't realized how much so, until recent weeks ever since he'd come to town.

Mike was still watching her closely. "You had a law practice here?" He was surprised.

Diana nodded. "For two years, before becoming the justice of the peace when the last J.P. retired unexpectedly last January." She looked up at him. "I know you think I was too harsh with your kids—"

"But you don't think you were."

"No."

He nodded, suddenly seeing more than she would've liked him to see. "You're that way with all juvenile offenders and petty criminals that are hauled into your court," he summed up pragmatically.

She couldn't deny it.

He gave her a disapproving look and her spine turned rigid. She defended her actions hotly. "Imposing stiff consequences—even if it's in the form of community service work—is the only way to get through to kids who cause trouble and prompt them to change course."

He made a dissenting sound. "So now, instead of keeping kids out of detention centers, you send them there," Mike concluded in a tone that was anything but happy.

Diana froze, not liking the tone in his voice. "When there's no other recourse, yes, I do. It's always a tough decision, and one I've had to make very infrequently. I won't shy away from it in the future."

Mike's eyes met hers. It was impossible to know what he was thinking, just that his thoughts were focused on her—and everything she still wasn't saying.

"You're unfairly prejudiced against all juvenile defendants, aren't you?" Giving her no chance to respond, he continued, "Oh, you might want to deny it, but you can't hide the way you feel."

Diana took a deep breath, angry that she had trusted him. He had turned on her—and so viciously! She straightened to her full height. "Can you blame me? With the climate here hostile to begin with, it's like putting those three kids into a pressure cooker, Mike." There was no telling what they'd do, or vice versa, and the whole situation just spelled trouble to Diana. No matter how much Mike cared or might try to keep them under his wing. "In a big city they wouldn't stand out so much—"

"Big cities are too full of temptation," he said, dismissing her suggestion summarily.

"Well, so apparently is Libertyville." If they could judge by what had happened initially.

He let out an exasperated breath. "Look, I didn't follow you outside to argue with you."

But they had argued anyway, Diana thought, provoked. Worse, she had actually allowed herself to confide in him! Why, she didn't know, except that his eyes had been so kind, so encouraging, moments ago. He had such a soothing, you-can-tell-me-anything manner. And she'd fallen for it, hook, line and sinker.

They were farther apart now in viewpoint than they had ever been. "Maybe we should go back to the dance," she said finally, acutely aware of her disappointment.

Mike nodded curtly. The corners of his mouth curled downward in frustration. He looked tired and drained. "Maybe we'd better."

HE'D BLOWN IT AGAIN, Mike thought. Ended up alienating her instead of getting to know her better. Now he knew one reason she wasn't well-disposed to his boys: she distrusted them, considered them culled from that criminal class she'd helped get off scot-free, despite their guilt.

Still, they lived in Libertyville now. That wasn't going to change, no matter how much the citizens might wish it to. He would just have to keep trying. Maybe talk to Diana one more time. Smooth things over. Try to hammer out some type of tenable working relationship, despite their opposing views.

With that goal uppermost in his mind, Mike stayed to help with the cleanup, figuring he would offer Diana a ride home after the dance. Unfortunately he wasn't watching her diligently enough, and she got out the door before he had a chance to ask her. Wanting to make sure she got home all right, and maybe take advantage of another chance to talk to her, he drove in the direction of her house.

As he'd hoped, he saw her walking briskly toward her house. Curiously though, she didn't turn up the front walk when she reached it, but strode straight past it, acting as if she didn't live there at all. Mike stared at her, his instincts shouting that something was wrong.

He pressed down lightly on the gas pedal and guided his car closer. In the yellow glow of the streetlight, he could see that something was indeed wrong, for although her steps were unhurried, her face was white and strained. Acting immediately and protectively as he would for any woman in trouble, he pulled over to the curb and opened the passenger door.

Before he could speak, she'd hopped in and pulled the door shut behind her. "Thank God you happened by!" She heaved a sigh of relief, fear in her eyes. "Don't look now, but there's a man on my porch."

"I don't see anyone." Mike hazarded a casual glance back as he put the car into park and left it running.

Diana gripped the handles of her purse tightly. "He's around the side, near the back."

Mike's heartbeat picked up. "You're sure?"

She nodded stiffly, briefly closing her eyes. "Mike, I saw him...." Her voice was a ragged whisper.

Mike's jaw jutted aggressively as every protective instinct went into play. "You don't know him?"

"No," Diana said unsteadily, shaking her head. "I was going to call the police."

Mike hazarded another glance back. Frustrated at his lack of vision, he made an impatient sound and threw the car into reverse. Backing up, he stopped when he had a full view of the porch. Sure enough, there was a man skulking around it. Seeing the car, the man stared at it a second, then pivoted on his heel, leaped over the railing edging the veranda and headed into the backyard. Diana sucked in her breath.

"Stay here!" Mike commanded, already getting out. The culprit was obviously guilty of some wrongdoing or he wouldn't have taken off like that.

"But..." Diana reached toward him pleadingly. "Mike, let's just call the police." She was frightened for him, as well as herself.

"No time," Mike muttered swiftly. By the time the police arrived, the intruder would be long gone, and Mike wanted to know who he was. He wanted to know who was threatening Diana.

When the man saw Mike coming, he broke into a run. Mike picked up his steps aggressively. No way was this guy getting away from him. No way.

Mike caught up with him near the rosebushes bordering the back of Diana's property. Knowing it would be a waste of breath to yell for the intruder to stop, he made a flying tackle, hooking both arms around the guy's waist. They thudded heavily to the ground, Mike landing on top of him. Within seconds, Mike had his opponent flipped over onto his back, his forearm across the man's throat. "Okay," he growled, "tell me who you are and what you want. And do it now!"

If he'd come there to harm Diana, there was going to be hell to pay!

Chapter Four

"Calm down, man! You've jumped to the wrong conclusion! I didn't mean any harm!" the intruder said in a clear but panicky voice as he tried to save his own skin.

It was all Mike could do to contain his temper. "Who the hell are you?" he demanded roughly.

"My name's Donald Griffin. I'm here to see Justice Tomlinson."

Mike tightened his grip on the man's collar. "What about?" he continued grimly, all the while noticing how clean-cut the intruder looked, almost sophisticated and well-to-do. Was it possible he'd made a mistake? he wondered as he kept a restraining hold on the intruder. But then if he had, why had the man run?

"It's a personal matter about my son, Kevin Griffin," the intruder answered reasonably, between attempts to get his breath.

At the mention of his foster son's name, Mike's protective instincts welled up at full force; unconsciously his grip on the man tightened.

"Look, do you think you could let me up?" the man choked out between gasps. "I can barely get my breath."

Mike stared at him, weighing the risks.

"I swear to you I won't try anything," the man continued to plead in a panicky voice. "Just give me a chance to explain, okay?"

For a long moment, a mixture of immediate dislike and distrust held Mike motionless. Knowing the man was no match for him physically, and was apparently unarmed, finally decided the issue. Slowly Mike released him and helped him to his feet.

Dozens of questions raced through his head, but preserving Kevin's location was, for the moment anyway, uppermost in his mind. He said only, "What does Justice Tomlinson have to do with your son?"

The tall blond man dusted himself off. Now that Mike studied him, he could see the resemblance between father and son—the similar hair, the slim angular face.

"I thought she might be able to tell me where he is. I know he's been placed in a foster home somewhere in this region," Donald Griffin continued stubbornly.

"How do you know that?" Mike asked, his eyes narrowing.

Before the man could reply, Diana had come forth from the shadows. "Mike, what's going on?" She hung back, standing slightly behind him.

"This is Donald Griffin. He's looking for his son, Kevin. He's in a foster home somewhere in this area—Mr. Griffin thinks." Mike sent Diana a brief warning glance. "I was about to tell him you can't help him locate him, that he'll have to go to the proper authorities."

To Mike's relief, Diana understood what he was trying to say. "That's right, Mr. Griffin. I don't have any jurisdiction over that."

"But surely, someone with your connections could help," Donald Griffin continued smoothly, his manners impeccable, his composure intact, now that he was on his feet.

"Have you talked to the social worker in charge of your son's case?"

Mr. Griffin's features hardened. "Yes, I have. Not that it did me any good." He paused, as if searching for the right words to explain his situation. When he spoke again, his voice was low, sad. "They don't think I've been much of a father to Kevin, and maybe... maybe they're right." His voice seemed to quiver with emotion as he continued to confess. "After my wife died everything fell apart." He gave Diana a candid look, then finished determinedly, "But I've got my life back together now and I want to see my son."

Something in Mike went very cold at the way Donald had glossed over the hell Kevin had been through, not to mention the fact Kevin seemed to want nothing to do with his father.

"Then I suggest you talk to the social worker in charge of your son's case," Diana said.

Glad she'd given nothing away, Mike put his arm around Diana's waist, drawing her close to his side.

Donald Griffin knew from the looks on both their faces that he had overstayed his welcome. Reluctantly he nodded his understanding and he bowed his head in disappointment, prepared to leave. "I'm sorry to have troubled you, Justice Tomlinson."

Before he could go, Diana asked curiously. "Why did you run just now, when you were on my porch?"

Donald Griffin hesitated only a moment before answering. "I was afraid my presence would be misunderstood. I'm on parole. I can't afford any kind of trouble."

"I see." At that bit of information, Diana was silent, her spine ramrod stiff against Mike's hand. He felt the tension in her and knew she was frightened, understandably so.

"I'm sorry I troubled you," Donald Griffin said. "It won't happen again."

It had better not, Mike thought darkly, still not trusting him.

DIANA WAS STILL TENSE when she let herself into her
house moments later. Although a couple of hours ago she
couldn't wait to be rid of him, Mike's offer to stay a while
was like a godsend to her.

Pretending an inner composure she didn't feel, she
flipped on all the lights. "Can I get you some coffee?"
she asked as casually as she could manage.

Mike was still watching her. "Please."

He continued to watch her as she measured coffee into
a filter and poured water into the machine. She had the
feeling he guessed how much she needed to be held at that
moment, and also that she'd resent it fiercely if he tried.
Any reassurances he could give her would have to be done
verbally. They'd be appreciated.

He leaned against the counter, his arms crossed loosely
over his waist. "Thanks for not revealing Kevin's whereabouts."

She switched on the coffee maker with more than the
necessary degree of concentration, then turned and finally met his gaze. "It was clear you didn't want me to."
She paused, fidgeting a little under his steady blue gaze.
"What's going on, Mike?" she asked nervously, her
voice a little scratchier than usual. "Why doesn't he know
where Kevin is? What haven't you told me?"

Aware the coffee had finished brewing, Diana opened
the cupboard and got out two stoneware mugs. She carried them back to the table and sat down opposite Mike.

"Kevin's mother died of cancer three years ago when
he was thirteen. Up until then, he had by all accounts a
happy normal childhood. He was a straight-A student in
school and continues to be so even now. But when Kevin
was fifteen, he had three trips to hospital emergency.

Doctors suspected abuse, but Kevin refused to admit that was true."

Diana was unable to suppress a shudder. She recalled the scars on Kevin's hands. To think that an adult might willfully inflict pain on another human being, his own child. "So authorities had no choice but to believe him," she said.

Mike nodded. "Until his father was arrested and convicted for embezzlement. I knew Donald Griffin was coming up for parole. I didn't know he'd gotten it."

"Will Kevin have to go back to him, now that his father's out of jail?"

Mike shook his head. "No. Not unless Donald Griffin can convince the court he's a fit parent, able to provide for him. And right now, given Kevin's state of mind—the fact he has avoided all contact with his father since he was sent to jail—indicates the chances are pretty slim."

Diana was silent for a moment, wondering what Kevin was keeping inside. Then she asked, "Does Kevin know his dad's out?"

Mike shook his head grimly. "No, and at this point, I'd rather he not find out. He's got enough to deal with as it is in adjusting to life at the ranch."

Diana agreed. She knew Kevin wasn't having an easy time of it, and despite her resolve not to get involved, she felt her heart going out to him. She sighed, thinking of the tasks ahead of her necessitated by Mr. Griffin's untimely visit. "I'm going to have to call Donald's parole officer."

Mike looked at her, an unhappy speculation on his face. "Then that makes two of us," he finished blandly, draining the last of the coffee.

Without warning, he stood and carried his empty cup to the sink. He set it down gently, then turned back to her. She made herself look at him, made herself hold his frank, steady gaze. The bond between them was tangible. Once again, because of circumstances linked loosely to his kids, they'd been forced to act as a team, rather than as opposing forces.

"Think you'll be all right now?" Mike asked casually, his expression inscrutable.

It was getting late. Too late for her to be sitting around, alone, with him. "Yes," she said with equanimity, "I'll be fine." She only hoped there were no more intruders. She didn't like feeling vulnerable or playing the damsel in distress to his Sir Galahad. It was enough to simply have to deal with him, never mind getting rescued by him.

"YOU LOOK LIKE you didn't sleep much," Mike commented bluntly to Diana the next morning after church.

Diana looked wearily over at him, not sure whether she was grateful for the attention or annoyed he'd been so ungallant as to point that out. Nonetheless, under that warm, attentive gaze she felt herself melting a little.

Glancing around, she noted that Mike had brought his whole crew with him. His three foster sons, Kevin, Ernie and Carlos, were standing in the shade next to the ranch's two counselors, Melanie and Jim. All three boys were suited up in their Sunday best—white shirts, dress pants, loosened ties. While Ernie and Carlos looked slightly uncomfortable in their new finery, Kevin looked as if he was born to wear a suit.

"I didn't sleep well," Diana admitted finally, when she realized Mike was waiting—no, expecting—a detailed report on her night. The truth was, she'd been up more than half the night just waiting for Donald Griffin to come back. He hadn't, of course, which made her feel all the more foolish the next day when she glanced into a mirror and noted the shadows beneath her eyes and the way her whole body was dragging. If the minister's sermon on the need for neighborliness hadn't seemed directed straight at her and other ungenerous people in the town, she probably would've fallen asleep. As it was, her conscience was stinging, because Diana knew in her heart that where Harrigan and his three boys were concerned, she hadn't exactly been fair. Not at first anyway. And she still had her reservations—about the boys being there at all.

"Got any plans for this afternoon?" Mike asked as he joined her, his soft voice sending tingles over her skin. He continued amiably, within earshot of the other parishioners, "If you're not busy, why don't you come on out to the ranch with us, have Sunday dinner with the gang. Melanie, one of the counselors, is a great cook. The dinner's already made—roast beef, mashed potatoes and gravy, just-picked corn on the cob, and strawberry shortcake for dessert. It'd be a good way for you to get to know us better."

And placate her conscience, Diana thought, all too aware of the fact that the minister would want her to accept and set a good example for the other townspeople.

"I do eat a lot of those diet dinners for singles," Diana murmured absently. While she was there she could at least unofficially check out the situation, see for herself if Harrigan's ranch was a good home for those wayward boys.

"Does that mean you accept?" Mike asked, his easy grin widening with something akin to relief.

"Yes, I accept," she said, smiling.

The drive out to the ranch was filled with small talk amongst the adults. Diana had plenty of time to regret her impulsiveness, as did Mike. Maybe this wasn't such a good idea, she reflected uneasily, watching the scenery whiz by. Maybe they were playing with fire, and maybe it was courting the possible loss of her next election. . . .

She closed her eyes. The thought of losing her job made her ill. She enjoyed her role as community peacekeeper. Mike seemed uptight, too.

If anyone else felt the tension, however, they didn't show it. Melanie and Jim were busy making up a grocery list for the following week. The boys were talking, too, but in such low voices Diana couldn't pick up much of what they were saying, except that it had something to do with riding horses on their free time.

Once at the ranch, Melanie and Jim went straight to the kitchen. The boys went along to assist and set the table. Diana got a personal tour of the ranch house, including the wing where Mike housed the boys and himself. All of the rooms were spacious and uniquely decorated, reflecting the personality of its occupant. Glad for the reprieve from her unsettling thoughts, Diana concentrated fully on the tour.

"Let me guess," Diana said, looking at a room that was filled with books, a small personal computer and a telescope. Charts of various galaxies adorned the walls. "This is Kevin's room."

"Right." Mike grinned at ease now that he was on his own turf. And why not, Diana thought, since he was obviously lord of the manor.

Next door, was a room filled with barbells, weights and various books and magazines on weight lifting, as well as a stack of *Mad* magazines. She had only to think of the physiques of the three boys to hazard a guess. Diana lifted a brow. "Carlos?"

"Correct again."

"Which leaves Ernie," Diana said. To her surprise, his room was filled with art supplies—an easel, stacks of art paper, bottles and jars of paints, charcoals and drawing crayons. The setup and amenities would've made any art major happy. "Ernie?" Diana asked in amazement. He had always seemed so clumsy to her.

Mike nodded proudly. "He's quite an artist. I've got a local artist driving over from Marble Falls to give him lessons once a week, starting next Wednesday. I think he might have real talent."

Glancing at a pencil sketch of the surrounding countryside, Diana could see that he did. "I'm impressed, Mike. You've made a real home here for the boys, far beyond what their funds from the state must cover." She had been prepared not to like the setup at the ranch, but as it happened, she couldn't find anything wanting.

Mike nodded, admitting, "Fortunately, I was able to get donations from various patrons. My parents have held several fund-raisers for me—the proceeds of which have helped buy the ranch and supplement the income the state provides for each child. I want the boys to be able to follow their interests. And the one sure way to keep kids out of trouble is to keep them busy."

Diana could see he had done that, and more.

The call came for dinner, and the group gathered in the dining room. To her surprise, the talk during the meal was lively and good-natured, with the boys rehashing a series of amusing pranks they had played on one another since their arrival at the ranch.

They lingered over dessert, their mood light and relaxed, like one big happy family. Diana had to admit to herself she was impressed with what Mike had been able to accomplish. And yet at the same time the cynic in her couldn't help but wonder, when it came right down to it, how long it would last.

"Can we go swimming this afternoon?" Carlos asked. To the rear of the house, visible through the open dining-room draperies, was a glittering blue swimming pool. Although it was cool inside the air-conditioned house, they could see the heat that shimmered from the concrete outside, a promise of a sweltering afternoon.

"Sure," Melanie said. "I'll be the lifeguard."

"Me, too. After this feast, I could use the exercise," Jim patted his stomach and glanced affectionately at his wife. "Honey, you've outdone yourself."

"I know," she replied, "and you're on for supper, so start planning your menu."

Jim groaned. Apparently he hated cooking, and everyone there was expected to put up with his inventive if not always edible efforts As the group exited the room, Mike began clearing away the dirty dishes, and Diana lent a hand.

For a while, they worked in happy silence, concentrating on the task of filling the dishwasher and wiping the counters. There wasn't room for the pots and pans in the dishwasher, so Mike washed those by hand while Diana dried.

They were a good team, not once getting in one another's way—until the very end, when they both turned to hang up their towels on the oven door at the same time and bumped into one another. Mike reached out to steady her, one hand lightly on her shoulder, the other at her waist. Diana's pulse skidded and quickened as he gently set her to rights.

Although he released her, Diana was sure he'd wanted to kiss her—and she wouldn't have rejected him.

Mike drove her home a little while later, after a surprisingly warm farewell from the boys. Both were quiet in the car during the ride back.

Judging from the unhappy look on his face, he felt the same sense of frustration she did. It was due to the knowledge that there was the potential for something to happen between them, but a wide chasm existed in their personal histories and viewpoints.

By the time Mike pulled up in front of her home, a tantalizing light came into his eyes. He leaned across the seat as she opened the door. "Diana. You should know...I think there's hope for you—for us—yet."

"Mike, please, I don't know," she said vaguely, and climbed out.

When she shut the door, he revved the engine before taking off as if he'd gotten in the last word after all.

BY THE FOLLOWING AFTERNOON, Diana found herself reluctantly dialing Mike's phone number, asking him to stop by the courthouse.

"Thanks for coming by, Mike," Diana began matter-of-factly as he seated himself in her chambers half an hour later.

"It sounded important on the phone." He looked worried.

Diana, too, was apprehensive. "It is," she began carefully, maintaining a businesslike attitude. She shuffled the papers on her desk and picked up the notes she'd made earlier. "I wanted to tell you what I found out about Donald Griffin. I talked to his parole officer. Apparently Donald figured he might be in trouble and reported in first thing this morning. He knows that what he did, coming by my place like that, was wrong, and he's agreed to work through regular channels to see his son. He's going to be getting counseling, and they think they have a lead on a janitorial job for him, so at least he'll be gainfully employed, if not in the style he was accustomed."

Mike's eyes narrowed and for a moment he said nothing. "How did he find out about his son being here in Libertyville?" Mike asked, his forehead furrowed with concern.

"That's the weird part." Diana sat back in her contoured leather chair. "He didn't know Kevin was here for certain and still doesn't. One of the social workers assigned to help him readjust to civilian life said something about his son being in a good home in the Texas Hill Country. Donald began visiting towns at random, asking about foster homes. Word of the foster ranch, Mike, has spread. My name, as the local J.P., came up in association with it. He put two and two together."

"Just luck," Mike said grimly.

"He's been counseled, now. He knows if he searches out his son's whereabouts again without permission, he'll be considered in violation of his parole. He'll be sent back to jail to finish out his sentence."

"And they think he's just going to leave it at that?" Mike asked irritably, unconvinced.

Diana'd had her doubts initially. Now she didn't. "Yes, they do. He's not an unreasonable man. He was just acting emotionally, and really under the circumstances I can understand what he did. If Kevin were your son or mine—" she began.

But Mike cut her off curtly, not interested in listening to excuses, no matter how reasonable. "If that were the case, Kevin would never have been neglected in the first place. But thanks." Mike stood restlessly and shoved his hands in his pockets. "I appreciate all you've done on Kevin's behalf." This, given unhappily, almost grudgingly. He was about to stomp out when Kay Reaves, Diana's secretary and court stenographer, burst through the door.

"Diana! Iris over at the diner just called. She said there's trouble with those three boys and you better come quick!"

"Hold it, hold it!" Mike shouted over the din of customers and onlookers crowding the diner. "What happened?"

"I'll tell you what happened!" Iris Lansky shouted, losing her customary control. "Those kids of yours put a rubber snake in the lettuce bowl at the salad bar!"

At a table nearby, Agnes McCarthy was still fanning herself weakly. "I'm the one who found it."

"And she almost had a heart attack when she did!" Iris continued, irate.

One of the boys snickered, and Mike turned around to glare at him. Carlos lifted his hands. "Hey, the way she looked when she lifted that snake with the tongs, the lettuce dripping off of it..."

Agnes stood, her strength suddenly regained. She looked as if she was about to grab Carlos by the ears.

Mike stepped between them, his attitude stern but protective. "Did you boys do that?"

"No!"

The denial seemed sincere, Diana thought, but surface emotions could be deceiving.

"Well, if they didn't do it I'd like to know who did!" Iris said, incensed at the disruption of her business.

Diana turned to Mike, holding her ground despite his furious glare. "She has a point. Everyone else here's an adult."

An uncomfortable silence followed. One thing was certain: everyone in the restaurant was sure Mike Harrigan's boys were guilty.

"If my boys said they didn't do it, they didn't do it," Mike continued gruffly. They had moved the conversation to the park across from the courthouse, where Diana had led them to escape the onlookers who'd made a rational conversation impossible. The boys were lined up on the bench. Whatever goodwill they'd exhibited toward Diana the previous day had vanished. All three looked surly and angry.

"What other explanation is there?" Diana asked, afraid that her worst fears were coming to fruition, turning her afternoon into a nightmare, from which there was no easy way out.

"I don't know. Why don't you ask the hundred and one people who were in that restaurant today?" Mike shot back angrily. "Half the town eats lunch there, and the other half eats breakfast there. Anyone, and I repeat anyone, could have played that prank, including a teen who has lived here all his or her life!''

"It happened while your boys—and no other kids— were in the restaurant," Diana said, fighting to hold on to her temper.

"Don't think that coincidence hasn't occurred to me," he shot back grimly. He closed the distance between them in seconds, regarding her with heat and passion. "Has it occurred to you that maybe someone who wants to get rid of the boys did this, knowing they would be blamed, that someone was just waiting for the opportunity to set them up?"

On the bench, the boys had stopped sulking and were looking quite pleased with Mike's defense of them.

"Oh, come on! Who'd go to that extreme!" Diana spit out, annoyed the boys seemed to be enjoying the high drama of the situation, even if they didn't enjoy getting the blame for serving as the instigators of it.

Silence fell between them as Diana and Mike squared off.

A tension headache was pounding at her temples. "I don't want this to happen again," Diana warned. In the meantime if she got proof…if she found out the boys had done this, then someone would have to pay.

Mike signaled to his boys. Taking in his serious expression on cue, they headed for the truck. "Then try to find the real culprit," he said angrily, not looking back.

Chapter Five

"Stop evading the question, Mike!" Linda Harrigan chided him late Monday morning. "I know something is wrong. I can hear it in your voice. So fess up. Tell me what's going on."

Mike lifted a bale of hay from the back of the pickup, and carried it to the farthest stall. The boys had cleaned out the barns before they left for their morning ride with the counselors. Upon their return, they would distribute the hay, see that the animals were cooled down, groomed, watered and fed.

Generally Mike went with the boys, but this morning, knowing his sister was on her way out to see him, he had stayed behind, grateful for the chance to see her.

He picked up another bale of hay. Although Mike had protected Linda constantly when they were kids, the situation had reversed itself once they were adults. She was always trying to mother Mike and his older brother, Tom. Tom was close to their parents, but for Mike, who had never really been able to talk to his parents much—they'd always been too busy with one of the other kids in the family—his sister's gentle intuitive interest was a godsend. He knew he could tell her anything, and more than that, she would understand. "The problem is, I haven't won over anyone yet."

Linda's blue eyes softened. "That must be hard for you. You've always been so popular and gregarious."

"I still am a people person, only here, because of what I'm doing, no one will give me a chance."

"Well, heaven knows being the local rebel isn't new to you."

Mike tossed her a wry glance. He always had liked doing the unthinkable. Partly for the challenge and the attention it garnered him, and partly because what people hadn't done, or were afraid to do, needed to be done. Take raising homeless boys, for instance. Few would dare to try that, and yet there was a crying need for such social services. A need Mike knew in his gut he could fill. "No, it isn't," he said dryly, tossing down one bale and striding back to get another.

"Still, it must be hard for you." Linda followed his every movement, her blue eyes filled with concern. "Are you dating anyone?"

"Nope." Mike took off his leather work glove, and wiped the sweat from his brow.

"Why not?"

He gave her a droll look. "Because the one woman I want to go out with won't give me the time of day."

"So?" Linda smiled slowly. "Change her mind."

Mike frowned, and slammed the tailgate of the pickup truck with a bang. "I only wish it were that easy." But the things that separated him and Diana weren't liable to go away. Yes, she was kind, but she still tended to put her own needs and concerns first, although he could see her softer side. She seemed to want a quiet, respectable life with all the accoutrements of comfort, and to support only winning causes, not causes that might deepen her character and really challenge her. He was attracted to Diana, but he couldn't see them ever being anything more than friends. Not unless she changed her outlook, became more of a humanitarian, a supporter of the underdog, the way he was.

They walked back to the house together. "I guess you're not going to tell me who this mystery woman is," Linda said finally.

Mike slanted her an amused glance, aware she was fishing, yet not minding her probes at all. "You guessed right."

She scowled and sighed. "I guess I'll just have to find out."

That stopped him. Mike grabbed her arm and sent her a warning glance. "Don't you dare." Each word was enunciated through gritted teeth.

"Still like to keep your private life private, I see," she teased.

"Yep."

Linda followed him into the house via the back door, and watched him take a pitcher of Gatorade out of the refrigerator. "What about that justice of the peace?" she said, continuing her genial inquisition. She frowned, trying to figure out what was troubling him. "Diana something, wasn't it? Is she still giving you grief?"

Yes, Mike thought, *but not in the way you're imagining, Linda.* More like she was haunting his dreams.

His mood had soured, and his tone got a little gruffer. "It's Diana Tomlinson." Linda's eyebrows rose, and he softened his voice with effort. "And she's okay, although a little narrow-minded where the boys are concerned." Briefly, Mike went on to explain some of the recent events: the snake-in-the-salad episode, and later a break-in and theft at a local gas station. No one had accused his boys directly of the robbery, but Mike knew they were the chief suspects.

Linda was silent, taking it all in. "But this Diana is a leader, right? And if she changed her mind about you and the boys, the townspeople would follow her lead, wouldn't they?"

Mike thought so, too. "I'm working on that," he said wearily, not enthused about his prospects for success.

"How hard?" Linda grinned, her blue eyes glimmering with teasing lights.

He lifted a brow in her direction. "I'm not going to court her for underhand purposes."

She held up both hands in exaggerated self-defense. "Hey, I didn't say that!"

"No, but you were thinking it!"

Linda grinned and shook her head. "Not true, brother. Although the idea does have merit," she said slowly, "if you were to go after her in a completely commendable way. You know—try and become friends or something."

Exactly what Mike had thought initially. Now he wasn't so sure. He'd started wanting more from Diana than simple friendship. He wanted her approval. Her interest. He wanted her in ways that went far beyond simple camaraderie.

Lightening his mood, he chucked his sister on her dimpled chin. "I want to get cleaned up and then we'll go into town and have lunch," he said. "Besides I want to hear all about your classes at UT, and how you're adjusting to college life after all these years in the work force...."

THAT SAME AFTERNOON, Diana found herself unable to concentrate. Deciding to take a break, she crossed the street to the Country Kitchen.

It was midafternoon, and the restaurant was empty save for Myrtle Sims and Iris Lansky. Setting Diana's iced tea and fruit salad in front her, Iris grinned. "Harrigan and his sister had lunch in here today. Attractive. You know, a live-wire type."

Diana chuckled. "Like her brother."

"Even more so," Iris said with admiration.

After a moment Myrtle said, "Diana, we've been talking. Maybe we haven't given Harrigan a fair chance."

She and Hal always had been a soft touch, Diana thought.

"Well, I think we've been more than generous," Iris said as she cleaned the grill. She scrubbed a little more vigorously. "If Harrigan feels unwelcome, maybe he should take the hint and leave, or at least give up his idea of running a foster home."

Myrtle frowned. "That's not a very neighborly attitude, Iris. Libertyville's always been such a friendly place! Looking at how we've treated Mr. Harrigan, it makes me ashamed."

Diana, too, felt a pang of guilt. She pushed it away defiantly. "We have to protect ourselves first."

"Well," Myrtle said with a sigh as she prepared to head back to the hardware store, "I'd say we've done that. And now maybe it's time to go forward and treat Mike Harrigan the way he would've been treated if he'd moved into the area without the foster kids...."

Over the course of the next few days, Diana vacillated, unable to decide what to do. Her conscience was bothering her. She knew Myrtle had a point. However, she didn't actually make up her mind until the following Saturday when she joined the group working together on a Neighbors project, tackling the interior of a house on Ivy Street. Watching Mike interact with the others, she could see he was a people person, gregarious to the core. Unfortunately, thus far in Libertyville, except for his work on the Neighbors project, he'd had little opportunity to socialize with his peers. She knew, as one of the town leaders, she could easily help that to change if only she was brave enough to set an example.

Taking a deep breath, she pulled him aside on one of the breaks and invited him to have dinner with her—as a friend. But to her surprise he wasn't at all gracious about receiving the invitation.

When she pointed this out to him, he said, "Why? You're one of the people ready to believe anything about my boys whenever something goes wrong in this town."

"Look, Harrigan." Lightly grabbing his arm, she turned him around. "I'm trying to be civil to you."

"I noticed," he said dryly, his eyes scanning her face and remaining confused about what he saw. He didn't want her doing anything out of guilt. He didn't want her doing anything that was less than one hundred percent honest. If she really wanted to be with him, fine. If not, he'd rather they didn't pretend.

Diana realized she was still holding on to his arm as her fingers warmed to the skin beneath. Startled, she dropped her hand, then wiped the tingling appendage on her jeans.

Mike was silent, watching her, taking it all in. And she knew at that moment there was absolutely nothing he didn't see about her. Maybe that wasn't all bad, though: maybe she needed to stop regarding his intuitiveness as a threat. After all, everyone needed to be understood.

She saw him begin to give a little, and her voice gentled. "I'm trying to hold out the olive branch," she said softly.

"All right," he said after a moment, holding out his hand. "Since you put it that way, I accept." He shook her hand firmly and gave her a crooked smile, letting her know he was willing to let bygones be bygones. Slowly, he released her hand. "Just name the time and place."

"Not the Country Kitchen!" The last thing she wanted was Iris's reading of the invitation.

"No," he agreed.

"Hmm." She considered all the options thoughtfully, glad to see he was open to just about anything. "Want to drive into Marble Falls? Or there are some other places, around Lake LBJ...."

"Something unpretentious would be fine." Now that he'd had time to consider the idea, he warmed to it immensely. "I'll pick you up at eight?"

How like him, she thought, to want to have the upper hand. "I can drive."

"I'd rather drive, if you don't mind."

She supposed this once she could live with that, but the next time she'd insist. "All right," she said slowly, "eight it is."

UNFORTUNATELY HER WORK ran late that afternoon, and Diana didn't have a lot of time to be ready for eight.

Weary from her day but excited about the prospect of getting to know Mike better, she jumped into the shower and washed her hair, then soaked in the tub for fifteen minutes to luxuriate in a perfumed bubble bath. By seven forty-five she was a bundle of nerves, and looking more gorgeous than she ever had before in a sleek black dress. By eight, she was dancing around the living room impatiently, looking out the curtains every five seconds. Eight-fifteen found her edgy. Nine found her madder than a wet hen. It slowly dawned on her that she'd been stood up. Was he paying her back? she wondered, then immediately discarded the thought. Mike wouldn't do that. If he hadn't wanted to go out with her, as a friend, he would've said so.

He'll call, she thought, sure there was some reasonable explanation. Either that or he's just running late.

But he didn't call. Not at nine-thirty, nor at ten. When, at ten-thirty, she finally gave up trying to appear casual and tried to phone him to find out what had happened, his line was busy.

And it stayed busy for the next hour. Worried that something might have happened to him, she called the police dispatcher and the closest hospitals. Nothing out of the ordinary had been reported; in fact they hadn't had any calls that night in the area.

Diana was by turns worried and angry. Mike should have called with either an explanation or an apology. His insensitivity where her feelings were concerned was just too reminiscent of her past. A past Diana would sell her soul to forget.

Around midnight, she fixed herself a can of vegetable-beef soup, a plate of cheese and crackers, and settled down to watch the late-night movie. When that failed to take her mind off Mike, she tried reading a few pages of a thriller she'd bought on her last shopping trip called *Crossbones and Terror*—to no avail, despite the exciting nature of the prose.

Too much reminded her of the past—getting excited about some promise, then being let down. First her father had been the source of disappointment then her ex-husband. She'd told herself when her marriage had ended that she would never let herself be taken for granted again. But she had. Well, she didn't have to concede to a similar situation again.

She'd simply never again consider going out with Mike Harrigan.

Her decision made, Diana turned on her answering machine. When the phone rang at two in the morning, she was a room away.

The doorbell sounded twenty minutes later. Diana ignored it. It rang again. And again. And again.

Throwing on her silk robe, she stomped to the door and flung it open. Mike didn't wait for an invitation. He stormed in, brushing past her, not stopping until he was standing in the center of her living room. "Diana, I knew you were in and I had to talk to you!"

Diana shut the door behind her, hoping no neighbors were awake or had seen him arriving at her house in the middle of the night. When she spoke her voice was gritty and unpleasant. "What about?"

"You're mad," he said, taking in her flushed face, angry eyes, and something more....

"No. I'm disappointed."

He blinked, incredulous. "You think I stood you up and that it was on purpose?"

"It doesn't matter," Diana whispered, feeling unutterably weary. She was tired of Mike Harrigan, tired of being hurt. The whole point was he only cared about his boys, and Diana was too emotionally injured to put up with a situation that repeated her past. "Look, Mike, I'm tired. I want to call it a day."

"Let me get this straight." He glared at her, refusing to leave. "You think I intentionally stood you up, because I have a habit of standing up women!"

She just stared at him, trying to draw air into her lungs.

Mike's face changed, his expression subtly changing—to what? Probably guilt, since her unspoken comments were no doubt on target. Suddenly she looked at him closely, inhaling the spicy scent of his after-shave, saw how closely he had shaved. He was dressed for a date. As if he'd intended to be there all along. Had she made a mistake, not giving him a chance to explain?

She didn't move, waiting for him to take the first move. Slowly he stepped toward her and pulled her into his arms.

She gave in to the warm feeling of her softness against his strength, the depth of her own need to be held, to be loved, to be touched, heart and soul. "Mike..." Suddenly her voice, her whole being, was trembling.

"This is my fault, I know," he said in the same velvety voice he'd been using since he arrived in the dead of night. His head slanted, his mouth moving directly over hers, so close that their breaths meshed, their scents mingled. He was no longer willing to let her back away. "For not showing you sooner, how things could be between us. For not insisting..."

She had wanted warmth, passion, and she got it. He didn't hold anything back, kissing her until she was dizzy and helpless, floating on a cloud of sweet sensation, the hot pressure of his tongue making her tremble. She yielded to him briefly, returning the delicious caress, sinking into the madness. She hated the fact that he knew she wasn't always as cool and contained as she pretended to be. Hated the fact that he could make her feel so much. So soon. And yet she savored the way he held her close, enveloping her in his warm scent.

Feeling stunned and off balance by the wealth of feelings he'd engendered, by her pliancy, not trusting herself to halt if the embrace continued, she gathered her strength and shoved away from him, her breasts heaving. Needing some equilibrium himself, he grinned at her; then wordlessly slid a gentle hand under her chin, lifted her mouth to his, and went in for the second round. He pressed his lips against hers, gently now, persuasively, until he felt her whole body soften.

She'd never felt anything more potent, should never have aspired to anything more wonderful than this moment. Suddenly it was more than she could take. Her heart pounding, she gently pushed away firmly this time. "No, Mike. Not now. I just...just can't."

His blue eyes glittered darkly, for a moment showing the tenderness he was capable of, the untapped reservoir of feeling deep inside him. He wanted her, yes; but he wasn't immune to the problems or the differences between them. "Damn us both," he muttered, and then turned on his heel and stalked out the door.

"HI, DIANA," Melanie said from across the aisle in the supermarket late Sunday afternoon. "You know I was going to invite you out for dinner again, after church today."

But Diana hadn't been there. "I went to the early service this morning." So she wouldn't have to see Harrigan and crew.

Melanie rolled her cart closer. "Is everything okay with you?" she asked in a low confidence-inspiring tone. "Mike was awfully upset last night."

It was all Diana could do to keep herself from flushing guiltily. "I know." Despite her trembling nerves, she managed to keep her voice calm.

Melanie gave her a closer look. "Even more so when he came back from your place."

Diana knew that, too. Not wanting to talk about it, though, she looked pointedly down at the shopping list in her hand and made no comment.

Melanie refused to give up. "Mike had a good reason for missing that date last night, Diana," she continued patiently.

For a moment hope soared in her heart. Then she recalled all the times she had been let down. "Really," Diana muttered skeptically, beneath her breath. "Well, he didn't say anything to me."

"Did you give him a chance?"

Diana's head lifted. Actually she hadn't. But then he hadn't tried very hard, either. No, all he'd had on his mind by the time he'd arrived was first battling it out, then holding her in his arms; both behaviors of which he'd been very good at. Too good for her own peace of mind.

Melanie made a face and said nothing. Finally Diana's curiosity got the better of her. "What happened?" she asked.

Melanie bit into her lower lip, for the first time looking uncertain. "Maybe it's not up to me to say. Mike's private life is his own."

So Diana had learned. She sighed and shoved her cart forward. This just proved that she and Mike were a bad match, regardless of the way she felt when he kissed her—which was terrific. Mad, vulnerable, but terrific. "Thanks a lot." Thanks for nothing. She paused in front of the dairy case and added a small carton of low-fat milk and large container of cottage cheese to her cart.

Melanie followed her, reaching for a carton of nacho cheese to add to her already overflowing cart. "I'm not trying to hassle you, Diana. I just think you ought to talk to Mike. Really. He...he had his hands full last night and, well, we all did." Knowing she'd finally caught Diana's full attention, Melanie said, "Aside from that, I really can't say anything else. You understand. As you know, it's his ranch. It's his life, and it's up to him what he wants you to know, but I really think if you'd give him just half a chance he'd more than explain everything to your satisfaction."

Chapter Six

There was absolutely no reason she should give Mike Harrigan another chance, Diana decided as she pulled her car into the driveway of her house. Slamming the car door, she walked around to unlock the trunk and pull out the two sacks of groceries, which would do her for another week. She'd let herself rely on him, begun to count on seeing him again, and what had happened? He'd let her down so badly she hadn't slept a wink all night! He'd been on her mind all during church, all during her shopping, and now it looked as if he was going to ruin what little was left of the weekend!

But try as she might, Diana couldn't get the handsome renegade off her mind, and by six-thirty that evening she knew it was either give Harrigan one last chance to explain and save his skin where she was concerned, or end up obsessive about him, during what remained of the weekend and beyond.

So, she got back into her car and drove out to his ranch, figuring an impromptu meeting would serve her purposes better. She didn't want him having too much time to think up great excuses before she got there, or to work up his anger again. And besides, with the boys as an audience, he was bound to be on his best behavior.

There'd be no grabbing her and kissing her senseless again!

She arrived just as the boys were finishing up their evening chores outdoors. Seeing her, Mike strode over to her car while the boys, casting curious glances her way, headed indoors after Mike instructed them to go wash up.

"Never thought I'd see you again," he said. His expression was inscrutable.

She had known he wouldn't make it easy on her, after the way she'd vented her temper the night before, but somehow Diana had hoped he wouldn't go out of his way to be difficult, either. It appeared, as she got out of her car, shutting the door behind her, that her wish would not be granted. "Well, I'm here," she responded with weary curtness. Melanie had better not have sent her all the way out there for nothing, she vowed silently.

Wordlessly, he stared her down. Then, apparently coming to some decision, he took her arm and led her toward the corral, well out of earshot of the house. Prying eyes could see them, but no one would be able to hear a word they said. Fine with Diana. Privacy was something she relished, too.

Suddenly nervous, Diana turned to the corral and watched the movement of the horses. The scenery was quite peaceful, not exactly mirroring the look on Mike's face at the moment. His expression troubled, he began harshly, "Look, if you're looking for an apology for last night—"

"For kissing me or standing me up?" Diana interrupted, not about to let him have the upper hand after she'd taken the initiative and gone out there to see him. She ought to get something for her trouble.

His mouth compressed into a thin white line. "I already apologized for one, and as for the other..." Slanting her a sidelong glance, he rested one booted foot on the bottom rung of the corral fence. "Well, it'll be a cold day in you-know-what before I take back all that!"

Strangely enough, that was a relief to her. She didn't want him "taking back" his kisses. Deciding they'd sparred more than enough already, Diana got straight to the point. "I saw Melanie earlier, at the supermarket. She hinted there was a good reason for what happened last night, but she wouldn't tell me what it was."

His dark brows lifted sardonically. He gave her a smile that didn't reach his eyes. "Willing to listen to me now, are you?"

She hated his sarcasm almost as much as she'd hated his behavior the night before. "I may not be if you keep it up," she warned darkly.

Silence.

He sighed deeply, the fight leaving him as abruptly as it had come. He stared out at the horses, his tone gentling, "What Melanie said was true. There was a good reason for my missing our date."

Some of his calmness transmitted to her. "Then I'd like to hear it."

He pivoted to face her, a new tension in the lines of his face. "Kevin ran away."

"What?" She stared at him in rigid disbelief.

"You heard me," Mike repeated gruffly, the anguish he'd felt now showing in his face. "He ran away right after I got home. It took me until almost midnight to find him, and when I did, well, suffice it to say I needed to talk to him, to show him that I'll be here when he needs me."

Diana took a moment to absorb what he'd said. When she had, she found her mood had calmed. "Why didn't you tell me that last night?" she asked quietly, a little embarrassed now that she'd heard the truth. If only he'd called her right away, when she hadn't given up on him, then maybe this misunderstanding could've been avoided.

It hurt to be neglected. And she couldn't help but wonder if that was a sign of trouble to come, if she let herself get any more deeply involved with him.

"I guess I should've had someone call, and I apologize," Mike said. "Things were happening so fast."

Guiltily Diana realized he was right about having to waste no time tracking Kevin down. Knowing further recriminations would serve them no purpose at that point, except to get them arguing again, she pushed for more details. As J.P., she needed to know certain facts. "Did Kevin tell you why he ran off?"

"No." Mike scowled in frustration.

"He's been silent lately. He's such an introspective kid, I didn't think much about it. It wasn't until I was getting ready for our date last night that Carlos sounded the alarm that Kevin was missing. The boys had been out feeding the horses and he just disappeared. The other two didn't see where he'd gone, but you know how much acreage the ranch is on." He lifted a hand at the unfolding countryside. "He could've been hiding anywhere."

For a moment, Diana suffered along with him, realizing the trauma he'd been through. "Why didn't you call the police?" Diana asked. "Also if you'd phoned me, I could've helped."

For a moment his eyes narrowed. "Because I figured to do so would be to admit failure where Kevin was concerned. I don't want the state taking him away from me. And to tell you the truth, with you being the justice of the peace, I felt it might place you in an awkward position professionally. So, I just let it pass."

He had been thinking of her, after all! Diana thought, overjoyed. "But you're telling me now," she said slowly, wondering exactly what he felt had changed. Was it because he had kissed her and she had responded? Or simply because he'd had more time to consider?

"I'm telling you now because the situation has been resolved satisfactorily, and I trust you not to use it against me." He was silent a moment, glancing over her face almost penitently, before finishing steadfastly, "I also want you to know the truth."

Diana nodded, glad Mike had confided in her. On a professional level, though, she almost wished she didn't know about Kevin's attempt to run away. It reminded her of her duties. "Where was Kevin when you found him?" she asked.

The grim lines around Mike's eyes tightened at the shortness of her tone. "He was still on my property, in a grove of trees near the stream beyond that next hill. I found him around midnight, just sitting out there."

"And?"

Mike shrugged, expelling a long breath. "As usual, he wasn't very communicative. I didn't know whether to be furious with him or just relieved. In any case, he wouldn't talk to me." Mike's disappointment was evident in his voice.

"He must've given you some explanation," Diana protested.

"He just said he had needed to get away, to think."

"And that was it?" Diana asked incredulously. Whatever Kevin's problems were, it wasn't like him to be deliberately hurtful, or try to cause someone undue worry— at least not from what she'd seen of him. He was sullen and moody a lot, but never hurtful—without provocation. Of course, he did have a temper—quite a temper, as she'd seen in her courtroom.

Mike nodded. "Anyway, it was right after I talked to him that I tried to call you. And got your machine."

"Sorry."

"So am I for not getting in touch with you sooner, and you're right, there is no excuse for me leaving you hanging that way, but it was just unavoidable."

"I understand, sort of."

He studied her, picking up on all she wasn't saying but was still feeling—the hurt, the exclusion.

"Next time I'll know better," he said, genuinely apologetic. He needed to know that she was feeling okay about the incident; he understood her reaction, empathized. But he also wanted to know that she empathized with his position; that she was the kind of woman who could understand his concern for his boys, his sense of responsibility.

"Forgive me?" he said.

After a moment, Diana smiled. "If you forgive me for refusing to answer your call last night."

He smiled, thought he saw some understanding. At least they would have to leave it on this note—a temporary truce. If she could make the effort to understand his stance—even when it meant she had to sacrifice—just a little, he wouldn't complain, or push.

"Well, it's all over now." Aware she'd been there talking with him for at least half an hour, and that the others were probably also aware of that, she lifted her free arm and glanced at her watch. She really should go, even if she didn't want to.

As if on cue, Carlos trod out onto the porch, waving his arms. "Hey, Mike! We got the VCR all set up."

Mike looked at Diana, her expression affable, if a bit remote. "Want to stay awhile?" he asked casually. "I rented a couple of tapes for the boys earlier today. One's a sci-fi film, the other's a comedy. We're going to make some popcorn and nachos and just generally pig out."

"Sounds like fun." She paused, knowing even before she spoke that she'd decided to take that ultimate leap of faith and get even more involved with him—even if she was just going to be his friend. "You're sure I wouldn't be intruding?" He had suffered a crisis with one of his kids last night, after all.

"Positive." He put a relaxed arm around her shoulders and turned her in the direction of the house. His confidence was catching. "The more the merrier."

TO MIKE'S SATISFACTION, the evening was as entertaining and fun as he could've hoped; the boys were relaxed and sociable. Diana fit in nicely—almost too nicely, judging by the faintly disturbed look on Kevin's face every time he looked over at Diana, who was seated on the sofa. Mike was sprawled at her feet, his back against the sofa base. After she left, he decided to call Kevin on it.

"About last night..." Mike began.

"I told you," Kevin said briskly, "I needed to be alone."

"But?"

For a moment, Kevin didn't say anything. When at last he did speak, his voice was discouraged, barely audible. "If you get involved with Diana, what happens to us?" he asked.

Mike wondered if Kevin resented Diana's coming to dinner the previous Sunday. Was that it? Had Kevin deliberately tried to sabotage Mike's date with her by running away?

"What do you mean?" Mike asked casually.

Kevin turned a dull shade of red. "Suppose you two hit it off and you decide you want to live with her or something...."

"First of all, I don't believe in just living together. I want commitment—"

"All right, suppose you marry her," he interrupted impatiently, needing an answer.

Mike stared at Kevin. Incredibly he was threatened by this!

"You haven't answered my question," Kevin persisted darkly. "What happens to us if you decide to marry someone?"

He deserved an honest answer. "I don't know," Mike said slowly. "I guess if I did marry—and to be perfectly frank I'm a long way from a relationship with anyone at the moment—then she'd have to come out here to live with me."

"With us," Kevin corrected. He looked at Mike as if he thought he were the most naive person ever to walk this earth. "You don't really think a wife'd go for that, do you? What kind of woman wants to be stuck with a houseful of boys?"

The self-condemning note in Kevin's voice made Mike angry; he couldn't stand it when the kids belittled themselves. "The only kind of woman I'd marry," Mike said quietly, making that plain. He regarded his foster son thoughtfully. "Is this what your running off last night was all about?"

Kevin shrugged and didn't answer. Mike knew he'd hit the nail on the head.

"Look, can I go now?" Kevin said, indicating with a sweeping gesture of his hand that the kitchen was all cleaned up. "I'm tired and I want to get some sleep before tomorrow."

"Sure," Mike said. Silently, he watched him go.

"MIKE, BRACE YOURSELF," the social worker began the next morning, over the phone.

Mike frowned. After the evening he'd had with Kevin, he didn't need more bad news. The social worker went on, "Kevin's father has requested visitation with his son. Formal approval has been given."

Mike felt as if he'd been punched in the solar plexus. He sat down behind his desk. "The officials know the whole history? That Donald Griffin just got out of jail and violated conditions of his parole trying to locate Kevin? That Donald may very well have been the person who abused Kevin?"

"Yes. They're also convinced Mr. Griffin loves his son, and they feel he should be given a second chance. With the supervision of social services, of course."

"Will the visits be here, in my presence?" Mike asked. If that was the case, he could still protect Kevin, make sure Donald caused him no harm.

"No. You know that's not how it works, Mike. Donald will get Kevin for a day. During that time, they can do anything they want within reason, short of leaving the state."

Which meant, Mike thought grimly, that there was no way in hell he could protect Kevin. They were asking the impossible of him and the boy! They were acting rashly, with typical bureaucratic tunnel vision. Mike was silent, trying to figure out what this would do to Kevin. "If I protested the decision..." God, how he wanted to do just that!

"I wouldn't try that, Mike," the social worker was quick to advise. "You are, after all, only providing temporary care for Kevin. You know how the department feels about foster parents who overstep their bounds and try to alienate kids from their birth families."

Mike knew. "If I did that, they'd think I was acting selfishly and remove him from my care."

"Exactly. I don't want to see that happen. So I'm advising you, officially, to go along."

"And privately?" Mike asked, sighing his dismay.

"Privately," the social worker responded grimly, her tone mirroring Mike's feelings, "I have my doubts about the wisdom of it. But rules are rules, and in this case, not to be broken."

"YOU WANTED to see me?" Kevin asked half an hour later, standing in the doorway to Mike's study.

Mike gestured for Kevin to come in and have a seat. He wished he didn't have to do this, but he did, so they might as well get it over with. He leaned against his desk, his arms crossed at his waist, fighting to keep his tone tranquil. "Yes, Kevin, I did. I had a call from the social worker in charge of your case. Your father wants to see you." With effort, he kept his voice calm, unemotional.

Kevin said nothing.

The hardest part of being a foster parent was knowing the kids weren't really your own, that some had parents they might one day go back to. In this particular case, Mike didn't want to acknowledge that fact, or even abide by it, even though he knew he had to. Aware Kevin was watching him with bated breath, Mike went on, as if talking about something no more devastating than the current weather outlook. "They've set up a meeting a week from Saturday."

Ten days from now would give Kevin plenty of time to adjust to the idea. It might not be enough for Mike, however. He still didn't trust the man.

Silence followed. "Was this my dad's idea, or the social worker's?" Kevin asked impatiently, moving past Mike to the bookcase, where he stood looking at titles.

"Your father's." Mike paused, reading the hesitation in Kevin's face and wondering about the emotions he was keeping under wraps. If only the boy would talk to him! "Is there some reason you don't want to see your father?"

Kevin turned to him, almost defiantly. "Why would you think that?" he demanded.

Mike kept a lid on his own worry and gestured evasively. "I don't know. You haven't kept in touch with him...."

His face blotchy with patches of red and white, Kevin shrugged. "That's just our way. We never were much good at writing letters." Mike said nothing in response. Kevin glared at him, daring him to say more.

Mike sensed he had pushed Kevin as far as possible. Like it or not, for Kevin's sake, he had to back off right now. He stood, signaling that the conversation had come to an end, just as Kevin had indicated he wanted. "Right. Well, if you have any questions, or if there's anything you want to talk to me about in the meantime, you know where to find me."

Try as he might, Mike couldn't get the boy's troubled, faintly fearful expression out of his mind. And knowing he had to do something or go crazy thinking about it, he sought out the best legal counsel in Libertyville later the same day.

"Is there anything we can do to stop the visit?" he asked Diana after he'd filled her in. He knelt next to her as she continued weeding the begonias that lined her front walk. Her flower gardens were a show piece, almost as nice as the ones in front of Agnes McCarthy's house.

She shook her head slowly. Unable to give him advice officially, she was glad to talk to him off the record, and render an educated opinion. "I don't think so, Mike. Not unless Kevin has told you his father abused him or gives us something concrete to work with." In shorts and knit top, she looked flushed and pretty, slightly disheveled. She was also very interested in what Mike had to say.

Mike exhaled slowly, venting his frustration. "Well, he hasn't done that, nor is he likely to before the visit." His mood somber, Mike watched as she capably dug out a few more weeds. Her arms and shoulders were bare, her smooth skin aglow with a light sheen of perspiration. "He's very protective of his father."

Diana paused, resting her weeder on her thigh. "Is it possible someone else abused Kevin?" she asked thoughtfully, after a moment. "Maybe a friend of the family, or..."

Mike knew that happened sometimes, but he didn't think the theory was applicable in this case. "I doubt it. From what the social worker said, Donald Griffin alienated everyone after his wife's death. Kevin was all he had. And he was all Kevin had."

Diana's expression darkened. "Maybe Kevin got the brunt of Donald's anger, and grief."

Mike nodded. "Maybe. It would make sense, in terms of family dynamics in a period of great stress. We also know that Donald had money problems. Big ones. Which is reputedly why he embezzled from his company." In any case, Mike thought, Donald wasn't a candidate for Father of the Year. And maybe Mike was being possessive, but he couldn't help but think Donald didn't need to be anywhere near his son. The idea seemed to trouble Diana, too, and Mike couldn't help but feel a twinge of satisfaction. It was nice to know they agreed on this, and that she was at heart a kind and caring person no matter how professionally removed she tried to be.

Mike continued watching her, hoping against hope she'd be able to save them all by coming up with some sort of legal miracle.

Her demeanor subdued but thoughtful, Diana went back to efficiently rooting out weeds, picking up the green stalks with her gloved hand and placing them in a paper bag next to her. Finally, she shook her head sadly, still perplexed but resigned to what was about to happen. She sat back on her heels and looked up at him. "I wish there was more I could do, Mike, but unless you can get Kevin to talk to you or give us something concrete, our hands are tied. Like it or not, we have no legal grounds to prevent his father's visit.''

She'd said "we," not "you," Mike noticed. It pleased him to know she was beginning to consider herself a guardian angel, however distant, to his foster kids. Which went with his theory that most people, no matter how hard-hearted they viewed themselves, were not immune to getting involved in someone else's difficult plight.

"What about the fact that he's been in jail?" he said, returning his attention to their present dilemma.

Diana scowled. "I don't like it, either, but that's irrelevant." She shrugged and continued matter-of-factly, "As far as society is concerned Kevin's father has paid his dues by serving time in jail and liquidating his assets to pay back the money he stole from the brokerage firm." Finished with her chore, she stood up. "He's made restitution, Mike. We may not like it or trust him, but we have to accept it. As does Kevin." Mike sighed, wondering if maybe he was becoming too emotionally involved, losing his objectivity where Kevin was concerned.

Impulsively Diana took Mike's hand in hers and squeezed it gently. He found himself responding to her warmth, the softness of her hand, the commiseration he saw in her eyes.

"I don't know what else to tell you." Regret was etched on her face. "Just try and take it one day at a time, okay?"

"Okay," Mike said. But he had a feeling it was going to be easier said than done. And again, he found himself reluctant to leave, even though he knew her ability to help him—legally, anyway—had come to an end.

Silence fell between them once more. The moment drew out. He realized how nice it was to have someone to share his problems with.

"Thanks for being here for me," he said softly after a moment. He wanted her to know how much he appreciated her patience. "I really needed someone to talk to tonight." A woman who cared about him. . . .

Certainly he knew that Diana didn't approve of everything about him, his life-style. And that bothered him at times because he needed a woman who could and would support him every step of the way. But he also knew they had a lot in common, and the more he knew about her, the more he liked. He wanted to know more.

Diana nodded, graciously accepting his compliment as she retained her pressure on his hand, letting him know by her touch alone that she was his friend. "I only wish, Mike," she said softly, "that I could do more."

"HI. I WOKE YOU, didn't I?"

Diana blinked and glanced at the clock. Eight o'clock. Her first Saturday to sleep in, in two weeks, blown by the ringing of the phone. And yet, because the caller was Mike, she didn't mind.

"I'm sorry," Mike's gravelly voice rumbled over the wire.

"That's okay." She pulled the phone base into bed with her and sat up against the pillows. "Is everything okay?" She really hoped nothing was wrong, that no other gas stations had been robbed, or snakes put in salad bowls. She felt as if she'd handled enough crises this summer already. She just wanted peace. More time to get to know Mike. More time to be with him.

He was quick to reassure her. "No, everything's fine. I was just wondering, since there's no Neighbors project going on this weekend, if you were free."

Now this was a surprise—a pleasant one. "Well, yes," she said, fairly beaming.

"Great. I'm taking the boys to the county fair this afternoon. I thought you might like to come along."

A group outing. Not the one-on-one she'd had in mind. As Diana contemplated the invitation, she lifted her heavy mane of her hair off her shoulders, her mind speeding on ahead, her emotions in turmoil. "With all of you?"

She didn't mind spending time with Mike. In fact, she rather enjoyed it. But taking on that whole crew of his at one time, especially in so chaotic an atmosphere, was another matter indeed. She didn't know if she was quite up to that.

"Sure," Mike said persuasively. "It'll be fun."

Fun—well, maybe. An adventure, a trying adventure—certainly. "Are Melanie and Jim going, too?" She smothered a yawn, a little in awe of how easily he took all this on, as if it was the most natural thing in the world. Maybe for him it was.

"No, they're away—they've got the weekend off," he responded cheerfully. "It'll be just me and the boys."

Diana was about to beg off, and ask if they would do something together—alone—another time. But then she realized the dynamics of what he was proposing, and she viewed the outing from another perspective—that of Libertyville's justice of the peace. Whether he realized it or not, Mike needed help managing those boys at the fair. Like it or not, she would have to go—if for no other reason than to help insure the boys stayed out of trouble. "That sounds fine," she said finally.

He paused at the lack of enthusiasm in her voice. "What's wrong?"

"Nothing." It just wasn't exactly her idea of a date, but then maybe it wasn't meant to be.

"The kids won't give us any problems," he said softly, reading her mind. "You'll see. It'll be fun. And I want you to get to know them better."

Diana wasn't sure she wanted to get to know them better, but she also knew it was probably a sacrifice she'd have to make if she wanted to become better friends with

Mike. And she did want that. Pushing her reservations from her mind, she agreed to meet him out at the ranch.

When she pulled into the drive, some time later, he was standing at the window, waiting. Her eyes held his briefly and he smiled. Despite her decision to play it cool, her heart sped up a little as she got out of the car and started up the walk.

"You look gorgeous," he said, greeting her with a light kiss on her brow. Diana's pulse sped up a little more. She caught a whiff of his after-shave. It was rich and mossy, unutterably masculine, different from the scent he usually wore. New, maybe?

"You guys ready to go to the fair?" Mike called over his shoulder, to the rear of the house, his hand resting lightly but possessively on her spine.

No sooner had he spoken than the three boys appeared in the hallway. All were dressed in clean and pressed shorts and shirts, their appearances immaculate. Looking at them, Mike beamed with pride, and for just a second, Diana thought she knew how he must feel. When the boys had first arrived, they'd been something of a ragtag group. Although they'd managed to maintain their individuality in the way they dressed and wore their hair, the boys were beginning to blend as a unit more. It showed in their body language, the relaxed easy way they moved when they were together in a group. These were people who cared about each other, she thought. Theirs was a solid family unit—and one she admired.

The drive to the county fair was accomplished swiftly. Once there, Mike went over the ground rules in a firm but protective way Diana both liked and respected. "We stay together," Mike began, making eye contact with each boy. "I don't want anyone running off. I'll give you each ten dollars to spend on tickets. How you use them—to go on the rides or play carnival games—is up to you."

While Mike and Diana watched, the boys went on several rides, then tested their skills in dart throwing and ring tossing. Although they had some limited success, no one could manage to toss all three rings over the bottle. To Diana's amusement, Mike decided he'd been a spectator long enough. "Let me show you guys how an expert wins a game," he said, jokingly elbowing them aside.

The boys guffawed and groaned, but agreed to watch. "I hope you are good at this," Diana said, laughing, "because if you're not you'll never live this down."

"She's right about that!" Ernie said, his mood ebullient.

To their mutual surprise, Mike managed not only to get the ring around the bottle every time, but win a stuffed animal. He looked at Diana magnanimously. "Your choice."

She decided on a teddy bear. "Ah, isn't that sweet." Carlos grinned. He looked at some of the attractive teenage girls at the next booth, then back at Mike speculatively. "I don't suppose you could do that again, could you?"

"And give you the stuffed animal?" Mike guessed.

Carlos assumed an expression that was all innocence. "Hey, I'd let you use my tickets."

"Forget it, bud. You want to impress a girl, you gotta do it on your own."

Carlos groaned and poked Ernie in the side with his elbow. "Come on, we might as well get something to eat. Can't exactly pick up any girls with Mom and Dad trailing along." Carlos turned to Kevin, including him, too. "What do you want to eat?"

Later, Diana wasn't quite sure how it happened. One minute they were all seated at a picnic table under an awning, eating chili-cheese dogs and French fries, discussing how to spend the rest of the evening, and the next minute Carlos was missing. Mike looked around, frowning, "He can't have gone far. Darn him."

He hadn't, as it turned out, but he might've wished he had. "I see him!" Diana crowed, standing up. "Oh, no…" Dread filled her voice as she realized why he'd run off.

"What?" Mike, Ernie and Kevin all looked in the direction of Diana's gaze. Too late, they saw Carlos flirting with Agnes McCarthy's niece, Martha. Worse, the two teenagers were within easy sight of the knick-knack booth sponsored by the Libertyville Historical Society and manned by—of all people—Agnes. "If she sees them together, she'll cause a big scene," Diana moaned.

"Then she'd better not see them," Mike declared.

Of one mind, they all took off at a fast clip. Diana headed straight for Agnes, the men heading for Carlos and Agnes' niece. "Hi, Agnes!" Diana skirted a group of rowdy, unchaperoned children and came to a stop in front of her.

"Hello, Diana." Agnes gave her a warmer than usual smile.

"How's business?" Diana asked, doing her best to appear chipper.

Agnes frowned and leaned forward conspiratorially. "Not so good actually. And for the life of me, I can't understand why. I mean look at all these beautiful china plates we have for sale—all decorated with Texas wildflowers."

Diana saw what the problem was right away. The plates were priced too high. At thirty-nine dollars each, few fairgoers could afford them.

"What's the money for?" a childish voice piped up.

The group of unchaperoned children was back. Grubby and dirty, they pushed and shoved around Diana, each jostling the other to get a better view of the plates. "Hey, stop pushing!" one shouted, giving yet another mean-spirited shove.

"Children, please!" Agnes cried, just as one of her plates went sailing over the heads of the children like a frisbee. Agnes and Diana gasped, both reaching in vain for the flying plate.

It sailed on past. A quick-thinking Kevin reached out and caught it. Meanwhile, the unchaperoned children vanished amid squeals of excitement. Kevin walked forward to hand the plate to Agnes. Mike, Ernie and Carlos weren't far behind, and Diana was relieved to see that Martha wasn't among them.

"Why, thank you, young man," Agnes said with difficulty. She picked up a tea towel and began polishing the plate.

"You're welcome," Kevin said quietly, without dropping his gaze. He knew precisely what Agnes thought of them; he resented her opinion.

Carlos surprised them all by striking up a conversation with Agnes. "Do you have anything cheaper for sale? Like a cup or something? I'd like to buy one, but I've only got about five dollars."

"No. We don't," Agnes said stiffly.

Beside her, Myrtle Sims said, "You know, that's not a bad idea, Agnes. Maybe we should lower our prices on our keepsakes...."

"You should have some cups with paintings of the Hill Country on them, too," Ernie said to Myrtle.

Agnes peered at Ernie resentfully. "Well, that's a wonderful idea, young man. As it happens we've already thought of it. Unfortunately, we have no money to finance a project of that magnitude."

"What's to finance?" Carlos said dryly, challenging Agnes on her own turf. "Just buy some cups. They don't have to be real china. And let Ernie do the painting."

"He's good," Myrtle said, before a red-faced Agnes could interrupt. "I've seen his stuff. And the boys are on to something, although I think you should forget about the cups and just sell Ernie's paintings of the Libertyville countryside. Maybe the Historical Society could take a percentage of the profit for marketing them, if Ernie would agree, of course."

"Yeah!" Ernie looked both stunned and excited. "I'd love to help out." He cast a quick look at Mike. "That is, if you think it's okay."

"Sure." Mike shrugged. "Agnes?"

Quite a crowd had gathered. Persuasively Mike added, "That's the good thing about charity. You find yourself getting help from people from all walks of life. Helps bring them together, if you know what I mean."

Agnes was silent. Aware a crowd had gathered—a crowd that might buy their wares—she said pleasantly, with a politeness only Diana seemed to notice was forced, "Bring the paintings by. We'll have the committee vote on them." Her decision made, she moved to the back of the booth.

Mike and Diana turned away. "I don't think she's ever going to accept the boys," Diana murmured.

"Maybe she'll come around yet."

Wishful thinking, Diana thought, but not wanting to argue with Mike, she said nothing more. The boys were anxious to try some more rides. But this time Mike and Diana kept a closer watch on them, Carlos especially, who flirted with every girl he saw when standing in line. Under their gazes he didn't wander off again. Diana and Mike were exhausted when they finally started home at eleven.

"Well, guys, what'd you think?" Mike asked, as they pulled into the ranch driveway.

"Smaller than Six Flags or Sea World," Kevin said, yawning, "but okay."

"I thought it was fun!" Ernie said.

"Lots of pretty girls," Carlos murmured dreamily. "Lots of pretty girls..."

The group trooped to the front door. "Want a cup of coffee before you start home?" Mike asked Diana lazily.

She nodded. "Maybe I'd better. All that yawning Kevin has been doing has been making me sleepy."

They'd gotten no farther than the living room when Diana realized that something was wrong. At first she couldn't put her finger on exactly what it was, then she saw what had eluded her initially.

For the boys it was another matter. They sucked in their breaths simultaneously, looking at the empty spot next to the wall.

"The TV," Carlos moaned.

"The VCR," added Ernie.

"We've been robbed!"

Chapter Seven

"Calm down everybody," Mike said, taking control. He stepped slightly in front of Diana, gesturing everybody to stand back. Reaching for the phone, he picked up the receiver and dialed 911. "This is Mike Harrigan, at the Harrigan ranch outside of Libertyville. We've been robbed. Yeah. Thanks a lot."

"Maybe you all should wait outside while I check the house out," Mike said.

"No way," Diana said. She wasn't letting Mike go off alone. What if the burglar was still back there somewhere, hiding? What if he was armed? What if...?

"I'm coming with you, too," Carlos said grimly.

"We all are," the boys said in unison, though Ernie was shaking visibly. Kevin looked white as a ghost. If truth be told, Diana didn't feel much steadier.

They went first to Mike's den. His steel box of ready cash was missing. In the kitchen, the microwave was gone. All four bedrooms had also been targeted, and Kevin's computer was gone, and his telescope and all the software and games were stolen. Carlos was missing his "jam box," and a whole carton of cassette tapes. They'd even taken Ernie's paints and brushes, his supply of clean canvas, as well as every painting he'd finished.

Devastated, the group looked at one another. Diana was both furious and heartsick. Who could have done this?

Sirens blared as the sheriff's deputy came up the drive.

To the group's mutual dismay, an inspection of the house didn't uncover any clues to the robber's identity. The back door had obviously been jimmied open, but there were no fingerprints. The burglar could have been anyone. And out in the country, at night, a burglary was fairly easy to accomplish.

But there was one oddity. "This bedroom window," the deputy said, coming out of Carlos's room. "Was it unlocked when you left?"

The boys all looked at one another.

"I don't know," Carlos said. "Maybe. I didn't check it."

"Well, it doesn't matter," the deputy said, "since it doesn't appear that anyone came in or out this way. Still, you need to be more careful in the future."

"Yes, we will," Mike said. Then to Carlos, "Don't worry about it, son. Whoever did this was determined to get in one way or another—the way they butchered the back door proves that. Ten to one, the thieves didn't even realize your window was open."

Carlos nodded, but still didn't look too happy.

"Maybe you should think about having a security system installed in the house," the deputy advised.

"I'll look at some systems," Mike said grimly, "but I have a feeling the cost will be prohibitive."

"Yeah, I know what you mean," the deputy commiserated. "I'm on a budget, too. Still, there are some relatively inexpensive gadgets you can buy to make your home burglarproof. I'll leave you a pamphlet about them when I leave."

"Thanks."

Beside him, the boys stared unseeingly at the place where the television had been. "They just better not come back," Carlos threatened direly.

Kevin nodded darkly. "Or there'll be hell to pay."

But as far as Mike was concerned, that wasn't the worst of it. "Talk about timing," he muttered, when the boys had gone back to rearrange what was left of their rooms. "My folks are coming tomorrow afternoon." He turned to Diana incredulously. "Can you believe it?"

"I'M GLAD YOU COULD COME," Mike said late the following afternoon as Diana got out of her car. She handed him a home-baked apple-cranberry pie, and then picked up another from the front seat to carry in herself.

Diana smiled. "Happy to oblige." She winked, unable to resist teasing. "You know us singles. We're always panhandling for a home-cooked meal."

"Yeah." He smiled back, his glance holding hers warmly before falling to the treats she'd brought with her, his brows raised in admiration. "Speaking of home-cooking, those pies you brought look wonderful."

"Thanks."

She was glad he had invited her; it pleased her that he liked her enough to want to introduce her to his family. And maybe meeting them would give her some insights into the private side of Mike she'd found so impenetrable. He'd become much more friendly and relaxed around her, but he still wasn't telling her nearly as much about himself as she would've liked. Maybe his parents would inadvertently drop some clues. Just meeting them was liable to give her some new understanding and appreciation, she thought.

Beside her, Mike examined the chocolate-curls-and-whipped-cream topping of the pie in her hands. "Chocolate cream?" he guessed, giving her a pitiably hungry look.

"With graham-cracker crust, and it's for the boys."
She slapped his hand playfully when he tried to steal a
fingerful of whipped cream. "Watch it."

"Yes, ma'am!" Mike saluted her comically.

"Are your folks here yet?"

Mike nodded. "Out back. Dad's manning the barbecue. Mom's in the kitchen heading up operations there."

Diana noted that although he had company and a
houseful of people to feed, he didn't seem to have anything on his mind but her. "So, what are you doing?"
Supposed to be doing, she should have said.

He shrugged nonchalantly. "A little of everything,
helping out here and there." His eyes darkened seriously. "Mostly trying to avoid talk of the break-in yesterday. Any more word from the sheriff?"

Diana wished she had better news for him. "No. They
asked around, but no one saw anything unusual anywhere in the vicinity last night. Of course most people
were at the county fair, either working in a booth or just
enjoying the carnival. It's unlikely the burglars'll try to
fence or sell the goods here, so I doubt we can catch them
that way, but the Houston, Dallas and Austin police have
all been alerted. It's a good thing you had those serial
numbers engraved on your television."

Mike nodded, his visage sad but accepting. "Let's not
talk about it anymore, okay? I don't want my parents
upset."

"Sure." She was pleased he was so considerate of his
parents' feelings.

That settled, he led the way inside. A slim woman with
silvery blond hair, wearing an apron over a cotton sundress, came out to greet Diana. Although comfortable in
the rural setting, she looked pleasant and sophisticated;
and Diana was glad she had dressed up herself in a gathered skirt and white voile blouse. A look of pride on his
face, Mike made the introductions smoothly.

"Nice to meet you Diana." Mrs. Harrigan took the chocolate pie and slid it into the refrigerator. "Mike said you were bringing dessert, but he failed to mention you were a master chef."

Diana blushed. She had slaved over those pies, to make sure they turned out just right; apparently Mrs. Harrigan knew that and approved. "Thanks." She looked around industriously. "Is there anything I can do to give you a hand?" She wasn't sure why it was so important— especially at this stage of their relationship; she just knew she wanted to be accepted and liked by Mike's family. She also knew it would be easier and quicker for them to become acquainted if they were involved in some mutual activity, rather than just struggling idly to make awkward conversation.

Mrs. Harrigan smiled, relieved and, again, approving. "I just got started on the potato salad. How are you at peeling potatoes?" she asked genially, in a way that let Diana know right off where Mike had gotten most of his charm.

"As it happens, peeling potatoes is one of my specialties."

It didn't take Mike long to make his exit once Diana was settled in the kitchen, an apron on over her clothes, working alongside his mother. "How long have you known Mike?" Mrs. Harrigan asked.

To Diana, it seemed like forever. And then again, not nearly long enough. "Just six weeks, since he moved the boys out here." She made her voice casual, and so inscrutable Mike would've been pleased.

"You're not..." Mrs. Harrigan hesitated, almost afraid to speak. Composing herself, she started over, "He had some trouble with the law when he first got out here...."

So Mike hadn't told them quite everything, she thought. "That's me." Not bothering to hide her amusement, Diana met Mrs. Harrigan's startled glance. "I'm the local justice of the peace."

"Oh. My. How interesting." Mrs. Harrigan flushed slightly. "I guess I put my foot in it that time."

"Mike mentioned me?" Diana said. Obviously that was an understatement.

"Originally in less-than-glowing terms. Then we didn't hear anything else except that everything here at the ranch was fine—until we arrived today and he told me about the break-in and that he'd invited a date." The corners of her mouth turned up mischievously. "I suppose I should've made the connection, but I just didn't."

Slightly embarrassed herself, Diana glanced out the window. It figured somehow that Mike would tell his parents as little as possible. He loved them, but kept them at arm's length. Pushing aside the disturbing thought, she counseled pleasantly, "Don't worry about it." As she reassured Mrs. Harrigan, Diana glanced again out the kitchen window. Outside, Mike and his dad were standing in the shade, next to the grill, talking. It would have been a peaceful sight for a Sunday-evening barbecue if not for the three boys roughhousing in the distance.

"Oh, no!" Diana gasped, her mouth widening in alarm as Carlos charged Kevin, tackled him about the waist and threw him to the ground. Ernie started yelling immediately. Diana and Mrs. Harrigan dashed outdoors just as Mike ran over to break it up.

"All right, you guys, that's enough!" he said, insinuating himself between the two of them and forcibly pushing them apart. Mike's dad stepped in to help, pulling the still-struggling Carlos off of the equally furious Kevin. Ernie stepped back, sobbing.

"What started this?" Mike demanded, his tone surprisingly calm in the sultry summer air.

Sweat streamed down Kevin's face. A thin stream of blood was coming from the corner of his mouth. He glared at Carlos and said nothing. Carlos glared back.

"Boys, I want an answer," Mike demanded. "Now!"

They said nothing.

Frustrated and angry, Mike looked at Ernie. "What happened?"

Ernie looked fearfully at his foster brothers, then back at Mike. He decided it would be easier to have his foster brothers mad at him than Mike. "They were fighting about the VCR. Kevin said it was Carlos's fault it got stolen because it was his bedroom window that was left open."

Mike looked at Kevin incredulously, his disappointment apparent. "You know that had nothing to do with it. The back door was jimmied open."

"He still shouldn't have left his window unlocked! That was just stupid. An open invitation to get the house broken into."

"Whoever did this came out with the intention of breaking into the house. I doubt they even tried any windows."

Kevin had no answer.

"Then they took off with everything they could carry or sell," Mike continued, conjuring up the probable series of events.

"And everything that meant anything to us," Carlos said defiantly, pressing his hand gingerly to the swelling along his jaw.

"I want you two guys to shake hands and apologize to one another," Mike said.

Truculently, the two boys did as ordered. "And I don't want you worrying about the stuff you lost. I called our insurance agent this morning. We're covered. It may take a few weeks to get a check from them, but when we do, we'll replace everything."

"You can't replace my paintings," Ernie said.

Mike patted him on the shoulder. "No, but the paints we'll get right away."

"Hey, man, that's not fair. I miss my jam box, too!" Carlos said.

Mike sighed, knowing Carlos had a valid point. "All right, we'll talk about this later. I'll try to work out something that's equitable. Kevin? You listening to all of this?"

Kevin nodded, but didn't say another word.

Predictably dinner was a desultory affair. The boys were unusually quiet. Mike was clearly disappointed in their less-than-exemplary behavior, as were his parents. When the boys went off to do evening chores and tend to the horses, the Harrigans confronted Mike. "I don't like the idea of your being way out here alone with those boys," Tom, Sr., began. "What if one of them got violent?"

Mike was not alarmed. He sat back in his chair, reminding them of the back-talking hell-raiser he had been in his youth. "What if I got violent when I was growing up? Or Tom had? Or Linda!"

"It's not the same thing and you know it!" Tom, Sr., shot back irately. "You boys were our own kids." The men were silent, glowering at one another, and Tom, Sr., continued, a tad more placatingly, "Dammit, Mike, it'd be different if you had adopted these boys at birth or they'd had less . . . troubled backgrounds, but they don't and I've seen for myself how . . . surly they can be."

Diana knew Mike didn't need her help, but she found herself stepping in anyway, hurrying to give what reassurance she could. "I know how you feel, Mr. and Mrs. Harrigan. I had the same reservations. But I've been around the boys for six weeks now. This is the first time I've ever seen them go at one another that way, and I'm sure it's only because of what happened yesterday.

They're still upset about the break-in and they have every right to be. Everything that meant anything to them was taken. I think they're scared, and maybe even just a touch bored or at loose ends." At least she hoped that was all it was, and not some sort of general backsliding.

"Well, we can't have that," Tom, Sr., growled. "Mike? Got any ideas how to take their minds off the break-in? Preferably something that would work twenty-four hours a day."

"If I did, I'd have them doing it by now, Dad."

Mrs. Harrigan interjected. "You know, Mike, we've still got quite a collection of board games and mitts and bats and footballs at home in the attic. Do you think the boys would be interested if I sent the stuff up by courier tomorrow?"

Mike smiled his gratitude. "Thanks, Mom. That's a good idea. I'm sure they'd love it."

"Consider it done, then, darling."

Mike was quiet a moment, and he looked so vulnerable Diana's heart went out to him. She longed to go to him and put her hand on his arm—to do something, anything, to let him know she cared and would be there for him if he needed her, like the night he'd been there for her when she'd found a trespasser on her porch. But with his parents there, she couldn't do that, not without risking that her gesture would be interpreted as something more. And knowing how private a person Mike was, she felt a move like that on her part would annoy him more than it would soothe him, so she stayed her ground, watching quietly and knowing her hands were tied.

When at last Mike spoke again, his voice was subdued, and aching with disappointment. "Diana's right, you did see the boys at their absolute worst today. But maybe it wasn't just the break-in that was upsetting them; maybe it was also the fact they knew I wanted to impress you. They may have been testing me, to see if I accepted them through thick or thin. It's a pretty common thing with foster kids.''

"I've read about that," his mother added, still trying to help make peace between father and son.

Tom, Sr., sighed. "I still wish you were doing this on some sort of nine-to-five basis, Mike."

So did Diana. More so than ever after today.

"I know, Dad. But that wouldn't work with these kids, and I've already explained why."

Tom, Sr., didn't agree. "You always were a reckless kid," he said heavily.

Mike grinned unrepentantly. "I still am, Dad. Some things never change."

"I'M GLAD you could come over," Mike said the following evening. In knee-length surfer-style swim trunks, his short-sleeved shirt open to the waist and a towel slung around his neck, he met Diana at the door.

At six o'clock the house was blissfully silent except for the ceiling fan whirring overhead. "Did the boys get off okay?" Diana asked casually. Mike had mentioned they had plans with Melanie and Jim, who had returned from their weekend away with renewed enthusiasm and energy. And although she jumped at the chance to spend time alone with Mike, she was also nervous about it, unsure about where their relationship was heading or where she wanted it to go. This seemed more like a date than anything they had done so far, although both of them had carefully avoided referring to it as that.

His free hand touched her shoulder lightly as he reached behind her to close the door. "Yeah, they left about half an hour ago."

"They were going to Austin?" Very aware of his nearness, she followed him into the living room and on toward the back of the house.

Mike nodded. "They were going to see the new Rambo movie and grab something to eat."

"That'll be a nice treat for then." Why was her heart suddenly pounding? She had known it would be just the two of them when he had called and issued the invitation.

"Yeah. I think they needed to get out. So, how are you?" He turned, his gaze lingering on her upswept hair in a way that told her he liked the casual style. "Surviving this heat?"

Diana fanned herself dramatically. The temperature had soared to one hundred and five that afternoon. "After living my entire life in Texas you'd think I'd be used to this heat."

"No one ever gets used to it being this hot," Mike murmured consolingly.

"I just hope it doesn't stay this way the rest of the summer."

"Me, too. We could do without the usual drought."

And without any more trouble, she thought. Any more robberies or pranks.

Mike looked at her curiously, uncertain of where her thoughts had drifted. Realizing she'd anger him if she did so, she said nothing to enlighten him, instead looked at him expectantly as she waited for his lead. There was no reason for her to think about problems this evening. She had only to relax, to enjoy their time together, this oasis he was offering from worry and the sweltering summer weather.

"Ready for that swim I promised you?"

Diana nodded, following him through the kitchen to the patio out back. She would be glad for the physical activity. She hadn't realized when she accepted the invitation how nervous she'd feel later about swimming with him. Keeping her gaze averted, she kicked off her sandals as soon as she hit the deck and draped her towel on a nearby lounge chair. "All I have to do is take off my shorts and shirt—" she was energetically unbuttoning as she spoke "—and voilà!" Anxious to get in the water, Diana slipped off her shirt and stepped out of her knee-length shorts. Beneath was a one-piece suit of turquoise blue.

Mike gave her a warm, appraising glance. "You come prepared, don't you?"

He likes my swimsuit. He likes the way I look in it.

"You bet." The only thing she wasn't prepared for was the way their relationship seemed to be changing—without warning going from an easy casual friendship to something more intimate.

Suddenly the thoughts were too much for her. Diana needed just to escape. "Last one in the pool is a rotten egg!" She dashed by him and, arms stretched above her head, dived into the pool. When she surfaced in the deep end moments later, Mike was beside her, his hair a sleek dark cap around his head. "How'd you do that?" she demanded rambunctiously, pretending irritation. "I had you beat by a mile!"

He laughed and with the flat of his palm teasingly splashed water up into her face. His attention was completely on her. "I'll never tell."

Her mood playful, Diana laughed and stopped treading water and went back under the surface. Mike went with her, his movements mirroring hers.

What followed was a merry game of chase. When at last they were breathless and exhausted, they turned to a more mundane pastime. Mike got icy colas from the cooler on the deck, and they sat in Styrofoam-based floating chairs. For a while both drifted lazily, enjoying the coolness of the water and the warmth of the early-evening sun.

"This is heaven," Diana murmured after a while, swirling one foot in lazy circles. She hadn't had so much fun in ages. She hadn't felt so at peace with herself and with him. True, there were still problems, but she was beginning to hope they could work everything out if they were just patient enough.

"I know what you mean. And so quiet." Mike gave a contented sigh. "Sometimes I forget what it was like before I took the boys in."

She knew what a busy life he led and wished he could experience private time more often. "Ever miss having your own life, with all that free time? Being a single person with few responsibilities except to yourself?" Diana asked.

"Sometimes," he admitted softly, his eyes on her.

Their chairs floated together, so their arms brushed, then slid away.

Needing to change the subject and wanting to find out more about him, she asked casually, "What were you like as a kid?"

"Hardheaded, something of a hellion. I got into a lot of fights trying to prove my mettle. I won most of them, too." Mike cupped his hand and sent a playful splash in her direction, watching as the water splashed up over her knees.

"Is that why you chose to work with adolescent boys?" Diana shifted her legs and gave him a tiny splash back. She knew him well enough to know he would have ended up in some sort of work with people regardless; she was curious, though, as to how he'd narrowed in on his choice of a field.

"I guess that's part of the reason." Mike's expression sobered. "I understand what it is to constantly be asked to prove yourself, or to be disapproved of."

"It hurts you when your parents don't support you, doesn't it?" she guessed softly.

He nodded. "Yes. Probably a lot more than they realize, but then again, I know they mean well."

"What about the rest of the people in your life?" she found herself asking. "Are your friends supportive?"

Briefly Mike looked troubled. "Most of them," he said slowly, "because if they're not, they don't stay in my life."

There was something so final about that. Diana swallowed.

Mike shifted the subject back to his work and the boys. "Anyway, that's one of the reasons I bought the ranch, and moved all the way out here. I'm trying to give the kids a solid base—similar to what my parents gave me." His voice gentled reflectively. "Because I think that's the major reason I did turn out okay, that and the fact they loved me through thick or thin, regardless of the irascible way I sometimes behaved."

Just as he wanted to be loved now by the people in his life, Diana thought. By his friends, by his woman. And if she couldn't do that—stand by him through good times and bad—he would have no use for her. But how much of the bad times could she stand? she wondered. Her childhood had been tumultuous enough. As much as she liked Mike, she didn't want to go back to that unsettled way of living, with disaster of some sort waiting around every corner, never being able to completely relax, always bracing for the next catastrophe....

Unaware of the nature of her thoughts, Mike glanced at his watch, then down at the lower half of him still immersed in water, noting they'd been in the pool well over an hour. "I don't know about you, but I'm turning into a prune."

"Me, too." Relieved to be able to forgo any more swimming at that moment—she found she was no longer in the mood to play—Diana slipped off the pool chair and stood up in the waist-high water of the shallow end. She was more than ready to get out of the water.

"Want to go in and get something to eat?"

What she really would've liked at that moment was simply to run and hide somewhere so that she wouldn't have to face Mike or his questions or the complications that were whirling around, unsolved, in her head. But she couldn't do that without seeming impossibly rude, especially since he had mentioned dinner as part of the invitation to his home. So, like it or not, she had to stay. Then ... well, maybe she needed more time. Maybe she needed time to think this situation out before she got in any deeper.

Making her voice light and pleasant, she said, "Sure." Swiftly, not looking at him, Diana toweled off and wrapped the beach towel around her waist. Long and thick, it covered her from torso to ankle. Mike did the same.

"Everything okay?" he said, as they walked into the house. "You seem a little subdued."

"I'm just tired," Diana lied. "It's been a long day. The heat and all."

"Sure, I understand." Still, he wondered.

But Diana couldn't elaborate, not without giving too much of her feelings away. Instead she said nothing and kept her guard up.

A bowl of chicken salad was already in the refrigerator, and they split the chores of putting dinner on. While she set the table, he poured them glasses of iced tea and heated crusty French bread in the microwave. She rinsed the lettuce while he sliced tomatoes. Fortunately neither activity required much conversation.

Several times Mike glanced at her curiously but said nothing further about the downturn in her mood, and they ate in companionable silence, talking a little about local events, people they both knew, nothing heavy. Yet the tension was heavy between them and mounting with every second that passed.

She had to get out of there, Diana thought. She had to think. She had to decide if this was really what she wanted. Or if she was just falling into it because deep down she was lonely, because she missed having a man in her life. Or because of the chemistry between them, which seemed to feel more right every time she saw him.

"How about dessert?" Mike offered casually, as they began stacking their plates in the dishwasher. "We've got fresh peaches and vanilla ice cream...."

His voice was so soft, so gentle and sensual. He seemed willing at that moment to do anything, to be anything, to please her. The thought thrilled even as it disturbed her, because she felt herself giving way to the same sort of vulnerability, found herself beginning to need to see him. She tilted her head back, looking up into his face.

If only they could have more evenings like the one they'd just had, more time alone, she thought wistfully. But she knew wishing for that was like wishing for the moon. Because the reality was that this interlude was an exception to the rule. The reality was that Mike Harrigan didn't have time for her any more than her husband'd had time. Not really.

He had commitments, obligations that superseded his devotion to her. And she wanted more out of a romance than just an occasional date. She wanted constancy and time from the man she loved. She wanted his undivided attention—not just once or twice a week, but for at least a small amount of time every day.

She wasn't unrealistic, and she knew that might be as little as half an hour on some days, hours on others. Maybe that was selfish, but it was the way she felt. The only thing was, she wasn't sure he could give it to her. And until she was, nothing more serious than what they'd already shared was bound to exist between them. She'd been second place to her husband's work, and she didn't want to be second place to Harrigan's boys.

"No, no dessert for me," she said finally, her mind made up. "That was delicious, and thank you—for everything, but I really have to be on my way."

I SHOULDN'T HAVE LET her go, Mike thought, long minutes after Diana had left. Not like that. Part of her wanted to stay longer, he knew it. And part of her had been scared silly of what was happening between them.

She knew he was aware of that. Which was, of course, precisely why she had run. She hadn't dared to be that close to him.

Mike frowned, wondering if her skittishness had anything to do with the socially committed way he'd chosen to live his life, to the fact he would never be well-to-do, nor choose to live the good life. Somehow, it seemed more than just money keeping them apart. He wondered if she was afraid of intimacy in general, or just intimacy with him. Not the physical part of it, but the emotional side that was the most engaging. He knew what it was like to risk everything and go for broke only to have it come right back in your face. He knew what it was like to feel humiliated, rejected.

But he didn't think that was her problem.

But dammit, he just didn't know for sure. He did know he was fast becoming obsessed with Diana Tomlinson and that he would never really rest until they had resolved this tension between them one way or another.

LATER, MIKE WASN'T SURE what had awakened him—the sound of a door opening and shutting, very, very quietly, or the sound of footsteps moving stealthily across the cement.

He got up and drew on his jeans, and grabbed his shirt, shoes, and since there was no time to put in his contacts, he grabbed his glasses from the dresser. He moved barefoot through the kitchen and slipped soundlessly out the back door. At the edge of the patio, he recognized Kevin. Being careful to remain in the shadows, Mike followed him to the barn.

When he was within earshot, he stopped and slipped on his shirt. Voices floated out—first Kevin's, then a man's.

"I thought I told you not to come here!" Kevin scolded, upset.

"Settle down, son. How else was I supposed to see you? You warned me not to try and see you in town again."

Mike froze as he realized Donald Griffin was back—in violation of his parole. Dammit, he'd been right not to trust the man!

"Yeah, and for good reason," Kevin continued in an anguished tone. "We almost got caught at that painting party a few weeks ago. If someone had seen you talking to me—"

"I know, which is why I want you to go away with me—now," Donald ordered.

"I can't. You'll get in trouble," Kevin whispered back.

"Do you think I care about that? There's nothing here for us."

There was a silence in which Mike could hear his heart pounding. His foster son's decision would not only affect Kevin's life, but the future of Mike's flagship program. Mike knew he could interrupt now or let things follow to a natural conclusion. Though it was risky, he elected to do the latter. It was the only way he would ever know what was really going on in Kevin's heart.

"I thought you had a job," Kevin continued, arguing with his father. Staying in the shadows, Mike crept closer.

"Yeah, sweeping out a warehouse after hours!" Contempt echoed in Donald's tone.

"I know it's not what you want...."

Donald evaluated his son wordlessly, unhappy with what he saw. "Is Harrigan turning you against me?" he asked harshly.

Silence followed, then Kevin, reluctantly, almost defiantly, said, "He's been good to me."

Donald Harrigan hissed his displeasure. Mike found himself balling his hands into fists. If that man so much as took one step toward his son . . .

"Listen to me, Kevin. Harrigan's just a spoiled Houston rich kid who's found a new plaything. When he gets tired of you and this rinky-dink ranch, he'll abandon you, the way he has everything and everyone else in his life!"

It was all Mike could do to stand still. "Mike's not like that!" Kevin defended his foster dad fiercely, in a way that made Mike proud.

"Oh, yeah?" Donald countered with silken venom. "Don't notice anyone else around him, do you? Any wife or kids?" An unhappy silence followed. "I'm your father, Kevin. Your mother would want you with me."

Mike knew it was time. Kevin had been through enough. He'd heard enough. He stepped into the barn. "I don't think so, Mr. Griffin. I think Kevin's mother, if she were here, would want Kevin to stay right where he is—with me. At least for the time being."

Donald and Kevin turned to him in unison. Donald swore and, recognizing Mike, took off at a run. Obviously, he wasn't about to risk another one-on-one confrontation, Mike thought in contempt.

"Kevin, c'mon!" Donald yelled over his shoulder. "C'mon."

To Mike's relief, Kevin stayed where he was.

Behind them the lights in the ranch house were beginning to be flicked on. Obviously the noise had awakened the others. Knowing that arrest, or at the very least a charge of parole violation was imminent if he stayed,

Donald swore again at his son and disappeared into the night. In tense silence they watched him go.

Mike turned back to Kevin. He saw the teen's distress and his heart went out to him—being put in an impossible situation, let down so many times. It was no wonder he worked so hard not to feel anything. "Why didn't you run?" Mike asked.

Kevin's jaw thrust out. He looked at Mike angrily, as if blaming him for the latest conflict. "Because I don't want to get my dad in trouble," Kevin retorted tersely. "And if he takes me with him when he doesn't have permission from the social welfare people and the parole board, it'd be considered kidnapping. You get sent to jail for that."

Given the scars on Kevin's hands, Mike wondered if that was the only reason Kevin hadn't run off with his father.

Silence. Mike sensed Kevin's loyalty had been pushed to its limit; he wouldn't question him any more about his father, not that night. "What he said about this being a lark for me isn't true," Mike said quietly.

If anything, Kevin's jaw hardened skeptically. He still didn't trust anyone, Mike thought, disappointed, but given his father's behavior, that wasn't hard to understand. Mike inclined his head at the house. "Let's go back inside."

Kevin paused warily, clearly wanting to bargain. "Are you going to call the police?"

Mike nodded slowly, unable to cut any deals, no matter how much it cost him. Any ground he lost with Kevin over this would just have to be regained. He faced Kevin implacably. "I'm sorry. I have to."

Chapter Eight

"Sorry to wake you up like this, Justice Tomlinson," the sheriff's deputy said as Diana wrote out the warrant for Donald Griffin's arrest.

"It's all right. That's what I'm here for." Finished, Diana briefly inspected the document for errors, then handed it to the deputy. Expressing his thanks, the man headed for the door. Aware there'd be talk if he evidenced any undue familiarity between them, Mike started to follow; but Diana, needing to talk to him more than she needed to preserve her reputation, stopped him, a light hand on his arm. "Mike, would you mind staying a minute?"

The deputy shot them both a curious look.

Dropping her hand, Diana continued with as much formality as she could muster. "I'd like to talk to you about the overall situation."

"Sure." Mike backtracked, his demeanor careful, civil.

"Well, if you don't need me, I'll be going." The deputy touched a finger to the brim of his hat, gave them both another speculative glance, then was off.

"How's Kevin?" she asked the moment they were alone.

When she'd gotten the call from the ranch, informing her of trouble, she had put on a pot of coffee. Now she poured them both a cup, all too aware that it was four in the morning and she hadn't had nearly enough sleep. But sleep was impossible now. Not when she'd seen the troubled look on Mike's face. All she wanted to do was help, be there for him the way he'd been there for her.

Mike sighed and sat opposite her, in a wing-back chair that faced her sofa. His dark brown hair was tousled, his cotton shirt was rumpled, and his blue eyes were rimmed with fatigue. "He seems to be dealing with it okay."

Diana took another sip of her coffee and found it tepid. "How are the other boys?"

At the mention of his other foster sons, Mike brightened slightly. "Thankfully they're coping fine. In fact, Ernie and Carlos were both very supportive of Kevin after his father left. So were Melanie and Jim. He'll make it, Diana."

With Mike caring so much about the boy and what happened to him, she didn't doubt it. She did wonder, however, if Mike really had room in his life for anyone else. "I'm glad he has all of you."

Mike frowned, taking little comfort in that comment. Glancing at his watch, he stood and frowned thoughtfully again. "I better get a move on. I've got a rough day ahead of me."

She gave him a blank look.

Realizing he'd said nothing of his plans to her when they'd been together the day before, he said vaguely, "I have to go to Dallas later this morning. I, uh, I've got some pressing business there."

Diana noted he didn't say what kind of business. Although he was a private person, it wasn't like him to be almost secretive about his plans. It wasn't like him to avoid her eyes. The lawyer in her reacted immediately—telling her he was up to something and didn't want her to know just what. Irritation stiffened her spine. Telling herself she was being silly—what business was it of hers what he did?—she fought back the wave of annoyance and managed to keep her voice civil. "When will you be back?" She needed to know, she told herself, just in case there was any more trouble in his absence.

Mike shrugged. "I'm not sure. Maybe tomorrow, or the day after. Sooner if I'm needed."

He still didn't say what his plans were, Diana noted with frustration, and she hated being shut out, but she now knew him well enough to trust his actions.

By dinnertime the following day, there was more bad news. Diana received it first, via the bailiff. She debated whether to call the ranch or go out in person. In the end, she knew this was one task she couldn't shirk. Like it or not, she was involved with Harrigan's foster kids.

When she arrived the setting was as tranquil as ever. The aroma of simmering spaghetti sauce filled the house. Melanie ushered Diana inside.

In one corner of the living room, Ernie was sitting with Jim. He was reading backward through a mirror. "Ernie's dyslexic," Melanie whispered in Diana's ear. "That's just one of the exercises he does to improve his skills." Sweat streamed down Ernie's brow as he slowly, painstakingly, sounded out each word.

"Is it working?" Diana asked.

"Yeah," Melanie murmured back. "He's improving—slowly—day by day."

Progress, Diana thought. Was the folly of one sorely misguided man going to take all that away from them?

"So, Diana," Melanie continued cheerfully when they were alone in the kitchen. "What brings you out here?" She'd known from Diana's serious look that it was a private matter, one that needed to be handled carefully.

"I need to talk to Kevin. Is he around?"

"Yeah, he's out back with Carlos. They're swimming. Want me to get him?"

Diana nodded. "I'll need to talk to all of you eventually, but right now I want to see Kevin—alone, if that's okay."

"Sure," Melanie said, picking up on Diana's distress. "Have a seat at the table. I'll get him."

Short minutes later, Kevin came into the house. His blond hair was damp, smelling of chlorine. He had pulled on a long, baggy T-shirt over his suit. He looked at Diana warily. "What's up?" His voice was curt.

At that moment, Diana wished she was anywhere else in the world. "It's about your father."

For a second Kevin went very still. "Has he been arrested?"

"Not yet, but he will be. Kevin, he...he robbed a bank in Beaumont late this afternoon." She understood and shared his disbelief. "There's no doubt it was him. The whole thing's on film."

"Beaumont," Kevin repeated dully, shocked.

"Yes, that's over by the Texas Louisiana border. About three hundred miles from here." She paused, trying to be as gentle as possible with the distraught boy. "We're afraid he may try to come back for you again now that he has a good deal of money. Kevin, he's considered armed and dangerous."

"He has a gun?" Shock layered upon shock.

"Apparently. He doesn't, however, have a permit."

Tears misted Kevin's eyes. He knotted his hands into tight fists and placed them on the table in front of him. "What'll happen if the police find him?"

"They'll ask him to surrender."

"And if he doesn't?" All the color drained from Kevin's face.

"I think he will, Kevin. It's very important to all of us that no one get hurt." And most of all Diana wanted Kevin, and everyone else at the Harrigan ranch, to remain safe.

Kevin blinked. When he spoke again his voice was rough with the husky threat of suppressed tears. "He didn't hurt anyone at the bank, did he?"

"No, thank heaven." She paused, wishing she knew better what to say to him, how to comfort him. "Are you going to be all right?" she asked softly.

Kevin nodded. Diana continued, wanting him to know there were options for him. "You don't have to stay here if you don't want to, you know. We can have you moved elsewhere—just temporarily, until this is over."

"No. I want to be here with Ernie and Carlos and Melanie and Jim." His head lifted. His brow furrowed with concern for his foster dad. "Does Mike know?"

"Not yet. That's one of the reasons I came here. I hoped to call him before he heard it on the news."

"Melanie knows where he is." Kevin got up and went into the living room.

Melanie and Jim returned to the kitchen. Kevin stayed in the living room, to talk to his foster brothers.

"I need a phone number where Mike is staying so I can call him," Diana said, once she'd filled the two counselors in on the latest developments.

Melanie and Jim exchanged a glance. It seemed to Diana they were hiding something. Again, she wondered where Mike had gone, what he was up to. Was it possible he had a girlfriend stashed away somewhere? A lover? And why were Melanie and Jim looking so concerned?

"You do know where he is, don't you?" Diana asked.

Jim nodded. "Yes. He's at the social-services department in Dallas. I'll get the number for you."

Diana tried him there, but no luck. He'd already left, but the receptionist suggested Diana try the architectural firm of Lance, Costigan and Wolrab. "What would he be doing there?" Diana asked. She turned to the counselors. "Is he planning some renovations?" As far as she could see, the ranch was in perfect shape.

"Uh, you'll have to ask Mike about that," Jim said evasively. "We're really not at liberty to say."

Diana got hold of Mike at the architectural firm, and to her relief, he promised to return to the ranch right away. She had no chance to ask him what he was doing in Dallas, but she vowed to find out at the first available opportunity.

When Mike arrived at ten that night, the ranch house was quiet. The boys had all retired early. Two deputies were keeping watch on the place. All had been quiet for some time.

"Thanks for coming over here personally to break the news," Mike said, the moment he had her alone in his study. He sat on the edge of his desk, while she took the wing chair in front of it. "I appreciate it."

"With you out of town that responsibility fell to me," she said carefully. Now that he was back in town again, she realized anew how hurt she was by his secretive behavior. Try as she might, she couldn't mask that hurt.

He looked at her as if sensing the barrier that had gone up between them since the last time they met. Still, he offered no explanation about his urgent business in Dallas, although he knew how and why he was hurting her.

"Well, I guess I'll head on home." She stood awkwardly, feeling embarrassed.

"You're mad at me, aren't you?" His low voice stopped her at the door.

"Why would you think that?" she said coolly.

He lifted one shoulder in a careless shrug. "The chill in your eyes." His glance narrowed analytically. "Is it the fact I went to Dallas so soon after Kevin's father appeared here?" His lips thinned unhappily as he continued tersely, "Do you think I abandoned the boys, Kevin especially?"

That was part of it, Diana silently allowed. "Didn't you?"

"No." He looked at her without apology. "I had business there."

"Specifically?"

He was silent for a moment, apparently debating with himself whether to level with her or not. "I want to expand the ranch. Build facilities to house an additional ten or so boys...." Still fidgeting, he stuck both hands in his pants pockets.

She gasped.

His voice swept over her, both rough and smooth, like raw silk. "And cabins for other married couples who'll work here as counselors and support personnel. Maybe eventually even a full staff of teachers."

She advanced on him without thinking, until they were a mere two steps apart. "Mike, that's impossible!"

"No, it's not."

"Yes, it is, and if you don't realize that, then you really are out of it!" In another world, maybe—a dreamworld.

He grimaced and his brows drew together like twin thunderclouds above his eyes. "I was afraid you'd say that." He paused significantly and frowned again. "Now you know why I didn't tell you or anyone else."

Agitatedly Diana swept a hand through her hair as she tried to figure out a way to make him see reason. "Mike, taking in three boys was problem enough, but to bring in a whole platoon of them... The community will fight you," she finished heavily. She disapproved, too. Didn't he realize he was making a personal life impossible?

He stood again, so that he was towering above her, all coiled energy and tensile steel. "No, they won't."

She watched as he crossed both arms defiantly over his chest. "Agnes—"

"Is an exception, as is Iris and Billy Reaves," he cut in stubbornly, refusing to back down or alter his opinion. "Everyone else gets along splendidly with the boys."

What about your own life? Diana wanted to say. What about me, and the relationship we were beginning to have? But she didn't ask because she already knew the answer. Mike was doing what her ex-husband had done. He was putting his work first—above her, above romance, above any chance for a lasting, satisfying personal life.

"Well?" he asked. "Aren't you going to say anything?"

Yes . . . no. "What's there to say?" she said stiffly. "You've apparently made up your mind."

"Yes, I have," he said with cold finality.

He was going to get what he wanted, and it wasn't her. "Then I hope you're happy," she said finally, ashamed of the asperity in her voice but unable to hide it. Because she sure wouldn't be happy, not if he went through with his plans to expand the ranch.

"MIKE, I LOVE YOU, but I need my sleep," Linda Harrigan groaned over the long-distance connection two hours later.

Mike propped his feet up on his desk. "Have a heart, kid. I need someone to pour my heart out to." Boy, was that an understatement!

Linda yawned audibly, showing no sympathy whatsoever. "Can't you talk to that J.P.—what was her name? Diana something?"

"Tomlinson, and no, I can't."

"Too bad. She was cute. Mom and Dad apparently thought so."

"They told you?" Mike asked, aggrieved. Why was it everyone in the family thought they had a right—no, a duty—to get involved in his personal life?

"Oh, yeah. In fact, they couldn't stop talking about her. So what's got you calling me in the middle of the night?" Linda asked around yet another yawn.

"What else but woman troubles." Mike leaned farther back in his swivel chair.

Silence. "Diana?"

"Yep." Briefly, Mike explained.

Linda sighed. "Well, you can't blame her for being hurt you didn't confide in her."

Mike sighed. He should've figured his sister would elect to play devil's advocate. "If I had told her why I was going to Dallas she would've gotten mad at me."

"She got mad at you, anyway," Linda pointed out patiently.

Mike growled in irritation, and taking his feet off his desk, slammed them onto the floor. "This isn't helping," he complained sourly.

"Do you want sympathy or honesty?" she shot back.

Neither, Mike thought. He wanted Diana. And the fact he couldn't have her, the fact they were hopelessly mismatched, was driving him crazy. "Okay, let me have it with both barrels," he said with a sigh. She would give it anyway.

"If you want her to forgive you for the duplicity, you have to offer an apology. And make it memorable."

Mike was silent. Was Linda right? Had he asked for this with his secretive behavior? "Candy or flowers?" he said finally, knowing that more important to him than his pride was being back in Diana's good graces. He wanted her friendship. He wanted . . . more than that, too.

Linda groaned and mumbled something he couldn't quite catch about the unimaginative male species being its own best case for deliberate extinction. She yawned before offering her final shot. "You're the hell-raising genius in the family. You decide. Just remember, if you want her back you better deserve to have her."

"MIKE?" DIANA CALLED HIM early the following morning, shortly after she arrived at her office. In a businesslike voice that was so starchy it grated on his nerves, she continued, "I thought you'd want to know Kevin's father was spotted in New Orleans last night. From there, he caught a plane to New York City."

"But he hasn't been picked up yet?" Mike was aware his frustration was coming through loud and clear.

"No. The FBI's in on it, of course, as are the New York police, but so far nothing. Frankly, with the amount of cash he had, he could get lost for quite a while."

Mike sighed. At the moment all his thoughts were on the boys. "I talked to the social-services department this morning. They want me to keep taking every precaution."

"They may have a point." She sighed, thinking. "Of course, as far as sheer probability is concerned, it's unlikely that Donald would show up here. He's a smart man, and he knows we'll be on the lookout for him here. Legally, Texas is the worst place for him to be."

"I know." Mike agreed tersely. His thoughts were much the same. "But we still have his son. And we've already seen what powerful motivation that is." Literally anything could happen.

She didn't disagree. When she spoke again her voice had gentled. "How's Kevin doing?"

Mike frowned, thinking of the pallor of the boy's skin and the dark circles beneath his eyes. "He had a rough night. I don't think he slept much."

There was a silence. "I'm sorry," Diana said sympathetically at last.

"Yeah." Mike's response was unnecessarily gruff; he didn't know what else to say. He hated his powerlessness to protect Kevin from his father.

"You'll let me know if anything else comes up?" she asked as carefully as if she were threading her way through a mine field. Mike wanted to do more than that, he realized. He wanted to see her, mend the rift between them. He hadn't realized just how much he had enjoyed seeing her until now. If only they hadn't fought. It wouldn't change the situation they were all facing, but it would make him feel much better. "Diana, about last night—" he began softly, needing to call a truce with her, mend the hurts.

But his apology was something she didn't want to hear. "Take care, Mike," she cut him off firmly but abruptly, telling him clearly that whatever friendship they'd shared was over. It wouldn't matter if he showered her with gifts; she wasn't going to forgive him, or support his plans to expand. "I'll talk to you later."

Mike was still holding the receiver in his hand when the phone clicked. While part of him said ending it now with Diana was for the best, the rest of him refused to admit it.

"YOU DON'T HAVE to do it, Diana," Iris said the following evening. They were all looking at posted assignments on the fire-station bulletin board for the latest Neighbors project. Harrigan had assigned Diana to work with him—alone.

"Get one of the men to switch with you. Hal will switch with you, won't you, Hal?" Iris continued.

Hal sputtered. Diana blushed. "It's not necessary. Really, we'll be fine." All they were going to do was pick up litter.

Iris stared at Diana thoughtfully. She pulled her aside. "You're falling for him, aren't you?" Giving her friend no chance to reply, she hissed, "Diana think! He's not the man for you!"

Diana knew. Oh, how she knew....

"YOU WANTED TO GET ME alone," Diana murmured, bending to pick up a bottle from the parched creek bed.

Mike arched a brow and didn't deny it. "If you didn't want to be here, you could've switched with someone else," he pointed out.

"Yeah. And really gotten tongues wagging," she said. He'd known he was putting her on the spot and he'd enjoyed it.

Mike smiled and shrugged, looking impossibly indomitable. "People are already gossiping. It's no big deal."

She let her breath out slowly and counted to ten. "Maybe not to you, but you're not facing reelection in another year."

He paused, his expression contrite. She could tell he was genuinely sorry. "I didn't think about that," he said slowly, upset. "We'll go back—"

"No," Diana said rapidly, before she could think. Returning now would only generate more questions she didn't want to answer. His brows rose as he misinterpreted her unwillingness to leave. Feeling the color flood her cheeks, she continued less hurriedly, "I mean, as long as we're here, Mike, we might as well just finish it." They were adults. They could handle working together even if they weren't getting along.

He held her glance a moment longer, as if testing the waters, then nodded in mute agreement. They continued along the shady enclave, on opposite sides of the shallow creek. Because of the lack of rain, the water had dried up, until only a two-and-a-half-foot-wide stream was visible. At the end of summer, the creek bed would be completely dry, Diana knew. Just as in hurricane season, when they received torrential rains, it would be filled to overflowing. But for now, it was a peaceful spot—a place apart. And she was alone with Mike.

Mike scowled as he bent to pick up a corn-chip wrapper. Diana collected a candy bar and an aluminum can. "Why do people litter?" she muttered in exasperation.

Mike shook his head, looking equally peeved. "I don't know. They're lazy, I guess."

"It takes just as much energy to hurl trash out the car window as it does to throw it into a trash barrel."

"Agreed." He paused. Their eyes met, and his look turned almost tender. She felt herself melting inside, wanting the tension between them to end. Fighting with him made her too unhappy. And like the littering, it was destructive.

Should she give him a second chance?

Despite her earlier reservations, Diana was beginning to think so. She knew she had missed talking to him, seeing him, since they'd argued.

Seeing no more litter on his side of the stream, but plenty on her side, he bounded across the water to join her. Moving on ahead, his strides long and purposeful, he began picking up the scattered papers. She appreciated the way he gave her plenty of physical space. Right now, she felt she needed it as much as she needed to sort out her feelings. Because right or wrong, Mike Harrigan was always in her thoughts these days on some level. She knew she cared about him more with every second that passed. And that he had the capacity to hurt her more deeply than anyone ever had, or maybe would have. What she hadn't figured out was whether or not she wanted to continue letting him court her. Already she felt too fragile where he was concerned.

Silence fell between them again, slightly less awkward now. As the time passed, Mike looked happier, more content.

The shadows were lengthening, Diana noted, just as her mood was mellowing. And the path behind them was blissfully clean.

"I like your hair that way," he said, after a moment.

She looked at him in surprise, warmed by the quiet intensity of his gaze. She'd just pinned it carelessly up off her neck. "Thanks." She gazed up at him amiably. She liked the way he looked in his dark blue shirt. A mosquito nipped her and she slapped her arm. She frowned, annoyed.

"Forget your repellent?"

She rolled her eyes and nodded guiltily. It seemed she always forgot her repellent. She never remembered until after she got bitten. So, she would grin and bear the misery and head straight for the Caladryl lotion when she got home. "It's too late, anyway. I already used cologne." And her cologne attracted bugs like the flowers it was made from.

Mike smiled. "It's never too late. Wait here." He dashed off before she could dissuade him.

"Do you always have to have things your way?" she grumbled when he returned, a can of insect repellent in his hand.

He grinned, not the least put off by her surly tone. "Whenever possible. Don't you?"

Yes. Which was another similarity between them.

He signaled for her to turn around. Figuring she might as well make use of the repellent since he'd gone all the way back to the truck to get it, she did as directed. She stood still while he sprayed the back of her. Finished, he handed her the can and she sprayed her front.

Finished, he tucked the can into the belt at his waist and they continued on down the stream, this time walking side by side, beginning to chat a little about inconsequential things. Diana realized what Mike must've known all along—that it was impossible for them to stay angry at one another if they spent any time at all together. As different as they were in so many respects, they still drifted inexorably toward one another.

Some distance away, a single flower was growing amid all the trash. "Oh, look, Mike!" Diana said, bending to touch the fragile violet blossom. "A dayflower." Her voice softened reverently. "It's incredible it could survive in all this trash." Just like it was incredible the boys in Mike's care could survive and come through their traumatic childhoods, their spirits and zest for life intact.

Diana paused. Was this how Mike felt when he found a foster child? Like he'd discovered some marvelous natural resource in the toughest survival zone?

"It is beautiful," Mike murmured.

He knelt beside her. Together, they picked up paper wrappers and empty bottles and cans, until the area around the blossom was clean again. He watched as she touched her nose to the violet petals and breathed in the subtle fragrance.

"You're not going to pluck it?" he asked, when she started to rise without the flower.

She was tempted. But she couldn't. "No. I'll leave it for someone else to enjoy." It would be wrong to remove it from its natural environment, she thought.

Aware that time was getting away from them, she stood and started on down the creek bed. This time he made no move to walk beside her. Behind her, she heard him mumble something, but to her frustration she couldn't quite make out the words. "What'd you say?" She slowed her pace, waiting for him to catch up to her and walk beside her again.

For a second she thought he wouldn't answer. "I was just thinking how nice it would be if you could exhibit the same generosity of spirit toward my boys as you do toward everything else."

A tall order. She couldn't pretend she didn't have reservations about the wisdom of what he was doing. "You really want me to like them. Why is that so important to you?"

He shrugged. "Because they're good kids. And you're a good woman."

Was she? She frowned and moved away from him slightly, although they were walking abreast as she'd wanted. "You don't know anything about me." Not really.

"So tell me." He moved closer.

Trying hard not to be unnerved by his nearness, she said evasively, "Tell you what?"

"I don't know." He gave her a beguiling smile. "Everything. Anything. Start from the beginning."

"Well, let's see," she drawled. "The day I was born—"

He laughed. "Not that far back."

She shrugged. There wasn't a whole lot of difference between her childhood and the childhoods of the boys Mike cared for. Was that why he was so drawn to her? she wondered. Because he could sense the unhappiness in her past?

Briefly she told him about her social-worker father, his early death and the difficult financial straits of her childhood, glossing over the worst parts as if it had been, in retrospect, a much appreciated character-building exercise, instead of the hand-to-mouth hell she remembered.

"Where is your family now?" he asked gently, when she'd finished.

"My mother married a retired refinery worker. They live in Corpus Christi now. My brother is a systems engineer. He's married, has a couple of kids. He and his family live in North Carolina."

"What about you? Are you happy leading the single life?"

Diana picked her way carefully through an overgrown area, peppered with weeds. "Most of the time. Sometimes it is a little lonely."

"I know what you mean."

Looking up at him, she could see he did. Another similarity between them.

"Do you ever think about getting married again?"

"Sometimes. I probably would if I could find a man I could count on through thick or thin," she admitted softly.

Her answer surprised him. "You're not turned off by your divorce?" He had half thought she was.

She shook her head. Enough time had passed for her to put the whole episode in proper perspective. "No, there's no reason I should be. The fates were against us, that's all. My ex-husband was a workaholic. He needed his work more than he needed me. I won't make that mistake again." If she married again, she would choose her mate wisely.

Finished with the cleanup, they turned back.

"What about you?" she asked as they retraced their path, enjoying the clean, uncluttered vista. "Have you ever been married?" Now was her chance to find out more about him, too.

His blue eyes clouded. "I was engaged once." His voice was flat, noncommittal.

"What happened?" she asked.

"She found out I intended to spend my life ministering to the needs of the less fortunate rather than try to make money hand over fist. And she left."

No wonder he hated criticism of his chosen profession—it probably reminded him of his ex-fiancé. "I'm sorry," she said, meaning it. He must've been very hurt.

"I'm not." He sent her an honest glance. "It never would've worked." Thus, it was easy for him to accept the end.

Now it was her turn to probe a little deeper. "Do you still want to get married?" She wondered if maybe his broken engagement was at least partially responsible for his total commitment to the boys. Would Mike have insisted on this twenty-four hour involvement with the foster kids if he had a family of his own to go home to every night? Would he then be content to run the ranch days, and spend nights with his wife and child, or children?

It was an interesting possibility, one she couldn't quite discard without mulling it over more.

Having reached the place where they'd started, they crossed the stream again and headed up the bank, back to the road.

In answer to her question of whether or not he would marry, Mike shrugged. He met her gaze for a long moment. "I don't really know. I might marry—someday. But only if I can find a woman who not only understands what I want, but will help me to achieve my goals—and I'd do the same for her—because I think for any marriage to be successful the two people involved have to be mutually supportive."

Diana agreed with that theory. Certainly the fact that her own marriage didn't have those qualities was the reason for its downfall.

She wondered, though, if Mike would ever find a woman strong enough and giving enough to take on what he was asking of her. More to the point, could Diana meet Mike's requirements for a potential wife? Sometimes she thought so. At other times, she felt the whole situation was impossible, given her feelings in general for quixotic social workers. She supposed only time would tell, and until the answer was clear, she would just have to take it one step, one moment, at a time.

In the meantime, she and Mike had a party to go to, and if they didn't hurry, they would be late.

A prior arrangement had been made, after the cleanups were finished, to all congregate back at the fire station for a dance. It was nothing fancy, just a few records playing on a stereo someone'd brought in, a bowl of punch and assorted cookies. To Diana's surprise, Mike didn't go straight back to the ranch with the boys.

Instead, he delegated that duty to Melanie and Jim and stayed for the party. She took this as a positive sign. More and more he was beginning to think about himself, too, and not just the welfare of his foster sons. When the first slow song came on, he made his way to her side. "Want to dance?" The question was casual, yet there was a hint of renewed intimacy in his eyes.

I want to be with you, too, she thought. The heck with our argument the other day.

Across the room, Agnes was watching Diana with a look that said, *Don't you dare!*

The heck with her reelection. "Yes, I'd like that very much," Diana said softly, ignoring Agnes's unspoken warning.

"It seems not everyone approves."

"That's their problem, not ours."

He grinned, liking the reckless way she was thinking. Diana had to admit to herself it felt good. Maybe she'd been toeing the line too much, doing things because they were expected, not because they were what she wanted; adhering to conservative values that should no longer apply. After all, what did it matter whom she dated, as long as she did her job and did it well?

"Enjoy making a spectacle of yourself?" he murmured, his tone only half-teasing. He wanted to be with her, but he didn't want to make her life more difficult.

She liked the fact he cared about what happened to her, but right now, she didn't want to think about political ramifications. "I don't know," she retorted. "Are you?"

He grinned at her saucy tone, then said softly, "I don't know yet. Ask me when this dance is over." Hand on her spine, he guided her closer.

He held her gently, almost reverently.

She'd thought she was prepared for the sensation of her body bumping up against his. She wasn't. Every brush of knee or thigh had her tingling, had her appreciating again just how nice and ruggedly handsome he looked in that dark blue denim shirt. Deeper than the physical satisfaction was the emotional intimacy. She liked being held in his arms. She felt safe, protected, cared about. As if she finally had someone who not only cared about what she was feeling and why, but who was instinctively in tune with those needs. She and Mike might still disagree about a lot of things—especially his planned expansion of the ranch—but they were remarkably similar. Both were stubborn, committed to their work. They cared about the town. They wanted life to be as fair as they could make it. They wanted intimacy with someone they could trust.

Maybe he hadn't told her everything about himself, she reasoned, leaning her cheek against his shoulder, but he was opening up to her more with every passing day. And knowing firsthand what a private person Mike was, she felt that was a very good sign indeed.

The music ended. A fast song started.

They moved apart reluctantly, both sorry the spell had been broken. His gaze remained on her face, and try as she might, she couldn't bring herself to look away. Nor could he.

"Mike, I—"

"Diana—" he expelled a ragged breath "—what do you say we—"

Before Mike could finish, Hal Sims was at Diana's side. "Hey, Diana, looking great tonight. I've got something I want to talk to you about. You know those new parking meters? Well, at least two of them aren't working right, and so far this week, I've had nothing but complaints from my customers."

Diana smiled reluctantly at Hal as Mike moved back slightly. Both were aware he had been about to ask her to slip out with him, and she would have gone. But that was impossible now, especially as others were coming forward, clamoring around, hitting her with all sorts of town business they felt just had to be settled that night.

Diana sighed and forced a smile. Like it or not, she would have to stay and hear them out. The only question in her mind was whether or not Mike would wait it out, too.

MIKE STOOD in the corner, watching Diana converse with the citizens of Libertyville, one after another. It seemed everyone there tonight wanted her attention. So did he.

It defied reason, this yearning he felt for her. Yet it was there. Consuming him like a fever. Relentlessly burning into his gut. She knew it and felt it, too, he was sure of it. But whether or not she would act on it was another matter entirely.

While there was still much separating them, there was even more drawing them together. Oh, he knew she liked to think of herself as above it all, but deep down she was as softhearted as he was. She was beginning to care for his foster sons. She cared for the citizens in the town. And she cared for him, too. It was in her eyes when she looked at him—and sometimes even when she didn't.

He wasn't sure how she would respond to his equally weighty feelings for her. But he knew he couldn't sneak around anymore. That if they were going to get involved, he wanted it to be done properly, in full view of all the citizens, so that no one would ever be able to accuse her of acting underhandedly.

Even so, he knew there would be trouble if they did get involved. And that worried him. His instinct was to protect Diana, not throw her into the fire.

So what should he do? Move forward impulsively, as he'd just been tempted? Or continue to take things nice and slow?

With difficulty, Mike opted for the latter. Hence, when the party ended, he took several people home, not just Diana, dropping them off in order of their houses.

Diana was perplexed by his action, when he'd so clearly wanted to carry her off earlier, and yet she was relieved, too.

He knew he'd done the right thing, giving them both a little more time, not rushing it. Nonetheless, she remained very much in his thoughts the rest of the night, and she was still on his mind the following morning when Kevin answered the doorbell.

Federal Express had a delivery for him, from his father. Before anyone could stop him, Kevin had torn open the red, white and blue mailing envelope. Inside was a letter written on stationery from a Toronto hotel.

Kevin stared at the letter, reading rapidly, then handed it to Mike. Without a word, he bolted out the back door and across the yard toward the barn.

With Kevin still in his peripheral vision, Mike opened the letter and began to read:

Dear Kevin,
I guess this is goodbye. I won't be able to come and see you again, as the police are after me, and I'll be on the run. I love you, but then I think you've always known that. I loved your mom, too. I'm sorry for the way I let you down.

I wish you had come with me the other night. I wanted that so bad, but I understand. In your place, I'd have had a few qualms, too. You're almost grown up anyway, and with my criminal record, I couldn't be much help to you, so maybe it's better this way.

I'll be thinking of you. Stay happy.

                                             Your dad.

HOURS LATER, Mike sat staring at the figures in the ledger, his mood abysmal. Besides the continuing problems with Kevin, he realized everything had cost more than he'd figured. The hay and feed for the horses. The food and clothes for the boys. The repairs to the fences. The amount of gasoline it took to drive back and forth to town, and to run the tractor.

He needed more money. With his trust fund emptied to buy the ranch, the monthly stipend he got for the boys from social services all but gone, his own account precariously low, he would have to start fund-raising in earnest again.

He hated fund-raising. Begging for money. But if he wanted to continue his work, pull out all the stops and make this flagship program worth imitating nationwide, then he would have get on with it. And he'd have to ask his parents for more help.

He didn't mind accepting their help, but he hated asking. Maybe because it reminded him of his youth. His parents had always anticipated the needs of his older brother and younger sister, but had rarely seemed to notice his. Rather than pipe up, Mike had found it easier to do for himself. He still did. But easier wasn't always smarter. Especially in this case.

Mike frowned. There was only one way he knew to make this whole fund-raising process more bearable, and that was not to do it alone but get help and moral support from every possible source.

"A FEW DAYS in Houston will do you all good," Diana said to Mike days later at the Neighbors painting party, which had gathered to fix up the fronts of businesses along Main Street. Of late, real life had taken on qualities of intrigue and suspense.

The RCMP had received a couple of leads already on Donald Griffin's whereabouts in Canada, and it was felt he would be in custody soon. That comforted Diana, and Mike, too. However long it took, though, it didn't look as if Donald was making any effort to return to the United States. Rather, he was going deeper into Canada, heading for the wilderness area in Northern British Columbia.

"When are you leaving?" Diana asked Mike now.

"Late Thursday afternoon."

He was silent again. She found she had a hard time controlling the meter of her breath. She cleared her throat, fighting to quell the sudden buildup of tension within her, her reaction to the low, husky sound of his voice. "In the meantime, we'll keep watch on the ranch," Diana promised, "just in case."

It was county policy, once it had been established that the threat—in this case Donald Griffin—was out of the state, to cancel a protective watch.

"Thanks," Mike said affably, "although to be honest I'm really not expecting any trouble there. Just to be on the safe side, though, I've hired a private security firm to keep watch on the place in our absence."

"That's good. I'll be sure and let the sheriff know."

A silence fell.

"Listen," he said at last, remembering his sister's words. "I've got to go to Houston for a fund-raiser. It costs a bundle to buy hay and feed for the horses, and food and clothes for the boys...."

"Yes?"

"Well, I'd like you to go. It'd be at my parents' house in Houston."

Was that a roundabout way of asking her for a date? Diana wondered, excited but wary. How much could she trust him in the future to open up to her?

"A lot of your old legal buddies from the big city will be there, even some people from your old law firm."

If he meant to tempt her, he was doing a good job of it. But it wasn't the lure of seeing old friends that was making her want to go so much as the prospect of spending time with him, seeing where he grew up....

"I'd like to attend, Mike." Unfortunately her schedule wasn't nearly as flexible as his. "But I'm not sure at the moment if I'll be able to get away. My court calendar is booked solid for the rest of the month." She could reschedule, of course, but it would take some doing and a lot of work on the part of her secretary, Kay Reaves.

"Give it some thought," he said.

When he'd first come to Libertyville, she'd expected him to be a totally negative, disruptive force. He had proved just the opposite, bringing more good than bad to the community of late. She relaxed beside him, enjoying the easy chatter as much as the mildly taxing physical work. All in all, she found painting was a very satisfying way to keep in shape. More productive than, say, simply running, or walking to and from work. Mike seemed to be enjoying himself, too. She slanted a glance at him, appreciating how ruggedly handsome he looked in the softening evening light. "All packed and ready for your trip?" She knew he was leaving for Houston in the morning. What he didn't know was that she was planning to show up and surprise him.

"Not yet. We'll do that later, when we get home. Or if we're too tired, tomorrow morning."

Hoping to divert the attention away from herself and thus keep her own plans secret, Diana glanced around. She'd spotted the boys earlier. Now they were nowhere in sight. Yet, diligent workers they had all proved to be, she knew they were somewhere close by.

"Given any more thought to coming to Houston?" Mike asked laconically, his expression noncommittal.

Beside Diana, Kay Reaves and Iris both turned, their expressions incredulous. Kay knew how hard Diana had been working to clear her calendar. Up until now, she'd known only that it was because Diana had a party in Houston to attend.

Oblivious to the fact they were being overheard, Mike continued casually, "If it's a question of lodging, my parents can put you up."

She knew about his famous father and wealthy upbringing, and knew he rarely mentioned either. "Thanks, but should I decide to come, I'll, uh, find my own place to stay."

Kay and Iris were still staring at Diana—both in obvious dismay.

Just then, Carlos came up behind Mike. He was splattered everywhere with paint. Even on his nose. "Hey, Mike," he said, "we finished with the shoe store and we already had our break. What's next?"

"I guess we'll find out," Mike said. "Let's go find Hal. He's in charge of the paint crews tonight."

No sooner had Mike disappeared, Carlos in tow, than Iris and Kay closed in on either side of Diana. "You can't seriously be thinking of going with him," Iris said.

Diana stiffened. She didn't want advice on how to run her private life. And until now Iris had never tried to give any. "I might."

"You can't—" Kay started emotionally, then bit her lip. Composing herself, she tried again. "Diana," she said softly, "think how people will respond to that."

Diana looked over her shoulder and saw Agnes McCarthy glaring at her from inside the office of the *Libertyville Press*.

She sighed, troubled. Yet for once her concern was not primarily for herself and preserving her place in the community, but for Mike. Just what would it take for him to win acceptance in this town? she wondered. For people to see that maybe there was more to him than they had at first thought? What would it take for them to give him a real chance?

"WALK YOU HOME?" Mike said several hours later.

Diana nodded. "That'd be nice, thanks." Darkness had fallen. Volunteers were still lingering in the park next to the courthouse, enjoying cold drinks and swapping stories, but for Diana it had been a long day. She was anxious to get home, run a hot bath and soak the tension and weariness from her aching muscles. She had a lot to do tomorrow if she was going to leave for Houston Friday morning. Which meant making it a very early night and saying goodbye to Mike at the door, rather than inviting him in.

"You know, if this kind of turnout keeps up, come fall we won't have much left to fix up," Mike said, as they started in the direction of her house.

Diana smiled, thinking of Libertyville in tip-top shape. She closed her eyes briefly. "Maybe we'll get some kind of award," she said dreamily, around a yawn.

"From the governor or state legislature? It's a thought."

"Or even Lady Bird Johnson. You know how big she was on beautification."

Mike glanced at her. His eyes touched her hair, then lingered ever so gently on her face. "She sure was," he said, continuing their conversation about the former first lady amiably. "Still is. And Texas has the wildflowers to prove it."

Diana smiled. "Speaking of flowers, I'll bet mine need—"

She was about to say "water" when her foot hit a clump of dirt and tangled root, and she stopped cold. Beside her, Mike sucked in his breath. Tears filled Diana's eyes as she took in the destruction of her front yard. Every single plant had been uprooted. The gutting was complete and terrible.

Unable to help herself, Diana began to cry, the tears slipping silently down her face.

Mike's arm went around her shoulders. For a moment, he simply stared at the devastation, swearing softly, virulently, saying all the things she felt but was too much of a lady to voice. And then he turned, and took her into his arms.

A few minutes later, he led her into the house and sat her gently down in a kitchen chair. "Feeling better?" Mike got her a glass of water and then, moving easily around her kitchen, put some coffee on to brew.

Still feeling shaken, incredibly violated by what had happened, Diana nodded. Tilting her head back, she closed her eyes. "Why?" she whispered hoarsely, thinking of the delicate blooms she'd slaved months over, planting, nurturing, weeding, watering.

"I don't know," Mike said slowly.

"Someone wanted to hurt me." Her hands trembled as she put down the glass.

"And they did." His blue eyes were grim and unforgiving, as he contemplated the perpetrator. Without warning, his expression turned even bleaker, and he turned away.

"You know something," she guessed. "Or suspect..."

He squared his shoulders and turned around to meet her inquiring look. His voice was steady, but unhappy, when he spoke, "I know who'll be blamed—"

"Your boys." Oh, no. No. Had they done this? Would they have?

"I also know they didn't do it, Diana." He firmly stood his ground. "They wouldn't."

She didn't want to think so, either. But she had her doubts. "Who else is there?"

"I don't know," he retorted heavily. "Suppose you tell me."

Silence fell between them. Diana hadn't exactly been popular since she'd championed Mike Harrigan and his causes. Nonetheless, no one she knew would do this.

Chapter Nine

I don't know what I'm doing here, Diana thought, walking into the Harrigans' River Oaks mansion Friday evening. *Just because Mike invited me doesn't mean I have to attend.*

But she had decided to attend, driving in all the way from Libertyville. She needed to see his boys again, try to figure out if they were as innocent in all the pranks as Mike had claimed. She needed to see Mike because, like it or not these days, he was on her mind more and more.

Then once in Houston, she'd decided that the formal she'd planned to wear was dated and had gone out to the Galleria to buy a new dress. The excursion had taken longer than she'd anticipated, and she'd had to rush back to her hotel, bathe and dress, before getting into the car Mike's parents had insisted upon sending for her. Now she was breathless and flushed, and just a little on edge. As her golden brown eyes fastened on the man she was looking for, her heart leaped.

The mixture of confusion and interest in his eyes—he obviously hadn't really expected her to show up—infused her with warmth. "Glad you could make it," Mike greeted her easily, before stopping a waiter and stealing two glasses of champagne.

Diana smiled as, his hand on her elbow, he guided her through a throng of ball players and their wives to a less-crowded spot in the living room. Once they were situated, he dropped his hold on her; still, his possessive touch lingered, reminding her how potently she responded to this man and probably always would. "Thanks. Looks like you've got quite a crowd here."

Everyone seemed to be having a great time, not that this was any surprise. The interior of the Harrigan home was opulent, yet comfortable, as warm and welcoming as the clan it housed. But the collection of antiques and art couldn't hold a candle to her host.

In dinner jacket, crisp white shirt, and bold-blue bow tie, Mike looked handsome, incredibly sexy, and at ease. She couldn't help but note he fit in here as well as he did in Libertyville; in fact in many ways this was probably more comfortable for him, more what he was used to than life on a Hill Country ranch.

"How's the fund-raising going?" Diana asked as evenly as possible.

"Better than I'd expected actually."

His blue eyes glittered warmly, then lingered on the soft, curling ends of her golden blond hair, before connecting again with her gaze. "I have my family to thank for that. Mom and Dad called in all their markers. Of course, it doesn't hurt that they throw a great party." He gestured toward a silver chalice stuffed with envelopes. "As you can see, donations are coming in even better than we projected." He looked incredibly happy about that.

That meant he was going on with his plans to expand the ranch and the number of boys under his care. Diana wanted to stay calm and collected, but she felt a chill go down her spine. She'd known the reason for the party, so why had she come? She didn't want to be annoyed with Mike, or disappointed, or the victim of these crazy ups and downs her mood had been taking of late. But not wanting to be a spoilsport, she plastered a smile on her face and prepared to move off, her eye already on a lawyer she'd known some time ago. She had to be happy for Mike; it was only right. "That's great, Mike. I'm happy for you." She patted his arm dismissively, and ignoring the thinly veiled hurt and confusion in his look, started for her old friend.

Mike watched Diana move off, with effort hiding his unhappiness over her reaction to the party's success. No matter what platitudes she mouthed, she wasn't supportive of his plans for the future, he thought angrily. Knowing that, he ought to just walk away from her and any thoughts of a relationship, but he found he couldn't stop thinking of her.

"Diana's looking great tonight," Tom, Sr., observed, standing next to his son.

"Yeah, she is, isn't she?" Mike said dispassionately. She was wearing a black chiffon dress decorated with hundreds of closely placed gold appliqués. Long-sleeved and full-skirted, the gown was cut demurely in front but the back dipped down to her waist. Mike found the display of lightly tanned skin, her slim but curvaceous figure, incredibly sexy.

Reading his mind, his dad slapped him on the back. "If I were you, I wouldn't let her out of my sight."

Mike kept his eye on Diana, wondering jealously what she was talking so animatedly about with that wimpy-looking lawyer. What could the jerk possibly have that Mike didn't? "I don't intend to," Mike murmured.

His sister, Linda, joined them. "Want to go with me while I say hello to Diana?" she asked Mike.

"Why not? Now's as good a time as any," Mike muttered, as Diana finished her conversation and moved alone in the direction of the appetizers on the buffet.

"Careful, brother," Linda warned teasingly. "You're wearing your heart on your sleeve."

She greeted Diana cordially.

"It's too bad Tom, Jr.'s, not here," Linda said with a smile, pretending she didn't notice the complex welter of emotions simmering between Mike and Diana. "I know he wanted to meet you, but he's off on an author tour to promote his latest novel."

Diana blinked in surprise, turning to Mike. "Your brother's a writer?" She looked excited, Mike noted grimly.

With effort, he concealed his irritation. "Yes. Tom Harrigan, known to his fans as T. J. Stone or Harrison James—"

"Harrison James, why, he wrote *Crossbones and Terror*—!" Diana said, naming the book she'd been reading.

Mike nodded. "That's his latest work, and first hardcover novel." Mike winced at her continued enthusiasm.

Oblivious to his discomfort, Diana rushed on in befuddled delight. "I know. I'm reading it now." She stared at him, obviously wondering why he hadn't told her about his brother, that he wrote under pseudonyms.

Reading her mind, Mike explained, "The fact Tom's a writer isn't anything out of the ordinary to us anymore. I mean, at first, we were kind of bowled over to see his work in the bookstores. We used to go into a store and just stare at his name on the jacket. But now, it's old hat."

Linda smiled warmly. "Tom'll be interested to know you've read his stuff, though. He always likes to know his work is being read, and to find an enthusiastic reader who doesn't know him personally first, well, that's kind of a boon to his ego."

Diana looked back at Mike, some of the pleasure leaving her expression as she took in his stony facade.

He knew his jealousy was showing and it infuriated him. He'd thought he'd put those old feelings of sibling rivalry to rest years before. And he had—until this moment, this woman. Growing up, Tom had stolen the heart of every girl Mike had ever dated. He'd be damned if he'd let it happen again.

Nor would he stand there and act like a thwarted schoolkid.

"If you'll excuse me, I'm going out to the kitchen to see if Mom needs a hand with the caterers." Not waiting for either woman to reply, Mike moved off. He knew Diana was staring at him in puzzlement, that Linda was irked by his spoilsport attitude, but it couldn't be helped. Any more than he could change his feelings.

"DIANA, HAVE YOU SEEN Mike?" Mrs. Harrigan asked long minutes later.

"No, why?"

Mrs. Harrigan sighed. "I sent him up to the attic to dig out an old punchbowl. I was going to make some sherbet punch for those three boys of his, but he hasn't come back down yet." She cast an anxious look behind her, frowning slightly when she noticed several dishes on the buffet in need of refilling. "Darn. I guess I'll have to send Linda up after him. Have you seen her?"

"Uh, I think she's out back doing the limbo. One of the baseball players drafted her for his 'team.'"

Mrs. Harrigan rolled her eyes. She peered at Diana. "You weren't drafted?"

"They tried," Diana said. "I resisted." It wasn't that she minded a little fun, just that she'd been looking for Mike, too, wanting to talk to him, to smooth things over between them. He seemed angry with her, for reasons she didn't understand. "Look, I can see you're busy with the caterers. Why don't I go up and get him? If you don't mind, that is."

"Mind? Darling, you're saving my life. And getting there is easy enough. Just go upstairs, to the end of the south hall. You'll see a door and another set of stairs. And if you find him, tell him to hurry up! At the rate he's going I could just have easily sent the caterers across town to pick up their own extra bowl."

"Will do." Glad to help out, Diana started off in the direction of the stairs. Two minutes later she found the attic stairs. Her skirt gathered in one hand to keep it off the floor, she climbed the well-lit stairs.

The attic was surprisingly spacious, the ceiling a normal height and steepled in the middle. There were dormer windows, which at the moment were covered with closed venetian blinds. The wooden floor was bare, but scrupulously clean. Boxes and moving crates were stacked in one corner. Odds and ends of furniture, as well as several wardrobes and trunks were scattered throughout. Mike was seated in an old rocking chair, his tie loosened, the top buttons on his shirt undone; he was holding a photo album in his hands. "Any luck finding the punch bowl?" Diana asked wryly. So this was what was taking Mike so long. He was woolgathering.

Mike looked up in surprise, then grinned sheepishly, knowing he'd been caught, but not really minding. "Uh, no. Mom sent you up?"

"I volunteered." She regarded him warily, aware that in all the time she'd known him she'd never seen him look this down. The thought she might have prompted the emotion filled her with guilt. "About your brother," she began carefully. "I'm sorry if I acted starstruck."

"I'm used to it. Or at least I should be." At her uncomprehending look, he continued, "Tom has always been the star of the family because he was born first. He took the first steps, spoke the first words. That kind of thing is very exciting to new parents."

"And all these years, growing up, you've felt you were in his shadow?" she asked softly.

He was silent a minute, reflecting. "It was more like, with me, there were no surprises. It didn't matter what I did, Tom had always done it first, and therefore with me it wasn't that amazing or spectacular or even out of the ordinary. I guess I always felt a little bit like old news, or yesterday's newspaper—about that interesting."

He was serious, but not self-pitying. "That's a horrible thing to say," she said softly.

He gave her a level look. "It's the way it was." At her astounded glance, his voice gentled slightly. "Don't get me wrong. I'm not complaining. I'm a psychologist and I know all the reasons things happened as they did. Mom and Dad were busy trying to juggle all they had to do, and I was just born in the unluckiest place. On the other hand—" his eyes twinkled merrily "—I did have the advantage of having less pressure put on me to succeed. I didn't have someone looking over my shoulder every single minute of every single day, or always drilling me on what to do and what not to do. So I, uh—how should I put this—got away with some things that I never should have, and that Tom never could have, no matter how clever he was. They just watched him too closely."

She grinned at the return of his sense of humor. "You sound smug," she accused lightly. With a swish of her skirt, she moved closer.

"The devilish exploits of my youth recounted." He wiggled his eyebrows like a TV star mugging for the camera.

She sat opposite him on the heavy trunk. "Was there anything you wanted to do in your youth that you didn't get to do?" Diana asked, enjoying the intimate respite from the boisterous sounds of the party downstairs.

Mike shrugged. "Not really. You can see that financially we never had much to worry about, although being the son of someone famous can be a real cross to bear. I don't really like the limelight." He frowned thoughtfully. "I guess if there was anything I wanted...I would have liked more one-on-one time with my dad, more time for just the two of us to go camping and stuff." He shrugged.

"You like the outdoors?"

His blue eyes darkened sexily. "Yeah, don't you?"

Diana sighed. She could see how a night under the stars with him might be very appealing. "Thus far, the Holiday Inn is as close as I've ever gotten to roughing it," she admitted wryly.

His eyes gleamed. "Too bad. You'd probably like sleeping under the stars."

Maybe with the right person, Diana thought, then immediately banished the thought.

"Anyway, you're right, I was sitting up here feeling sorry for myself," Mike continued genially. "And," he added with comic emphasis, "I was doing a bang-up job of it until you arrived and decided to cheer me up."

Next to him was an open trunk, crammed with all sorts of memorabilia. "Is that what you were doing just now? Looking at one of your family's photo albums?"

"Yeah, but not for the purposes of comparing myself with Tom. Just to look back, remember. Sometimes just being here in this house, I get to feeling real nostalgic and sentimental, and I just want to remember."

She gestured at the album he'd left on the floor. "May I?"

He nodded. Diana began going through the pages, one by one. She saw pictures of Mike as a baby, walking, getting into things, wearing his father's hat and baseball glove. "You were cute, you know that?" She smiled, intrigued as she pored over the pictures. Finding one of him in his birthday suit when he was about three, she gasped and then grinned.

Seeing what she was looking at he promptly turned a bright red and confiscated the album. "Enough of that," he said firmly.

"Why, Michael Harrigan, I do believe you're embarrassed."

"Damn right." He crossed the attic to replace the album in the trunk.

She followed. Looking over his shoulder, she asked, "What else have you got in there?"

He yawned as if extremely bored, indicating she would be, too. "The usual certificates from school—for being on the student council and the football team. Handmade treasures from art class—"

"Did you make this mug yourself?"

"Yeah, in a ceramics class at school."

Diana handled it lovingly. It was a gray two-handled cup with the face of an elephant on the front. "Michael, it's beautiful! How old were you when you did this?"

"About eight."

She noticed he was flushing again, this time with pleasure.

She spotted a cardboard cylinder. "What's in here?"

"Oh, just a painting. It was displayed at the annual arts fair when I was in the tenth grade." He looked embarrassed again.

"May I?" He cringed even more, adding playfully, "You're determined to make this painful for me, aren't you?"

"I can't think of a better way to get to know what makes you tick," Diana murmured, taking the cap off the cylinder. It was also the first time she had ever seen him exhibit even the barest trace of shyness. Which went to show he was human, and as vulnerable as anyone else, after all. Somehow, she found that facet of his personality, and the fact he was comfortable enough to share it with her, most endearing of all. "Mike, this is beautiful!" Diana exclaimed, unrolling a landscape of the sea-shore at sunset, done in beautiful muted blues, pinks and grays on textured watercolor paper. "You have real talent."

"I liked the class," he explained modestly, as if that said it all, "although to be honest I only took it to meet the fine-arts requirement I needed to graduate."

She slanted him an admiring glance. She saw now why he was supportive of Ernie's talent. "But you were so good at it. Why'd you quit?" Her voice softened. She knew, had he still been painting, he would've said something about it to Ernie.

"'Cause the other guys said it was sissy," he said gruffly, looking mischievous again, "and I had other things on my mind."

"Such as?"

"Sports, cars."

"Girls?" she teased, before she could think.

"Mmm-hmm." He grinned back in a way that let her know he was every bit as aware of her as she was of him.

"It really is beautiful." With great care, Diana rolled up the watercolor and replaced it in the cylinder. "It's a crime to hide this in the attic," she said, putting the cylinder back in the trunk. "It really should be hanging somewhere."

He shook his head in disbelief. "Who would want it?"

"Your mother, for one." Diana pivoted to face him, her exasperation evident. "You know, you are much more wonderful an artist than you give yourself credit for."

She saw the first sign of a grin tug at the corner of his mouth. He lifted a sardonic brow in her direction. His eyes glittered at the fiercely possessive note in her voice—a possessiveness she could do nothing to quell, caught off guard as she was and goaded into speaking impulsively.

"Am I?" he said gruffly, clamping one arm around her waist, his other hand lifting her chin. "Then prove it to me," he dared in a silken way that stole the breath from her lungs. "And show me how you feel, Diana. This once, forget about all the things that separate us and show me that you care," he implored softly.

Then his mouth was on hers, taking, demanding, making her feel and respond. Diana wreathed her arms around his neck and stood on tiptoe, pressing every inch of her against every inch of him, taking every thrill he could give her and stretching it to the limit, and then returning that passion tenfold, yet tenderly, so tenderly. Only the sound of a spirited "Yoo-hoo!" from below, and footsteps clomping up the stairs forced them apart. Guilty, disheveled, they stood side by side to face their intruder. Mrs. Harrigan stood there, hands on hips, merriment sparkling in her eyes. "Michael Harrigan, where the devil have you been? And where is that punch bowl?"

Diana couldn't help but giggle when Mike said in his best Wally Cleaver fashion, "Uh, gee, Mom...I don't know..."

"NOW THAT WE'RE on good terms again," Mike said as he and Diana walked back downstairs again hand in hand, "I'd like to show you around. I'd like you to be my date for the evening—officially."

She liked the sound of that, and the possessiveness in his voice. Was it risky to her political career, to her personal well-being? Suddenly she didn't care. She knew only that she wanted to be with him, and that was all that mattered. "That'd be nice. Thanks." She was glad to see his good humor restored. She also suspected his earlier blue mood had less to do with old sibling rivalry than with the tension between them the past few days, with her suspecting his boys of mischief at every turn, and him unable to exonerate them completely.

"Any word on Donald Griffin?" Mike asked as they casually rejoined the others. They stopped in front of the buffet, which was now loaded with a variety of scrumptious-looking entrées and side dishes, and began filling their plates.

Quietly she told him what she'd been loathe to bring up earlier in the presence of so many others. "Yes, there is. You know they've been running his photo in Canadian newspapers. Well, someone in Calgary reported seeing him purchasing camping equipment there."

Mike paused, his expression concerned. "They figure he's headed into the mountains?"

Diana nodded, relieved that Griffin wasn't in their vicinity, yet knowing she'd not feel totally secure until he was locked up again or at least got some counseling. "It'd be a good place to get lost, and with all the national parks in that area . . . well, I can see him disappearing for quite a while."

Mike sighed, the gaiety he'd felt earlier leaving his eyes. "At least we don't have to worry about him coming after Kevin, not for the moment anyway."

"Yeah." Diana shared Mike's relief. "How is Kevin holding up?" she asked compassionately.

Mike started to respond then stopped. "See for yourself." He gestured toward Kevin, Ernie and Carlos as they walked into the dining room, obviously intending to refill their empty plates. All were in tuxedos and on their best behavior.

As Diana regarded them, an unexpected wave of pleasure surged through her. Despite everything that had happened back in Libertyville, she found a lot to like about the boys. In fact the more she saw of them, the more she cared about them, she realized with surprise.

And suddenly she knew instinctively that Mike was right. These boys couldn't have uprooted all her flowers.

Pleased the boys looked so happy to see her, Diana smiled back. Maybe this foster-parenting business did have its rewards.

"Hey, Diana!" As he neared, Carlos lifted his hand in greeting. "Glad you could make it."

"Hi, guys. Having fun?"

Ernie reached into his pocket with his free hand and pulled out a slim black leather book with his name engraved on the front. "And we've been getting autographs all night! From the Oilers and the Astros!"

"It has been pretty neat," Kevin said quietly, looking at Diana with a question in his eyes.

She repeated what she'd already told Mike. Kevin seemed relieved his father had not been picked up by the police, but made no comment.

Melanie and Jim came into the room. After greetings were exchanged, the boys went off with them, their refilled plates in hand. It was ten o'clock and the party was still going full speed.

Mike looked around for a quiet place to eat and talk, and finding nothing indoors, directed her out the French doors in the morning room. "Did I tell you?" he asked casually, leading her to a rear patio. "We had a news crew here earlier, interviewing the kids. They're going to run a spot on the flagship program and my plans for the ranch on the evening news. If the spot is successful, they predict it may go nationwide—air on one of the network-news programs."

No, he hadn't told her. "You seem pleased," Diana said cautiously. She hated to think what would happen to Mike's life if he became famous in his own right. Would he have time for her then? Or would their friendship fall by the wayside?

He nodded, taking a sip of his wine. He was so deep in thought he failed to notice her distressed expression. "I still have a long way to go before I realize my dream, but it's a start."

Again Diana's feelings were in turmoil. Part of her wanted what he wanted, and part of her felt excluded. Although she didn't want to risk spoiling their amiable mood, she knew there were things that needed to be brought out into the open. "Why didn't you tell me about your plans for expanding the setup at the ranch sooner?" Diana asked quietly as they seated themselves at a white wrought-iron table. She was still stinging over that.

The adjacent garden was gilded in moonlight, fragrant with the scent of magnolia blossoms and Texas roses.

Mike was quiet a long moment, his mouth forming an unhappy thin line. "I guess it had something to do with my last serious entanglement with a woman—you know, the fiancée I told you about? When she found out I didn't want to go into lucrative private practice after I graduated, she hit the ceiling. In her view it was fine to be compassionate during the day as long as we both came home at night to a cushy, carefree existence. Her needs had to be met first, and to hell with what my plans were. The bottom line was that she loved me for what I could provide, not for who I was. I'm not conscious of it, but I guess I've been a little leery ever since. I knew I'd never be happy unless I did have my dream, and so I haven't wanted anything to jeopardize that."

Diana knew how that felt. "My marriage left a few scars, too." Because she'd been married to a workaholic, she didn't want to get involved with anyone who prized something else over her, either.

His voice dropped to a mesmerizing pitch. "Since we argued I've gone over and over in my mind how I could make it up to you."

He already had, with just a few kisses. Diana didn't want to think about what that meant where her will-power was concerned. "And what did you come up with?" she asked, trying hard to keep the breathless excitement from her voice.

His mouth lifted in a half smile. "No answers, just a few facts. I care about you. I miss you when I'm not around you. The bottom line is I want to see more of you, and I'm confident if we both stay flexible, and make some adjustments to our respective schedules, we can work this out."

Diana sighed. She hadn't expected him to be so direct, but now that he had been didn't she owe it to herself to be frank, too? And if he was willing to try harder to save what they'd begun, shouldn't she? After all, an attraction like theirs didn't come along every day. She could live her whole life and never find that kind of chemistry with anyone else! It wasn't a risk she was willing to take, not without at least giving it a good shot. "I want to see more of you, too," she confessed softly, her eyes holding his. She paused, her mind returning involuntarily to the problems that had separated them in the first place. "But we still have these fundamental differences..." she said, then bit her lip.

"And fundamental desires." He stopped and put his hand over hers, warmly increasing the pressure, telling her with just his touch how much he cared. "Don't shut me out, Diana," he said. "Please."

She found strength in their closeness, being together.

"I'm not going back to the ranch until late Sunday night." He paused again, this time his mind made up. "I had planned to take the boys to NASA tomorrow with Melanie and Jim, but there's nothing they can't handle without me. And besides, it's time I had a few days off. Can you stay the rest of the weekend? Will you?''

"To do what?" she asked cautiously, willfully suppressing a joy that felt suddenly selfish.

But Mike had no qualms or second thoughts as he urged, "Spend time with me, of course." He touched her face gently, and the sexy caress of his fingers was as exciting as the caress of his lips. "With no one from Libertyville looking over our shoulders."

This was the kind of sign she had been looking for, that Mike wouldn't always put her second to his dream and the needs of his kids. That he would make time for them, too. Special time. Private time. "The answer is yes," she said, sliding closer to gently kiss his lips in silent promise. "Yes, yes, yes."

Chapter Ten

"You'd think I'd be able to manage lacing up a simple pair of ice skates," Diana complained Saturday afternoon at the Galleria Center rink.

Mike grinned at her frustrated moue, his own manner relaxed and confident. "Still too tight, huh?"

Diana wrinkled her nose and sighed in defeat. "No, this time I've got them too loose," she murmured in defeat, standing up and testing her weight on each thin-bladed shoe. For some reason today she was all thumbs, whereas Mike... Mike was all easy, predatory grace.

"Can't have that," Mike cautioned in a steady voice. He glanced at her skates thoughtfully. "You'll end up breaking your ankle."

Perish the thought! It was enough to hope, after several years away from the sport, that she would at least do well enough not to embarrass herself or him. She smiled ruefully at the next image that appeared in her mind—the two of them sprawled together on the ice, their limbs hopelessly, helplessly entangled.

"Losing your nerve?" he teased, reading the look on her face.

"No, never." If there was one thing she wouldn't be accused of, it was cowardice. "Just thinking." Her voice drifted off as she once again dwelled on the image of her body entwined with his, only this time not on the ice.

"About what?" he prompted lazily.

She wasn't going to tell, not now anyway, she thought. Quickly she moved on to safer territory. "That if I do fall, then you'll have to carry me back to my hotel," she retorted, laughing and giving him a playful glance.

His face lit up at the possibility. "I wouldn't mind that. But you're right—" he eyed her slender frame as if assessing her weight "—it is a long trek to the parking garage. I'd probably get so winded between here and there I'd have to stop for mouth-to-mouth resuscitation several times."

"At the very least."

"Oh, yeah." He nodded solemnly.

"And I bet you know just the person to give it to you." She'd meant her voice to be frolicsome not caressing; somehow it was both.

His eyes sparkled and then softened, and he looked as if he were enjoying the repartee immensely. "I admit I had someone special in mind. Someone very special," he said, his eyes holding hers for a long moment. Hand on her shoulder, he guided her gently back to the wooden bench. "Allow me, m'lady," he said with mock gallantry, kneeling in front of her.

"I take it this means you know what you're doing?" Diana queried lightly, all too aware he had managed to lace his own skates perfectly the first time around. She wondered absently if his dexterity would extend to other things as well. Like...well, never mind what.

"In every sense," he retorted, just as lightly. Unlacing the ties swiftly to the toe of the boot, he pulled the tongue straight, and then began systematically tightening the laces until they were just the right tension. He looked up quizzically, his hands resting lightly on the boot. "How's this?"

"Perfect," Diana said, managing to keep her voice level despite the subtle new tension thrumming in her.

Moments later he was finished. Diana tested her skates, and, as she had expected, found them to be perfect. Mike modestly brushed off her thanks and, her hand in his, led her to the edge of the ice. "It's always easier to lace someone else's skates."

"True." But he hadn't needed any help lacing his.

To her enjoyment, Diana found him to be as adept on the ice as he was at everything else. To her relief, she hadn't forgotten what to do. She glided along with him expertly, her hand still tucked in his, aware she felt more content now than she had in a long time, and it was all due to the man she was with. "Where'd you learn to skate so well?" she asked. It was a skill few Southern men had; but he appeared to have been doing it all his life.

"My parents have a condo in Vail. We used to go skiing every winter and I did a lot of skating there, too." He slanted her an affectionate glance and she noted his cheeks were ruddy from the cold in the rink. "I'll take you there sometime. What about you? Where'd you learn to skate?"

"I used to roller-skate all the time when I was a kid. Then when they built this mall, while I was in law school, some of my friends used to come here for exercise and a break from studying. It was a lot of fun, ice-skating inside when it was a hundred degrees outside."

"I know what you mean. Cold?" He looked down, noting goose bumps had risen on her arms.

"A little," she admitted. Both were dressed in walking shorts and short-sleeved shirts—not regular skating attire, but then they hadn't had the idea to go skating until they'd arrived at the mall and seen the other skaters having such a good time on the ice.

"Come closer." He wrapped a lone arm about her waist and held one of her hands with his free hand. "I'm freezing too. We'll have to skate faster to stay warm." As he spoke he picked up his pace and Diana followed easily. Locked loosely together, in the correct couple's skating style, they circled the rink several times. When they were winded, they went over to have some hot coffee and a doughnut from one of the vendors in the mall. "This is the best afternoon I've had in a long time," Diana confessed, "and I can't wait to see how your painting looks when they get it framed."

"I can't believe you talked me into that," Mike said, rolling his eyes.

"Oh, you know it's good!" Diana chided warmly. "It's damn good!"

His face flushed with pleasure at the sincerity of her compliment. "I know you think so anyway. And that means a lot."

To Diana's disappointment, however, by the time they got to the shop to pick up the painting, it had already been wrapped in protective brown paper and string.

"Unless you've got X-ray eyes, staring at that heavy brown paper won't do you a bit of good," Mike teased as they started for the mall parking garage.

Diana stomped her foot in exaggerated frustration. "I can't help it. I'm dying to see what it looks like framed."

"All right. You can take it up to your hotel room and look at it before you change for dinner." They had reservations at Brennan's.

"Don't you want to see it, too?" Diana asked, as they made the short drive to her hotel. She didn't see how he could not want to.

"Sure—" Mike shrugged as if it didn't matter much to him either way "—if I'm invited up to your room. If not—" he glanced at her in a way that let her know it was okay "—I'll just wait for you in the lobby." From there, they would go back to his parents' house so he could dress.

"You come with me," Diana ordered passionately. "I want you to see this, to appreciate what you've done."

No sooner had they entered the room than she was tearing off the string and paper. Diana had expected the painting to look spectacular; even so she wasn't prepared for how much it touched her. "Mike, it's magnificent," she breathed. "Truly, it is." It was incredible to think he'd had that much artistic ability in him at such a tough age.

"You think so?" He was looking at her expression, not the painting.

"I really do." Diana returned his ardent look. She touched the frame lovingly. "And the natural oak frame you picked out is much better than the gold-leaf one the store owner kept trying to push.

"It'll go better with the furnishings in your house."

For a moment, the enormity of what he'd said didn't register.

At her quizzical look, he said, "You've got ten times the emotional investment I'll ever have in that picture already. I'm giving it to you."

For a moment she was so stunned she couldn't speak, but she had only to look at the serious expression on his face to know he meant what he said. Suddenly there was a catch in her throat and a welcome in her heart for this very special man. "You're sure?" she pressed, deeply touched.

"Very sure," he said softly, taking her into his arms. "You see things in me no one else does, Diana." He was grateful and smitten. "I want to hold on to that."

So did she. "It's a two-way street, you know," she answered gently. He had a way of making her feel generous and kind and giving. Qualities she wasn't used to associating with herself.

"Then we're two of a kind," he said tenderly, his thumb tracing the line of her cheekbone. The fingers of his other hand threaded through her hair. She felt the warmth of his touch infiltrate her entire being, and when he touched his mouth to hers, the unique taste of him flooded her senses. She moaned softly in response, feeling her knees go weak. Only when the languid caress drew to a halt did she try to speak. "Mike—"

"I know, I know. I'm asking for trouble." He admitted breathlessly, as unrepentant as if making love to her was his lifelong ambition. He kissed her again, a deep warm kiss that had her whole being trembling and her mind swirling. Feeling deliciously desirable, she wrapped her arms around his neck and continued the caress with leisurely sensuality, letting herself hope, and dream, as she never had before.

"*We're* asking for trouble," she corrected, when at last they'd stopped again to catch their breath.

His hands around her waist, he held her steady. "Maybe we are at that," he countered huskily, all the love he felt for her reflected in his eyes. "Oh, Diana," he whispered, drawing her close. He began to nuzzle her neck, sending frissons of pleasure down her spine. She knew then that she needed to be with him as much as she needed to breathe, and that her mind had really been made up long before they'd entered her hotel room, or gone skating together that afternoon. She'd known, at least subconsciously, that this had been what she'd wanted for a very long time. For them to be together. The need was urgent and powerful, the need to make their bodies one.

Feeling her surrender in the soft yielding of her body against his, he groaned. He kissed her hard and she opened her mouth to the urgent probing of his tongue.

"Diana?" His voice was strained and serious as he looked at her. "You're certain this is what you want?" As much as he wanted her—she could feel his want in the tense hardness of his thighs—he wouldn't take advantage, wouldn't ever let her do anything she'd later regret.

She knew it was time he heard how she felt. "I need you, Mike," she whispered back as her arms possessively circled his neck, her fingers threaded through the dark silk of his hair and caressed his cheek and lingered on the soft moist line of his mouth. "I need you. And I know what I want," she continued huskily, standing on tiptoe and giving her mouth back to his.

His eyes darkened with desire. "Oh God, Diana. I need you, too. You just...have no idea how much." Without another word he swept her into his arms and carried her to the bed. She could feel how much he wanted her as he stretched out beside her, fully clothed. And yet they had time, they both knew, all the time in the world....

"I think we're forgetting something," she teased, kicking off her sneakers, starting to relax, to feel herself fill with erotic anticipation.

He grinned lazily, drawling in a spine-tinglingly sexy voice, "Think so?" He sat up long enough to kick off his shoes and unbutton his shirt. Lying back down beside her, he let his eyes drift over her, murmuring, "I promise you we'll get to everything—in due time. But for right now," he said with a roguish smile, "I need to hold you...."

Diana felt as if she could lose herself forever in the splendor of that one unending kiss, and for a while that was all they did, his mouth caressing hers, his tongue intimately invading, exploring, simulating the evocative rhythm of the coupling to come. She relaxed against him, breathing in the masculine fragrance of his skin, aware she had never felt so safe or so cherished, so paralyzed by the hot river of pleasure that followed his questing touch.

As their kisses continued, passion turned to yearning, and she found all the things she needed in him—tenderness, concern, kindness, compassion. And yet to her satisfaction there was finesse, too—he knew just how and when and where to touch. He knew without her telling him when she was comfortable enough to more fully undress, and when she did, her breath caught as he caressed her breasts, his lips touching off fires on the silken curves of her flesh.

Impatient, tingling, she arched her back, lost in mindless pleasure, need, the sense they were meant to be together. Driven to make him feel, she touched him as he touched her, learning everything that aroused him, learning what was too much, what was not enough, until he was as excited as she.

"Make love to me," she whispered, trembling from head to toe.

"Yes, oh, yes."

His eyes dark with the depth of his desire, they moved to rid themselves of the last of their clothes. She sighed as he brought her to him once again. Touching length to length was a satiation in its own, arousing, binding them together heart and soul. Dreams of the future, of love, had been exempt from her life for so long, but she opened herself to them now as he slipped inside her slowly, silencing her gasp with his mouth. Still kissing, their hands touching, caressing, they moved together in a harmony that was stunning in its perfection. And yet even as he demanded, he gave until he, too, surrendered and they both lost themselves in the quiet splendor of their love.

"YOU LOOK SAD," Mike murmured early the next morning as Diana finished packing.

"I guess I am," she admitted on a sigh. It had been a wonderful weekend, a wonderful night. Now it was time to get back down to earth, back down to reality.

"Don't want to go back to Libertyville?" He laced his hands around her waist and nuzzled her neck.

Diana relaxed against him, wishing they had just one more day, one more hour. But checkout was eleven, and it was now ten forty-five.

"I guess I don't, as amazing as that is. I never liked Houston that much while I was living here—maybe because I was raised in a small town north of Dallas—but now that I'm here with you I don't find it so bad."

"Neither do I, and I admit I haven't been crazy about the city for some time—traffic, noise, pollution. I kind of like living on a ranch."

"So you're not looking forward to going back, either," she noted dispassionately.

"Not if it means I have to be away from you." His look was honest, intent. And asking things of her she just couldn't give, considering the circumstances of small-town life. Just the fact she was dating him was scandal enough.

Diana dropped her head, resting her forehead on the solidness of his shoulder, knowing she had to tell him what was on her mind. "I want to be with you, Mike, I do." If only he had half an idea how much! "But... it's just that Libertyville's such a small town—everyone knows everyone else's business there." She didn't want her sleeping with him to be common knowledge; somehow that would spoil it, make it seem tawdry when it was not.

"You think it'd be hard to carry on an affair discreetly." He sighed, disappointed.

"All you'd have to do is spend one night at my place, and half the town would know it by breakfast, the other half by lunch." Because she was an elected official, she couldn't afford that kind of scandal.

"And because of the boys my place is out of the question."

"It'd be just as obvious if we were always out of town at the same time, too." Diana sighed, seeing no solution. She liked sleeping with him, waking wrapped in the warmth of his arms, the intimacy of sharing breakfast and the shower, as much as making love. She'd been independent far too long to like the idea of having to carry on an affair under the restrictions as to what was proper and what wasn't. She wanted to do what she felt, what she knew in her heart was right, without worrying how others would see it or how it would affect her political career.

"Hmm." He narrowed his eyes thoughtfully. "I guess with the ramifications of your career we do have a logistical problem," he said slowly at last. One he hadn't really considered until now.

Diana nodded, her normal resolve returning. "But not one that can't be worked around if we put our thinking caps on." They could still be together, somehow, someway.

He grinned, pulling her near, touching his lips to hers, then pausing for a lingering kiss. "Lady, I like your style."

DIANA DROVE BACK to Libertyville alone, knowing Mike was not far behind her with the boys and that he would call her later that evening, once the boys were settled at the ranch.

Whistling as she walked into her house, she dropped her suitcases in the entryway, then went back out to the car for the painting. Shutting the door behind her, she went straight to the pantry for the toolbox she kept there.

She was going to hang the painting right away, and she knew just the place for it—right above the sofa in the living room. Opening the door, she looked in, then blinked and gasped simultaneously.

In seconds she found herself up against the wall, a knife at her throat. "Don't scream, Justice," a grubby-looking Donald Griffin warned. "Not one sound." He laid the blade against her throat, letting her know he meant business.

Beads of perspiration sprang out on her forehead, throat. Diana started to nod, then checked the impulse, the cold blade of steel reminding her not to move. "I won't," Diana promised, her heart pounding so hard she thought it would fly right out of her chest. There was a roaring in her ears, and a peculiar metallic taste in her mouth, and the feeling of abject terror was incredibly strong. "Please, don't hurt me," she said. She was surprised to hear herself begging calmly for her life, but not surprised she wanted to live. She had everything to live for, and she'd be damned if she'd let some ex-con take what she'd found with Mike away from her before she had a chance to really experience his love.

Griffin's eyes were wild, darting, crazed. "I have no intention of hurting you, unless you make it absolutely necessary. I don't want a murder rap hanging around my neck, too. So as long as you do exactly what I say, you have nothing to worry about," he said with a kind of manic civility. "Now move!" Grabbing a handful of hair, he guided her roughly to a chair in the kitchen and forced her into it. Diana landed hard on the oak seat, aware the knife was still at her throat. I'm dealing with a Jeckyl and Hyde, she thought. Sometimes the guy is rational, and sometimes he's not—

"Put your hands behind you," Donald ordered gruffly. "Do it!" he shouted when she was slow to move.

Diana did as she was told. He grabbed her shaking hands roughly, the knife clattering to the floor, and pulling a length of rope from his pocket, he began tying her wrists together. "Not so tight," Diana complained, aware she was perspiring now from head to foot.

"Shut up," he growled. "Shut up!" Finished securing the knots, he studied her face. "Now you're going to do me a favor. You're going to phone that ranch and get my kid over here. I don't care what excuse you use. Just get him over here and get him over here alone! You understand? Because anyone else who shows up here is going to get hurt. I'm not leaving without my kid." He tightened his grip on her hair until tears flowed from Diana's eyes.

"I understand," she said calmly, her mind working, although she was careful to keep her look blank.

She would do what he said, and somehow manage simultaneously to warn Mike of the danger. "But they may not be there," she continued quietly, wanting Donald Griffin to be prepared for any eventuality. "They were . . . they were in Houston this weekend, too."

Glowering, he walked over and punched in seven buttons on the kitchen wall phone. "You better not be lying to me, Justice."

It was ringing. The knife at her throat again, he placed the receiver next to her ear.

Diana almost sobbed when she heard Mike's harried voice pick up the phone on the tenth ring. "Hello—"

"Mike." Her voice was trembling and husky.

"Diana?" he asked, instantly alarmed by her unsteady tone. "What is it? Where are you?"

Griffin's face turned dark red with anger. He nicked the tender skin of her neck, and the knife had a drop of blood on its tip. Diana saw the wild desperation in his eyes, and she knew she had to make her call good.

She swallowed hard, fighting for control, and took a deep, measured breath. "Mike you're going to think this is silly, but I need to see Kevin this afternoon. You know how upset he's been since his computer was stolen. Well, you won't believe this, but one of the neighbors anonymously donated a used personal computer today, complete with software, and it had Kevin's name on it, and it's here, and well, I'd kind of like it to be a surprise. I know you have a lot to do. . . ."

"You're right about that." His voice was a mixture of bewilderment and annoyance. "You realize I just walked in the door and I haven't even been to the grocery store."

"Perfect then. You can drop Kevin off here, and go on to the grocery store, then pick him up later. And Mike, don't bring the other boys. I wouldn't want them to feel left out, and I haven't had a chance to arrange to get them any replacement items. You know how depressed Kevin has been about his father," she added for good measure, slightly emphasizing the last word, "so maybe this would be a good way to cheer him up."

Silence on the other end. Sweat was pouring down Diana's face, streaming into her mouth. She wanted to say more, to scream, but she was afraid. Wild-eyed, still wielding his knife, Griffin waited.

He was on drugs, Diana thought, getting a closer look at his face and realizing finally why he was so off kilter. He was high as a kite.

"All right. I'll be there as soon as I can," Mike said curtly. "Twenty minutes?"

As far as Diana was concerned, that wasn't a moment too soon. "Perfect," she said quietly.

The next twenty minutes were the longest in Diana's life.

She waited, her pulse pounding, while Donald paced. Only when her front doorbell rang, did Griffin move to untie her. "Remember, act naturally as you let him in. I'll be right behind you."

Grabbing her by the arm, he shoved her in the direction of the door. "Just open it and step back," he said, not letting loose of her arm.

Swallowing, Diana did as ordered. Maybe Kevin could reason with his father. Bring him back down to earth.

To her mixed feelings of relief and worry, Mike was beside Kevin, which was not what Griffin wanted. But it was too late, and Mike pushed on in without waiting for an invitation. As he did so, Griffin yanked Diana back. Before she could do more than stomp on his instep, he had his arm around her throat, the knife pointed at her heart.

Kevin was inside, too. "One wrong move, Harrigan, and she's dead," Griffin warned.

Utterly calm, Mike shut the door behind him. Kevin was white as a sheet, looking as if at any moment he might faint. "Dad," he croaked finally, anguished. "What are you doing?"

"What does it look like I'm doing? I came to get you."

"But I...I thought you were in Canada." Kevin blinked.

"I was. And I'm going back. I've got everything I need set up. I've got your computer up there, your telescope, everything...."

Mike turned to Griffin enraged. "You broke into the ranch."

"I knew Kevin would want his stuff when the time came. 'Course I had to steal some other stuff, too, like rob a gas station down on Main Street to throw the cops off the trail. Fenced most of it, except for Kevin's stuff."

So the boys hadn't robbed Billy's gas station, Diana thought.

Griffin turned to Kevin and shouted out the next order hoarsely. "There's a rope in the kitchen. Go get it!"

"Dad—"

"Dammit, move!"

Swallowing, Kevin fearfully went to do as bid. Mike stayed where he was, his eyes on the knife. "You don't want to do this, Griffin," he said calmly.

The man didn't loosen his grip on Diana. "The hell I don't! I lost my wife. I lost my job. I'm not losing my boy, too, and you can tell that to the state!"

Kevin was back. "Tie him up." Griffin pointed to Mike.

Mike looked at Kevin in silent entreaty. *Don't do this.*

Tears were streaming down Kevin's face. "I've got to," he said raggedly and motioned for Mike to sit down. Swiftly, Kevin tied Mike's hands and feet. During the grim procedure, Griffin hovered over both of them, his arm still around Diana's neck, almost choking off her breath, as he made sure the knots were viciously tight.

"Now her," Kevin's father ordered, shoving Diana at his son. He stayed close, waving the knife at Diana's face, canceling any hope she had of struggling to get free. "And get her farther away from him." He pointed at Mike. "I don't want them trying to untie each other as soon as we leave."

"You needn't worry about me," Mike interjected. "My arms are already going numb."

"Shut up!" Griffin growled, looking suddenly anxious, paranoid.

And it was then, in that instant, that Kevin shouted, "Dad! Behind you! Get down!"

There was nothing there of course, but the trumped-up diversion was all the opening Diana needed. She grabbed a poker from the fireplace and brought it down heavily on Griffin's arm, knocking the knife from his hand. He cried out in pain and lunged for it. But Mike had hurled his body out of the chair and knocked Griffin off balance. And then Kevin tackled his father around the middle, knocking him to the ground. "I'm not going to let you do this, Dad," he screamed, crying hysterically as he got his prone father in a headlock. "I'm not, I'm not, I'm not...."

THE SHERIFF LEFT several hours later, after taking a detailed report from Diana, Mike and Kevin. Kevin had been crying on and off throughout the questioning. He'd cried especially hard after his father was taken away in a squad car.

"How about some hot chocolate?" an exhausted Diana asked after they'd left.

Kevin shrugged at first, not at all interested in food or drink after what had passed, but then remembering his manners, he recovered and said politely, "Sure. Okay. Thanks, Diana."

"You're welcome," she said tiredly. Anything to get them back to some semblance of normality. "Mike?"

"Coffee, if you've got it."

"Coming up." Although Diana was still shaken, she took comfort in the routineness of puttering around the kitchen.

"What do you think is going to happen to my dad now?" Kevin asked quietly, once the chocolate and coffee had been delivered. He wrapped his hands around the steaming mug.

"I don't know. Probably he'll be turned over for psychiatric evaluation and drug rehabilitation," Mike said quietly, refusing to sugarcoat the situation. "My guess is he'll go to jail."

More tears slipped down Kevin's face. "Do you think they can help him?" he asked finally.

Mike met his gaze honestly. "I know they'll try. In the meantime, we've got to work on you. You've taken a giant step today in refusing to help your father. And I'm proud of you, incredibly proud. But emotionally you still have a lot to work out, and to do that you need to talk it out more," he said firmly.

"With you?"

Mike nodded. "And maybe a support group for teenagers who've been in similar situations. What do you say? Will you give it a try?" Mike wouldn't push, but they all knew what he wanted.

Kevin was motionless, dread whitening his already pale features. He swallowed hard, looking first at Mike, then

Diana, then back at Mike again. "I guess," he said finally. "If you want me to...."

"I do," Mike said softly, his own eyes moist.

"Will you come with me?"

Mike smiled and reached over and put a paternal arm around Kevin's shoulder. "I will."

Finally, Diana thought, because of Mike, Kevin had a chance.

Chapter Eleven

"I'm sorry," Agnes McCarthy said abruptly, moving away from her desk in the cramped quarters of the Historical Society, after studying for an inordinately long time Ernie's best watercolors, oils and charcoal drawings. "We can't use Ernie's paintings of the Hill Country here. Maybe you could try one of the art dealers in Austin, or that tourist trap—" At Mike's glare, she censored herself abruptly. "Er, gallery in Marble Falls. You know, the one that specializes in unknown artists."

Mike had hoped, when Agnes had called him to say she and the others were interested in looking at Ernie's work, that it meant a surefire deal for his foster son. So, he'd brought not just Ernie, but Carlos and Kevin, and now he was sorry he had. He should have known a self-righteous woman like Agnes wouldn't really do anything that encouraged the boys. No, she'd meant to humiliate them all along, and she had done a bang-up job of it in just fifteen lousy minutes, destroying with a few dismissive sentences a lot of the work he, and the art teacher he'd hired, had done for his charge all summer long.

Ernie sat beside him quietly, his posture slumped, the hope crushed out of him. It was as if, with his low self-esteem, he'd secretly figured a possible sale of his art was too good to be true. "Thanks anyway, ma'am," he said, beginning to gather up his work.

"Thanks for nothing, you mean," Carlos cut in angrily.

Agnes's chin lifted another notch. "You just stay away from my niece, young man. You hear me?"

"You're coming through loud and clear," Carlos shot back.

Wordlessly, Kevin helped Ernie pick up the rest of the stuff. "This don't mean nothin', man," he said, patting his friend on the back. Kevin paused to glare at Agnes— the only member of the Historical Society who had shown up for the viewing. He smiled slowly, as if formulating with great glee what he was about to say next. "This old biddy wouldn't know a good piece of art if it came up and bit her on the nose."

The other boys burst into laughter. Agnes's face suffused with blood. It was all Mike could do not to break into laughter himself.

"I see your hooligans still have no manners," Agnes leveled her verdict heavily, glaring at Mike.

Mike was tempted to say, "They only use them in the presence of a lady." But knowing to insult her so flagrantly would set a bad example for his foster kids, he only said in a calm, clear voice, "C'mon boys, let's get out of here. We've wasted more than enough time for one afternoon."

All three were grumbling as they left. "I can't believe what she did, man," Kevin was the first to comfort Ernie once they were alone.

"Oh, she's just trying to get back at you because of me and her niece," Carlos said.

"Have you been seeing her niece?" Mike asked.

Carlos paused. With effort, he assumed a look of choirboy innocence. "How could I do that?"

That was just it; Mike didn't know.

Later that evening, he told Diana about what had transpired. "She can be so mean spirited sometimes!" Diana exclaimed in dismay. "Ten to one, the other ladies in the Historical Society had no idea what she was doing, either."

"Maybe this incident will provide the ammunition they need to get her to step down from her position as president."

"I don't think so." Diana put a bag of sour-cream-and-onion popcorn into her microwave, and switched it on.

"Why not?" Mike spoke a little louder to be heard over the humming noise of the oven.

"Because Agnes owns the building the Society is housed in, and she leases it to them free of charge."

"Thereby guaranteeing her continued election as president," Mike concluded dryly.

"Something like that, yeah."

Mike sighed. "I had hoped by now to win everyone in this town over to the idea of the kids staying."

"And you have, with the Neighbors Helping Neighbors program. Everyone except Agnes, and a couple of her diehard friends. And I think even they might slowly come around if it weren't for Agnes's constant doom-and-gloom prophesying." Removing the popped corn from the oven, Diana opened the bag, and poured the contents into two large bowls. Feeling as at home in her kitchen as he was in his own, Mike fixed the drinks. Together, they went into the living room and sank down on the sofa.

Diana relaxed beside him, feeling cozy and replete in his presence, if a bit worried about the boys. "So how's Ernie doing?"

"He's fine. Depressed, of course, but he also knows Agnes did that out of spite, not out of a lack of appreciation for his art."

"Do you have any thoughts about trying to market his work elsewhere?"

Mike paused. "I don't know. This was so rough on him...."

Diana turned to him, animated. "What if they could sell a painting over at a gallery in Marble Falls? Wouldn't that be something?"

Mike frowned, considering. "I don't want to put him through any more trauma. As an amateur artist myself once, I know how much goes into every stroke of the brush. I don't want his feelings hurt, especially when his self-esteem is in such precarious balance."

Diana linked hands with Mike. "He's still having trouble reading?"

"Yeah." Mike's hand tightened over hers. "He's improving, but so slowly the change seems barely discernible to him. Most sessions leave him frustrated, and with the new school year starting in another month..." Mike's voice trailed off in discouragement.

Suddenly Diana had an idea. She sat forward earnestly, then swiveled around to face Mike, her knee nudging his thigh in the process. "What if Ernie didn't know we were trying to sell his painting?"

"What do you mean?" Mike cupped his other hand over her bent knee, absently stroking the place through the fabric of her slacks.

"Couldn't we just tell him I wanted it for my house? After all, I have one of yours hanging up." She turned to look admiringly at it. "That's not so farfetched, is it? He'd believe it."

Mike's eyes were troubled. "He probably would, but that's not the problem. Telling him that would be dishonest. And I've made it a rule to always be straight with the kids."

"I know," Diana soothed, touching his cheek with the back of her hand. The skin was rough with the beginnings of evening beard. "But I think this once we'd be better off shielding his feelings." She dropped her hand, continuing emotionally, "I just can't bear to leave it like this, with him thinking his art is no good. If it did sell, we could tell him the truth. He'd appreciate the fact that we cared enough to get another, more genuine opinion of his art. He wouldn't mind that, would he, particularly if it validated what we've all been feeling about him and his talent?" If not, they wouldn't have to tell him; he'd never know.

"I guess not," Mike said. "After what Agnes did, I think it's important we do whatever we can to help restore his self-esteem." He paused. "You really care about the kids, don't you?"

"Yes, I guess I do." Diana was silent. Her feelings weren't what she'd expected. In fact, she would've bet against them happening. But they had, and she was beginning to see she might fit into Mike Harrigan's life after all.

"WHAT'S THE BIG SURPRISE?" Mike demanded several nights later, as Diana drove him toward a mystery destination.

"If I told you where we were going, it'd spoil it," Diana insisted imperiously. "Now keep your eyes closed!"

"C'mon, can't I take a little peek?" he said gruffly, but with a note of amusement.

"No!" Through her laughter, she struggled to keep her voice stern. "Now keep those gorgeous blue eyes of yours closed, Michael Harrigan! You promised me you'd be cooperative!"

Mike groaned with mock indignation. "That was before I knew this surprise was going to take hours to be delivered."

"It hasn't been hours, silly. It's only been twenty minutes." She slanted him a flirtatious glance, all too aware of how handsome he looked this evening, his dark hair combed neatly into place, his clothes neatly pressed, his freshly shaven jaw scented with a rich, enticing after-shave. "You're not good at taking orders, are you?" she teased.

He slitted open one eye and aimed it her way. "And you are?" he asked, incredulous.

"Michael Harrigan, you're peeking!" Not that his brief view of the winding country highway would tell him anything of her plans. In fact she was betting he hadn't a clue. She'd seen to that, doing tons of things to throw him off the track, including wearing a dress and high heels.

"Okay, okay." He promptly shut both eyes again and leaned his head back against the headrest.

Minutes later, Diana guided her car carefully into the parking space she'd arranged for earlier. She switched off the engine. "You can open your eyes now," she said softly.

Mike blinked. In front of him was a solitary camping place, with a pitched tent and picnic table. "The cool-er's in the trunk, as well as some outdoor clothing for both of us. And just so you'll know, we're at Inks Lake." She'd asked for and gotten them the most private camp-site possible when she'd driven up earlier in the day to get everything squared away.

"This is... You set this up?" he asked, stunned.

She shrugged modestly, able to tell by the joy leaping in his eyes how happy he was. "You said you never got to go camping enough when you were younger. I figured the two of us could remedy that—starting now."

His grin widened and his eyes sparkled wickedly. "How many sleeping bags in that tent?"

She grinned back, getting out of the car. "One, and it's a double. We've also got enough food and beverage to feed an army.'' In his absence, Melanie and Jim would handle the boys.

"But no one else is invited," he ascertained quickly, circling around the front of the vehicle to her side.

"No one but you and me," she assured, standing on tiptoe to give him a brief, chaste kiss.

"Just the way I like it," he said, pulling her to him for a long, passionate kiss. When he finally lifted his head again, both were breathless. "And, Diana, thank you for this."

Diana smiled and wreathed her arms around his neck. "You're number one in my book, Mike," she informed him tranquilly, aware she had never felt so replete before, "and you always will be." She kissed him again, ardently this time. "Nothing else, no one will ever destroy what we have." She wouldn't let them.

"HOMEMADE PEACH PIE. You spoil me, Diana."

"I know." She smiled and seated herself on the edge of Mike's desk. Not that the special treatment was one-sided. Mike had been showering her with gifts for days now; he'd taken her dancing, to dinner, discovered her favorite perfume and then bought a huge bottle of it. At his ranch, she'd learned the rudiments of horseback riding, and though she was still far from expert, she was now capable of riding with him along the various winding paths around his property.

"I've always heard the way to a man's heart is through his stomach," she teased. "I thought I'd test the theory."

Mike dipped his finger into the sugary liquid pooling beneath one of the slits and offered it to her to taste, before sucking off the rest himself. "Hmm, it works. But that's not the only way to a man's heart," he teased back with a wicked grin that had her blood warming. His ardent gaze seemed to be tempting her to discover them all. And the sooner the better.

Aware they were at his house and could be interrupted at any moment, Diana kept her desire in check. Knowing a change of subject was in order if she was ever to get her mind off him and his exquisite lovemaking, she glanced down at the materials spread across his desk. "So." She cleared her throat dramatically, looking for safety in a more mundane discussion. "What are you doing?"

"Going over some files on other foster children. Now that my probation period is about to end, social services is going to allow me to take in three more kids, and if they work out, in another three months, three more, and so on and so on. I figure by the end of the year I'll be up to nine, maybe even twelve, if I'm lucky and they move up the date a little—What is it?"

Diana swallowed hard. This was like the return of a bad dream. Only it wasn't a dream, it was real. She shook off her feelings of jealousy and unease. "Nothing. I just..." Suddenly she couldn't keep her thoughts to herself. "Mike, everything has been so good here." She studied him, weighing the risks, and decided finally for both their sakes, for their future, that she had to be blunt. She took a deep breath and plunged on, heedless of the way his expression was darkening unhappily in anticipation of what she was going to say, "Is it really necessary for you to rock the boat now? Kevin's barely adjusted and..."

He kept his eyes unflinchingly on her face. "Diana, you knew this was my plan. You've known for weeks now." He curtly emphasized the last.

Yes, Diana thought, but she had put it out of her thoughts. She knew she had no right to stop him, but she couldn't help thinking, selfishly, *What about us, Mike? How will this affect us?* She forced herself to have a more positive attitude and stop looking for trouble where there might be none. "Tell me more about the foster children you've been looking at," she said briskly.

"They all have stories that break your heart just hearing them," he said, "but mostly I want to concentrate on the kids that are really hard to place. Especially now that I've had some success—"

"What do you mean?" At his description of what he was looking for, a chill slid down her spine.

Oblivious to her fears, Mike pointed at the photo set front and center on his desk. "Well, like this boy, for instance. Robby Allen. Like Kevin, he comes from a family with a history of drug dependency and abuse. His mother's in jail, his father's been gone for some time."

"Wait a minute. You're not thinking of bringing him to Libertyville?" Diana asked. Surely they'd been through enough trauma for one summer, indeed possibly forever!

"Why not? Diana, this kid needs a place to go. And frankly it wouldn't hurt for Kevin to be around someone who has been through what he's been through. That kind of support is invaluable."

"But he can get that at his group-therapy sessions."

Mike's jaw hardened stubbornly. "It's not the same."

No, it wasn't, Diana thought, still resisting the idea. She tried to reason with him, make him see the ramifications of what he was about to do. "By bringing in a kid like that, with a history like that, you risk the same kind of problems you had with Kevin's father."

She could almost hear him mentally counting to ten, but when he spoke it was in that same implacable, I-know-what-I'm-doing tone he used with the boys when they were misbehaving. "I don't think so. For one thing, the boy's mother is in jail, not his father, and she's voluntarily given up her rights as a parent."

The atmosphere between them now was almost hostile, rife with anxiety. "What about the others you're interested in?" she asked, deciding this once she wouldn't back down or ignore her instincts, which were telling her now that if he continued as planned they were all heading for disaster. "Are their parents criminals, too?"

He looked at her, his mouth set in a bleak line. "I don't like the way you're sounding!" he countered brusquely.

"And I don't like what you're doing!" she snapped, her voice rising with emotion. "Bringing danger voluntarily to this town!"

He stared at her stonily. "Is that the way you see it?"

"Yes. And it's the way you should!" Without warning, hot bitter tears were streaming from her eyes. She remembered all too well what they had just been through. "Dammit, Mike, isn't what happened with Donald Griffin enough?" she whispered hoarsely. "How many times do you have to put my life—and the life of everyone around here—in danger?" How many people, and problems, did he have to put between them? Was he trying to shut her out of his life, or was he doing it unthinkingly?

He stared at her as if she were a stranger. "You're being unreasonable!" he ground out.

"I'm being realistic, something you, for all your psychology classes and advanced degrees, apparently never learned to do!"

He stood up and put his hands on the table between them, palms down. "Selfish is more like it," he said menacingly.

Although her first instinct was to recoil from his furious presence, she valiantly held her ground. Aware they were nose to nose, she lowered her voice to a seething whisper. "Maybe I am selfish to want to keep this town safe from harm, from the invasion of criminals. That's why most of the people live here, because Libertyville is so safe!'' Her voice had risen emotionally again, despite her efforts to keep it down.

"And uptight!'' he shouted back.

A furious silence ensued. Her fingers curled at her sides and she itched to slap his face. "I won't let you do this,'' she said quietly. She wouldn't let him put any of them through a similar situation, not her, not Agnes—who certainly would use the episode to ride him out of town on a rail—and especially not Kevin, who'd suffered more than enough turmoil and terror.

His dark brows lifted in contempt. "Is that a threat?''

"It's a statement of fact,'' Diana said firmly, recovering her composure. "Bring in healthy, orphaned boys. Boys without heavy emotional problems.'' Everyone would support him in that.

Mike regarded her coldly. "And what happens to the rest of them?''

His tone grated on her nerves. She crossed her arms. "It can't be my problem, Mike. It shouldn't be yours, considering all else you're responsible for.'' He had his three foster sons to think of. He had them—himself and her—to think of, and their relationship, and if he brought in truckloads of troubled kids, they'd have no time together at all.

Mike circled around to the front of his desk. He was standing so close his sheer physicality overwhelmed her. He glared at her until her heart sank like lead. "Well, there we disagree, because unlike you, I take some social responsibility for the homeless kids in this world. And I'm not afraid of risk. I don't turn tail and run every time I see a potential problem. I don't shut others out.''

She looked at him, for once having no reply. She knew instinctively there was no way they would ever agree on this, no matter how much they talked about it. Neither would bend. Neither could see their way clear to switch to the other side.

Suddenly Diana had no appetite for peach pie, or the home-churned vanilla ice cream he had promised her earlier, when planning their weeknight date at his ranch, and she sure as heck knew she couldn't sit through the videotape of *Overboard* he had planned for them to see, now that he'd finally had his TV and VCR replaced.

They had said enough, hurt each other enough for one evening. She backed up slightly and away. "I've got to go," she said, brushing past him and out of the room, past the gaping faces of the boys.

She half hoped he'd come after her, apologize, or if not that at least ask her to stay a while longer. But he didn't. And she knew then the trouble between them was there to stay.

Was Mike right? Was she afraid of emotional risk? Diana wondered several hours later. Was she merely being selfish and ungenerous?

The question was still on Diana's mind as she walked out of the courthouse the following day and saw Ernie in the park across the street.

Spotting her, he waved.

She walked over to see what he was painting. His rendering of the limestone courthouse building was exquisite. "My art teacher told me to work on linear objects," he explained.

"It looks great."

"Thanks, Diana."

Because of Mike, Ernie was happy. Because of Mike, a "throwaway" kid had a chance at a decent life. Because of Mike, the buildings on Main Street were all gleaming with fresh paint.

She'd thought she couldn't be with him on his terms, but the truth was she couldn't be without him. Not when she knew now the magic of their being together. "Mike around anywhere?" she asked casually.

"Yeah. He said he was goin' over to your house and I could meet him there." Ernie looked suddenly worried. "Didn't he tell you?"

"No." Aware Ernie was watching her with concern, she touched the bottom right corner of the painting. "Don't forget to sign that. Someday it could be worth a lot of money."

"Sure it will," Ernie drawled, shaking his head. But his dark eyes were alight with pleasure.

Diana found Mike on his hands and knees in front of her house. He was planting pots of flowers in the ground. He looked up when he heard her approach. His eyes still on her face, he sat back on his haunches. "Someone should've done this weeks ago," he said.

"I'm glad you're doing it for me now," Diana said softly, closing the distance between them. "But it wasn't necessary."

"Yes, it was." Mike stood. He drew off his work gloves and let them fall beside him. He took her by the shoulders. "I want you to be happy," he confessed softly, his eyes searching hers. His voice deepened. "The past couple of days I realized I haven't devoted myself to that end—not the way I should, the way I intend to in the future."

"Oh, Mike, I am happy—at least when I'm with you," she whispered back, tears filling her eyes. "It's when we're apart that I'm miserable."

At her revelation, his eyes lit with hope. Then the hope faded. "Diana, my plans for the future haven't changed..." he warned in a husky undertone.

"Mine have. I need more, Mike. More than I've had in the past." She took a deep breath, knowing she had to tell him everything she had recently discovered. "You were right. I *have* shut myself off from others. But being around you has changed all that. I don't think I could go back to living life just for me if I tried." She knew too much now, felt too much.

"Does that mean . . . ?" His voice caught, he didn't go on.

"I love you and I want to be with you," Diana confessed, moving into his arms. "Whatever else happens," she whispered as he embraced her lovingly, "I'll adjust."

He held her close, then kissed her firmly. "We both will."

UNFORTUNATELY THE PEACE Diana found with Mike wasn't to last. At two in the morning the phone rang. She answered on the third ring.

"Diana! Agnes McCarthy. I've already called the sheriff, but I thought you should know, too. . ." she began shrilly.

"Know what?" Diana sat up in bed, her pulse racing.

"Those three hooligans of Harrigan's have been prowling around my house again, and this time with my niece! I caught them trying to climb the trellis to her room. 'Course when they saw me they took off, but I'm not going to let it go this time without pressing charges. You ought to see my rosebushes! Ruined, all of them!"

"Calm down, Agnes. I'll be right over."

By the time Diana reached Agnes's house, Mike had arrived too. His face grim and white as he inspected the sagging rosebushes. For once, Agnes wasn't exaggerating. They were badly trampled. "I'm sorry. I'll pay for the damages," Mike said gruffly.

Diana noticed he wasn't even questioning whether or not his boys might have been there, and that was a bad sign. "Where are the boys, Mike?" she asked.

For a moment he didn't respond, his expression inexplicably bleak. "I don't know," he said finally in a tone barely above a whisper. "When Miss McCarthy called me, I checked their rooms. They weren't there."

Diana stared at him, incredulous.

"They make a habit of sneaking out at night, prowling our city streets?" Agnes screeched.

Indignant, Mike turned to her. "No, of course not," he said, recovering. Then as an afterthought, he added, "I'm sure there's an explanation for whatever happened tonight. When I find them I'll discover what it is." He seemed to be trying to reassure himself, Diana noted.

"What about your niece?" Diana asked Agnes. She hoped to heaven Martha hadn't run off with the guys!

"She's still inside. Pouting because I interrupted a romantic rendezvous, no doubt." Agnes looked at the deputy, her expression turning more sour. "If you find those boys, I want them arrested!"

The deputy nodded, then started for his car. Diana followed, superseding the older woman's instructions with her own. "If you find them, I want the boys turned over to either Mr. Harrigan or the counselors at his ranch."

"Right," the deputy said.

Mike stood next to Diana. "Thanks," he said, watching as the deputy drove off. Diana looked at him. "What's going on, Mike? What haven't you said?" She'd known both from the boys' actions and the grim look on his face that he was withholding something.

"It looks as if they've done more than just sneak out," Mike said finally, sighing. His eyes were troubled as they met hers. "It looks as if they've run away."

By morning, there was still no news of Mike's foster sons. Diana and Mike had spent all night driving around the area, looking for them to no avail. When they returned to Diana's home, she fixed them both some coffee and sat opposite Mike at the kitchen table. "They may have hitched a ride out of town. If that's true, then they're probably in Houston or Dallas by now."

"And maybe they're just lying low somewhere—somewhere in the hills," Mike theorized, still hanging on to the theory that they hadn't really left, that this was all some sort of prank. After all, the boys had played practical jokes on him and each other before.

Diana harbored no such illusions. "Did they take any food with them?"

"No."

"How much money did they have?"

Mike shrugged, his expression dejected. "Not a lot. Maybe thirty dollars between the three of them, if that."

"What happened last night?"

His mouth thinned and he made an impatient gesture with his hand. "They had a stupid fight over chores, who was supposed to do what. I lost my temper and sent them to their rooms for the night. I admit I could've handled it a little better, but even so, that's no reason for them to run away," he finished with heartfelt conviction.

"Maybe it was more to them than you knew," she pointed out quietly.

He crossed his arms and glared at her. "I don't believe that."

She sighed in exasperation. When would he take off his rose-colored glasses and face reality? The reality that not everyone in this world could be saved or reformed with regular doses of tender loving care, that for some it might be too late? "Then maybe there's been more going on with Carlos and Agnes's niece than any of us realized."

His eyes filled with fury. "I don't believe that, either," he said flatly.

Then what? Diana wondered, searching her mind for other plausible explanations. "Is it possible the two could have planned to elope?" That would explain why he'd climb the trellis, the way lovers did in all the old movies. "That they just got caught before they could pull it off?"

Mike waved his hand in a dismissive gesture. "Carlos is only fourteen."

But as the idea germinated, Diana realized it had merit. "He's been without a family of his own for years. It's possible he could be trying to recreate that."

"Martha and Carlos hardly know each other."

"Maybe they know each other better than we think. How many times have the boys gone to the theater alone on Saturday afternoon? Do you actually know who else was there?"

Mike swallowed, realizing she had a point.

She paused, not wanting to hurt him but in this situation her civic responsibilities came first. "Mike, if we don't find them in the next eighteen hours or so, if they don't come back on their own, then you'll have to file missing-person reports with the police department, who'll put out an APB on them."

"I want to avoid that, if at all possible. Dammit, Diana, they left voluntarily. I have to believe they'll come home voluntarily—if we just give them half a chance."

"I want to believe that, too, Mike." The trouble was, she couldn't. If it hadn't been an elopement gone awry, if things at the ranch had been so dissatisfactory that the trio felt they had to run away, past experience told Diana they'd run away again. And again. Knowing this, too, the child-welfare department would have no choice but to split up the boys and place them elsewhere.

Unless the boys could be completely controlled, the parents of every teenage girl within the school district would be up in arms, afraid their daughter would hook up with one of Harrigan's hooligans and meet a bad end.

Like it or not, maybe it was time they faced the truth. "Mike, you tried your best. I know you did."

"Only my best wasn't good enough." He stood up, angry.

"Maybe those boys are beyond saving. Maybe they're too old for you to help!" It was the only comfort she could think to give.

He turned on her, as if seeing a stranger. "I don't believe that," he said gruffly, "not for a minute."

Diana was silent. She didn't want to argue with him now. They were both too upset: Mike, because he had obviously failed, and Diana, because she had foolishly let herself fall victim to the same impractical dreams as Mike.

"If the social-services department finds out about this, I could lose my license to run a foster home. All my dreams for the future—all dust in the wind." He swore profusely, slamming his fist onto the counter in frustration, worry and fear.

All his dreams? What about the two of them? Their dreams? Didn't they count for anything? Apparently not, judging by the miserable expression on his face.

Diana faced Mike tensely, a river of hurt inside her. She knew if those boys didn't come back, she'd have to urge Mike to give up the idea of running a ranch for boys from unfortunate circumstances. She would have to bring him down from the clouds and make him face the grim reality of the situation, and the long-range implications. That being the case, the situation between her and Mike would only get worse.

DIANA WAS IN HER CHAMBERS finishing up for the day, when Myrtle Sims rushed in unannounced, waving the latest edition of the *Libertyville Press*. Her face red as a beet, she handed the offending paper to Diana. "The old Biddy!" Myrtle cried. "How could she?"

"How could she what?" Diana said, unfolding the paper. And then she saw it, square on the front page, a scathing editorial entitled "Too little, too late." It was all about Mike's efforts to run a foster home for wayward boys.

"She says kids like Ernie and Carlos are beyond help!" Myrtle continued, incensed.

Diana knew how attached both Myrtle and Hal had become to Ernie, especially over the past three months; but she also knew, statistically speaking, anyway, that Agnes had a point.

"She even talks about Kevin's father in there, says Mike's actions are bound to bring in even more criminals!"

That viewpoint was uncomfortably familiar. Diana shifted uneasily in her chair. She didn't really like the idea that she and Agnes agreed on anything, but the fact was she knew that the spinster's objections were valid—at least from a strictly intellectual viewpoint. "Have you heard from Mike?" Diana asked. She knew he was keeping in close touch with everyone on the Neighbors Helping Neighbors project. Silently she prayed he had found the boys, worked things out. Because she didn't want to have to come down on him for not doing his job.

"No, he hasn't found the boys yet." Myrtle fell silent, depressed; Diana shared her mood. The longer the boys' disappearance went on, the harder it was on all of them. Mike especially.

"You know," Myrtle continued after a moment, "the way those kids have been treated by Agnes and some of her friends, it's no wonder they want to run away. With school starting soon, they probably don't want to be hassled."

"Do you think the other students would hassle them?" Diana asked, her interest piqued. Could that be why they'd run away? Because they feared the start of school and had been afraid to vocalize it?

Myrtle shrugged, then shook her head. "No. In fact, the few times they've been around other area kids—in the hardware store, for instance—they've interacted just great."

"So it has to be something else," Diana said. The question was what.

Chapter Twelve

"No word yet," Diana guessed sadly, when she saw Mike and the tired, drained look on his face. She, too, had spent an anxiety-filled day, alternately thinking about where the boys might be, wondering if they were all right, and being angry with them for putting Mike through this agony. Between her duties at the courthouse, she'd made some phone calls herself. People at the community church had been alerted, and they helped with other calls; also drove over country roads, looking, keeping an eye out for any sign of the three youths. All to no avail. Diana was deeply frustrated and puzzled. As justice of the peace, she knew there would be a penance to be paid for their thoughtlessness. If she, with her limited involvement with the kids, had suffered, Mike must have been in agony, and as the hours passed without any word, it could only get worse.

"None," he admitted gravely, stepping inside. In need of a shave, his dark hair askew, he looked disheveled and exhausted. "And frankly I'm about to give up hope."

She led him into the living room and sat down with him on the sofa. She covered his hand with her own, infusing his chilled fingers with warmth. For the hundredth time that day, she found herself wishing he had chosen another line of work. "How much longer until you can file a missing-persons report with the police?"

Mike's expression became even bleaker. "Officially, 2:00 a.m., but they said if I came in and wrote it up earlier, they'd put it into effect when the time came."

"So you went ahead and did it?"

He nodded, looking more unhappy. He covered her hand with his palm, so that her fingers were sandwiched between both his hands. "I felt like I was signing their death warrant, know what I mean? Because no matter what happens now, if they're found, they'll probably be sent elsewhere to live."

Diana found herself hoping that wouldn't be so. She knew how hard Mike had worked to create a sense of family for the boys, and he'd been successful. "Maybe not," she said slowly. "Maybe I could testify on your behalf. That is, assuming there's some logical explanation for the boys' action, and I'm really hoping there is." Because if there wasn't, it was all over. The boys would be taken from Mike, returned to social services. His flagship program would be down the drain.

Diana frowned. She just couldn't accept the fact they would let Mike down like this for no reason. He'd been too good to them.

"You'd do that for me—act as a character witness?" Mike's low voice brought her soundly back to the present.

She nodded soberly. "I want to help in whatever way I can." She wanted him to be happy. And right now he looked as if he could use a big dose of TLC himself. "Have you eaten anything this evening?"

He looked up, startled by the question. "Uh, no."

"Let me fix you something then. I haven't eaten, either."

While she quickly scrambled them some eggs, and fried up slices of ham and hash browns, he made toast and coffee and set the table. "Well, there's been some good news, anyway," Diana informed him as they sat down to eat. "Agnes sent her niece Martha home this morning. She felt she'd be better off in Dallas than here."

"Did you have a chance to talk to her?" Mike asked.

Diana shook her head as she spread her napkin on her lap. "No. Myrtle Sims did, though. Martha said she didn't know what the boys were up to. Said they fell off the trellis before they got all the way up—which is what alerted Agnes and Martha to their being there. Martha says she's as mystified by all this as the rest of us, and Myrtle believed her."

"Which shoots a hole in any elopement theory," Mike pronounced.

Yes, unfortunately it did. "It could be because of Ernie, the humiliation he went through, showing his paintings to Agnes, then having her reject them. All three boys were angry and hurt about that."

Mike grimaced, remembering. He spread jam on his toast. "She sure went out of her way to make them feel unwelcome in this town." He shook his head, remembering. "But there were so many others who tried hard to make them feel welcome, after the initial resistance."

And so many who hadn't welcomed them, too.

"I just don't understand why they'd take off like that," he said.

"I don't, either." Diana was pensive as she finished her meal. She hoped for Mike's sake the boys' explanation, when they were found, was a good one.

Mike pushed back his plate restlessly, then got up to carry it to the sink. "I guess we'll just have to wait and see what happens."

The silence drew out. He looked so beaten and hurt. A lump in her throat, Diana got up and moved to his side. She touched him, and when he turned toward her, she wrapped her arms around him, holding him tight, telling him wordlessly that she was there for him and always would be. His fingers combed through the silk of her hair. He rubbed his chin on the top of her head and then planted a fervent kiss there. "Oh, Diana," he whispered, sliding his thumbs beneath her chin, tilting her face up to his. She saw the quiet desperation in his eyes, the longing, the need. And then his mouth was on hers, seeking reassurance, some release, however temporary, from the unbearable tension they'd been under. Diana knew how he felt. She, too, had the feeling that everything they cherished was falling apart, and she clung to him as she wanted to cling to their love.

And for that moment, time stood still. There was nothing else, no one but the two of them and what they felt for each other. Helpless to resist, she kissed him back passionately, with growing ardor, letting her senses accept all the tenderness he had to give. She wanted to be with him through good times and bad. And she could tell by the way he kissed and caressed her he felt the same.

Later she couldn't remember exactly how they got to her bedroom. Or who had initiated it. Just that suddenly they'd been there, and that their lovemaking was quick, ardent, all-consuming, with Mike demanding more of her, giving more, taking more even as he drove her over the edge.

Only this time there'd been no lazy aftermath, no soothing words of love, only the crash back to reality. The gut-wrenching worry. And she knew then that for him the passion had replaced the tears he would never allow himself, no matter how much he hurt.

For long moments they simply held each other, lending comfort in the only way they could. Temporarily their world was a mess, Diana admitted to herself, but at least they had each other.

Finally they drew apart. Quietly she pulled on a robe. Mike was as tightly wound up as before, maybe even more so. She watched as he dressed and prepared to leave, knowing instinctively that he felt guilty for making love to her now, and that more than that he hated his helplessness where his kids were concerned. And so did she. Neither of them was used to this feeling of powerlessness, and yet short of sending out a full-state alert with all the accompanying media coverage—something she was sure that would drive the boys farther away—everything possible had already been done. They'd called everyone the boys might contact, and Mike and others had personally driven over every inch of road in the county. There was just too much wilderness in that part of the Texas Hill Country to cover it all. And the boys were old enough and smart enough to take care of themselves, at least for a while. Most frustrating of all was the thought that the boys probably wouldn't be found unless they wanted to be found, and right now, that didn't seem likely. Especially if they knew Agnes McCarthy was still after their hides for trampling her rosebushes. So what next? Diana wondered. Was there anything else to do but wait?

"Call me," she whispered, "when you know something."

"I will." He hesitated and then drew her back into his arms, holding her tightly against the length of him, and pressing a kiss to her temple. "And Diana," he whispered in a rough, emotional tone, "thanks for being here for me tonight." He held her harder, and there was a catch in his throat she'd never heard before. "I really... needed ... to be with you."

IT WASN'T UNTIL the next morning that they discovered what had happened to the boys. Diana got a frantic phone call, and it was a crisis she'd feared all along.

When she jumped out of her car, she hurried over to Mike's side as he faced his three foster sons on Agnes

McCarthy's lawn. "I don't get it," Mike was saying angrily. "Why would you do something like this? Why?"

Diana gasped as she glimpsed the cause of the uproar: multicolored graffiti had been spray-painted over Agnes's lawn, her flower beds, the four-letter words telling Agnes in no uncertain terms to lay off.

Traffic was stopping right and left; people were spilling out onto the curb sidewalk to watch.

"I found them out here, along with copies of my editorial!" Agnes cried hysterically, pointing to her article "Too little, too late," which had also been rimmed with a red and the crudely worded demand that she not air her prejudices so publicly again.

"You little hooligans!" she shouted at the boys, waving her fist in the air. "You're going to pay for this!"

"I told you something like this would happen when they first moved here!" Billy Reaves strode up to join the group.

"Billy, calm down," his wife, Kay, said, running up and clutching his arm, holding him back.

Iris followed close behind the Reaves. In the distance, others were heading their way, Diana noted with chagrin. Evidently word had traveled fast.

Iris looked at Diana. "Now are you going to do something? How much more trouble do these kids have to cause?"

Diana had to admit the boys looked guilty, even though Agnes had given them much provocation. Still, she had to be fair. "I want to hear what the boys have to say." *Please, let them have some explanation,* she prayed.

Mike's attention focused on the boys. "Well?" he demanded irately again, "What do you have to say for yourselves?"

Silence among the group.

"I told you they were guilty!" Billy Reaves scoffed.

Hal Sims came up behind Mike and said to the officer, "Look, the paint'll all grow out—eventually. Another week or so. No real harm done!"

"It's still vandalism," Diana said curtly. And the boys had to be held accountable for it.

Mike turned to his kids. "Why would you do something like this?" he demanded, still trying to understand, to hang on to what little patience he had left.

Ernie looked frightened by the growing rage he saw on Mike's face. Carlos, willing to bargain, "Hey, man, chill out. We—"

"We did it because she's a witch," Kevin's voice cut coldly across the other two kids'. He looked at Mike and then Diana, seeing the two of them standing together side by side, and something in him became even colder, even more determined to inflict as much damage as he could. "Because she had it coming, for hurting Ernie like she did, for treating Carlos as if he wasn't any better than dog dirt, for keeping Martha away from the likes of all three of us, like we might infect her or something—"

"Kevin, that's enough!" Mike's voice cut in gruffly.

Kevin flinched at Mike's tone, for the briefest moment looking incredibly hurt and as if he were about to cry. Then he toughened up again. "Yeah, you're right," he said with a sarcasm that had even Diana cringing, "it is enough. And that's why we ran away. To get the hell out of this one-horse town."

"Only you had to come back," Agnes interjected shrilly, "to get your revenge. Well, now I'm going to get mine, and I will personally see that all of you are sent as far from this town as is legally possible!"

"Fine with me," Kevin shot back, unperturbed.

Diana, staring at Kevin, felt as if she was looking at a stranger. Carlos and Ernie had moved in behind Kevin, their faces impassive, their eyes averted from Mike, and indeed everyone else.

Her heart was heavy as she realized they had been wrong about the boys, that their good behavior had been an act, and that they were probably responsible for just about everything they'd been blamed for.

The deputy pushed his way through the crowd. "Boys, I'm going to have to take you all in this time. Now everyone be quiet, while I read 'em their rights, and then clear out so I can collect the evidence. . . ."

DIANA WASN'T SURPRISED to see Mike in her office the moment she entered the courthouse. "Diana . . ." he began, before the door was even all the way shut.

She had hoped he wouldn't put her in this situation, or try to use his influence with her to sway her opinion. "Mike, this is my job. Don't make it any more difficult." Her control on her emotions ironclad, she slipped into her black robe. She was tired and exhausted, no longer sure of her ability to judge anything, least of all anything that had to do with Mike and his boys. Nonetheless, the task of doing so had fallen to her.

"You can't put them in jail," Mike insisted flatly, approaching her desk.

Diana took a deep breath, knowing it wasn't going to be easy for her to deal with Mike, maybe even cause his ruin. Remembering her duties as elected official, she said evenly, "I'm not going to put them in jail. After all, it's only a misdemeanor. But I will charge them. There'll be a fine, and of course it will have to go on their records."

Mike stared at her, angry and disappointed she was punishing the boys at all. "And then what?" he barked.

Diana's chin lifted in defiance. She, too, was beginning to get angry—at the situation, at him. "Then I call the child-welfare department before they call me. They have a right to know about this situation, and I promised earlier, when we had the initial trouble between the boys and Agnes McCarthy, I'd keep them informed of any further developments." She sighed tiredly and averted her gaze from Mike's astonished, chastising one.

If only this weren't so hard!

Maybe if the boys hadn't vandalized Agnes's lawn, if they'd just come back on their own and said they were sorry, it would never happen again, Diana might have been able to square it with her conscience and say nothing to the child-welfare people. But now she had no choice. And maybe, just maybe, she hadn't really had a choice before, either, Diana thought. Maybe her feelings for Mike were getting in the way of doing her job, to preserve the peace of the community.

"Diana, you can't do that. I know—" he held up an imperious hand, staving off her interruption "—they've slipped. But that doesn't mean I have to give up on them. They can and will straighten up again. They're just testing me. That's all it is, all any of this is."

Diana sighed, unable to believe Mike could be that naive. "I probably would've believed that if I hadn't seen them this morning, seen the destruction and the ugliness, and . . . and Kevin's defiance. You have to be realistic here, Mike. You have to accept things as they are, not as you want them to be, or envision they could be. Those boys are unhappy. The truth of the matter is they haven't blended in well here. We can't afford to be Pollyannas . . ." She knew she was hurting Mike with her bluntness, but she also knew that someone had to say it and that she was probably the only one who could.

Mike glowered at her. "I thought you were on my side?"

She wanted to be, he would never know how much, but she simply couldn't share his quixotic view of the world when the boys weren't upholding the law! "I am on your side," she shot back, both hurt and determined, "but I'm also on the town's side. I have to do what is right for everybody."

His mouth tightening, he shook his head in obvious disagreement. "Not everybody, the majority. No matter how much it hurts the others." He paused, blinking back the hurt, looking as if she had willfully betrayed him. Hurt him. When he spoke again, his voice was barely above a whisper. "Everything you said—" his glance accused her of lying, leading him on "—about being a character witness for the boys..."

Diana let out an anguished breath and dragged a hand through her hair. She was angry at him, too, for making them go through this now, for making her hurt him, when she would've liked nothing better than to be able to walk away, for them both to be able to walk away from this whole ugly mess. But they couldn't, and like it or not, she had to stay and sort this trouble out. As she was paid to do. "That was before they vandalized Agnes's lawn and got caught red-handed. Now, considering everything else they've done—all the pranks, my flower beds, the snake in the salad bowl—"

"We have no proof they did any of that!" Mike cut in furiously.

Didn't they? Maybe nothing that would hold up in court, but in their guts, Diana thought, they all knew. "Maybe we don't have proof," she said quietly, furiously, "but I think we all suspect them just the same." She watched him, her resolve hardening. She wouldn't let him make her feel guilty. "Mike, we have to do what is best for them," she began again, wishing he would stop taking this all so personally and understand she was just doing her job.

"Then leave them with me. Please. I am giving them the best." His voice was stony with resolve.

Diana swallowed around the ache in her throat. "I know you've tried your hardest, and that's what makes this all so sad. Don't you think this hurts me, too? It does. But I have to put their welfare first, and the welfare of our community."

He sighed and combed both hands through his hair. "Look, couldn't you sugarcoat all this a little, just this once?" He was asking her to help him. Begging.

She shook her head in silent refusal, affronted he'd even ask.

All pretense at civility stopped abruptly then. Mike glared back at her furiously, his blue eyes narrowed in disgust. "You're being unfair."

"You're being unreasonably empathetic."

"What's worse is that you do know them, Diana. And you should know that angry or not, they couldn't possibly have done that."

Diana sighed, but said nothing.

He was silent for a moment, too. "Maybe I do understand those kids," he said finally, his velvet-edged voice cutting her to the bone. He looked her over contemptuously, and his voice lowered even more, to a rough, indicting whisper. "Maybe it's because I was such a hell-raiser when I was a kid that I find it so easy to forgive the recklessness in others." He leaned across her desk and finished emphatically, "They can and will change, given time!"

But Diana had done all she could and then some. "You may be fooling yourself, Mike."

His mouth compressed in a thin, uncompromising line. "No, you're the one who's fooling yourself, Diana, if you think that you can do this to them and have a clear conscience—"

"My conscience is clear!" How dare he imply otherwise!

"Oh, is it?" A wealth of irritation underlined his words. "And I suppose the next thing you're going to tell me is that you've never, in your whole entire life, committed one damn mistake!"

She closed her eyes, thinking of the graffiti on Agnes McCarthy's lawn, the ugliness of the crude four-letter words written out for all the town to see. "Not like that, I haven't," she said distinctly, giving him a hard look that added credence to her words. "I haven't ever done anything destructive or vicious—"

"Oh, no? Well, there we disagree, because I call what you're about to do very destructive and very vicious!" His voice lowered insinuatingly. "Or maybe I should just say self-serving."

She recoiled from the contempt she saw on his face. "What are you talking about?" She had to search to find her voice. "What do you mean?" Suddenly she was filled with fear, not for the boys, but for them!

"Just this. It'd be very convenient for you if we did get those boys out of the way, wouldn't it? I mean, then you'd have a clear path to me. Maybe you'd even talk me into giving up my idea of taking in foster kids altogether, or if not that, then just some problem-free kids from lily-white backgrounds."

Diana swallowed hard, aware she was trembling from head to foot. She couldn't deny that possibility had crossed her mind. But what she was doing now had nothing to do with her personal wants for her and Mike as a couple, and he damn well knew it! "I want what is best for those boys," she continued doggedly.

"You want what's best for yourself."

Before she could speak again he had turned on his heel and left.

"I'M SORRY, Diana, Mike won't take your call," Melanie said several days later.

Diana sighed. She'd known Mike was angry with her, but she hadn't expected it to last. She had hoped he would see things her way, once he'd had time to cool off, but evidently she was wrong. "Has he...has he talked with the child-welfare people?"

Melanie's voice was laced with sadness as she replied, "They came earlier this afternoon. All three boys are being placed in other foster homes. They're being separated."

The knowledge that this was actually happening was like a knife in Diana's heart, and yet part of her knew that it was probably for the best. "How are they taking it?"

"About as well as you'd expect," Melanie continued sadly. "They all had stiff upper lips, but it was hard. I could tell they were trying not to cry." Melanie's voice grew choked as she talked, "Well, you know, you try to stay a little aloof in this business, for circumstances just like this, but it never actually seems to work that way."

To her surprise, Diana found tears had gathered in the corners of her own eyes; she blinked them back with determination, telling herself they had done what was best. "And Mike? How is he doing?"

Melanie sighed audibly, her concern evident. "He hasn't come out of his study all afternoon."

Diana was silent. Despite their argument, the angry words, she couldn't help but want to do something for him, to make this a little easier on him. "About his status as a foster parent..." she began.

"Unfortunately that's under consideration, too. His dad is doing all he can, from what I understand, but...I don't know. Mike may not get another chance. It isn't helping that the boys still won't tell us what initially prompted them to run away."

"You don't think it was because of anything the townspeople did?"

"Well, that's what they claim, but somehow Jim and I just don't buy it. Mike, either. I guess now we'll never find out."

Diana was silent, her heart pounding, her face flushed with heat. "I'm sorry," she said finally, meaning it. And yet she knew she'd just been doing her job, and if she had it to do all over again, she'd do exactly the same thing. She swallowed around the catch in her throat, distressed everything had turned out so badly. "I'm really sorry." She hesitated. "Tell Mike I called, will you?"

"I will, but Diana," Melanie said bluntly, after a moment, wanting her to be prepared, "I wouldn't count on it doing any good."

Chapter Thirteen

"Ms. Tomlinson? This is Patty Shaw, over at the Country Artists gallery in Marble Falls. I have some great news! That painting you brought in by Ernie Johnson? Well, I found a buyer for it, and I wanted to tell you if he had anything else available I'd be glad to show it, too."

"Well, that's...that's wonderful," Diana said. Stunned, it took her a moment to get her breath.

"Is Ernie there? I'd like to talk to him if I may," Patty Shaw continued genially.

This was much harder. "No, but I can get in touch with him," Diana answered carefully, some of her joy at the news being lessened by the fact Ernie was no longer there with them.

"Marvelous! When can I expect to hear from him?"

"I'm not sure. As soon as possible, though," Diana promised. The moment she hung up, she grabbed her car keys and bag and started out the door. It had only been two days since the boys had been returned to the custody of the child-welfare department, and she had neither seen nor heard from Mike. She kept expecting him to call, do something, anything, but part of her knew better. At any rate, they needed to get the news to Ernie.

Mike was just coming out of the barn when she arrived fifteen minutes later. He sent her a stormy look but didn't break stride as he headed for the garden hose next to the house. He turned on the water and began washing his hands. "If you've come to gloat..." he warned darkly.

It hurt her to realize he felt she might see this whole sordid episode as just an opportunity to say I-told-you-so, because the truth was, she hadn't wanted this to happen even in the beginning when she had so rightly feared it might. She kept her voice calm with effort. "The gallery called. They sold Ernie's painting. They want to see more."

Surprise rendered him temporarily speechless; then shock turned to joy, as Mike realized what a boon something like that would be to Ernie's self-esteem. "Hey, that is something to celebrate!" Mike said, for a second smiling broadly. Then his expression sobered. He offered Diana his back as he deliberately put physical distance between them. "Unfortunately I don't know where he is at the moment."

"The department didn't tell you?"

He turned to her, his expression giving nothing away. "They think it's better we not communicate, at least for a while."

That seemed cruel, and yet considering how things had ended, a reasonable-enough decision on the case. "How do the boys feel about that?"

Mike swallowed, and despite his efforts to look impassive, he couldn't hide his pain. "I suppose they're in seventh heaven. After all, they requested the ban on missives, et cetera, et cetera."

"Mike, I'm sorry."

Shaking off his hurt, he brushed past her rudely. "Why should you be?" he countered roughly. "You got what you wanted. I don't think you should come around here anymore, Diana. Not ever."

His words cut her like the slash of a knife. "You can't mean that," she whispered, beginning to tremble.

But he did. "Seeing you is only going to remind me of everything I lost," he said tersely. And he was in too much pain to handle any more.

Tears misted her vision, but she refused to let them fall. Diana still didn't want to believe it was over, but the stony expression on his face told her there was no chance to reconcile. "About Ernie..." she began finally, wishing there was something more she could do or say.

"I'll see he gets the news about the painting." Without a backward glance, Mike headed for the front door and slammed it shut behind him. The sound echoed in the dusky light, more final and annihilating than anything she had ever heard.

"You know, it's too bad about that Harrigan fella having to close down his ranch," the sheriff said to Diana early the following morning.

"He's not shutting it down!" Diana shot back fiercely, before she could think. Somehow Mike would get past this difficulty. She just knew it.

The sheriff lifted a brow and poured himself some more of the courthouse coffee. "He'll have to if he doesn't get any more kids out there to live, and from what I've heard, there's some debate going on now about whether or not he should be given a second chance."

"Of course he should be given a second chance!" Diana said hotly. "With younger kids." Kids who hadn't been so badly scarred, or gone so long without love.

"Age isn't going to make that much difference. Kids are kids."

"Yes, it will," Diana said firmly.

The sheriff looked at her curiously. "I suppose you told him that?"

Diana nodded slowly. "I tried, anyway. He wasn't buying any of it."

The sheriff sighed. "Well, like I said, it's a shame. They seemed like such a nice group, too, most of the time, doing all that community-service work with never a complaint. Of course that one—that Carlos—he was a bit of a Romeo, but Mike seemed to be keeping him well in hand. Until they tried to climb Agnes's trellis, anyway."

"They never did say why they did that, did they?" Diana paused, intrigued.

"Nope, and I don't imagine they will, either. Although the social workers involved would probably like to hear it. 'Course even that isn't going to matter much after what they did to Agnes's lawn. She's still trying to grow out some of those curse words they painted on the grass."

Diana sighed and poured herself more coffee. "I still can't picture them doing that to Agnes. Oh, I know she's an old biddy, narrow-minded as all get out and everything, but spray-painting! I mean, where'd they get the time and money to buy the paint in the first place? They would've had to plan it days in advance, purchased all that paint and then found a hiding place for it at the ranch—which would've been hard enough, not to mention there's only one place in town they can buy that type of outdoor paint that was used."

"Yeah, you're right. Seven cans would be hard to purchase without someone noticing and questioning it."

Unless they'd been stockpiling it for weeks, Diana thought. Buying one can at a time. "There's something else that bothers me, too." She took another sip of the bitter coffee, finding that it perfectly fit her mood.

"What?"

She looked at the sheriff curiously, wanting to draw on his expertise. "Why would the boys spray-paint the grass? I mean, have you ever known any kids to do that? Don't they usually aim for more permanent places—like highway concrete or rock walls or bridges or sides of buildings, not something that will just grow out.''

The sheriff frowned. ''Maybe they were just trying to lessen the damage. You know, maybe they figured if they just sprayed the grass and the flowers they'd get in less trouble. Or maybe they knew how much her yard meant to her and aimed to hurt her as much as possible.''

''Maybe,'' Diana mused, remembering what a fuss Agnes had made when the boys had just walked on her grass that first week in Libertyville. Nonetheless, it wouldn't hurt to do a little more checking, if for nothing else but her own peace of mind. ''Do you still have the cans?''

''Yeah, they're in the evidence room down in the basement.'' He sent her a quizzical, warning look. ''Diana, what are you up to?''

''Nothing yet. I don't know.'' Diana stood restlessly. ''Maybe everything. Would you mind if we took a look at those cans?''

The sheriff shrugged and sighed. ''All right, though what you're hoping to see . . .'' his voice trailed off as he hastily drained the last of his coffee.

''I'll know when I see it,'' Diana murmured, already leading the way.

Downstairs, the sheriff put on some plastic gloves and brought out the bag of evidence in the misdemeanor. Enclosed was the editorial denouncing the ranch, Agnes had written, outlined in red, and the seven empty paint cans and lids. Diana looked at them carefully. All carried price stickers that were labeled Hal's Hardware.

''That means Hal must know who bought that paint. It would be in his records,'' Diana murmured.

''Look, we already know who did it,'' the sheriff said. ''The boys were found in front of her house, at dawn, standing there with the empty cans in their hands. Agnes saw them from her window and called us; the boys were still there when the deputy drove up.''

"Yes, but did he actually see them painting?'' Diana pressed, realizing too late all the evidence had been very circumstantial.

"Well, no, but—''

"Isn't it possible they were framed, or just in the wrong place at the wrong time?''

He looked skeptical. "It's possible, maybe.'' He underlined the maybe.

"I'm going to see Hal.''

"Then I'm going with you.'' The sheriff removed his gloves and headed out after her.

Hal was behind the front cash register when Diana and the sheriff walked in the door. His face drained of all color. He knew something, Diana thought, something he wasn't telling them. "Hal, we need to talk to you about the paint that was sprayed on Agnes's lawn. We know it was purchased here.''

Hal gulped but didn't seem that surprised.

"Hal, we want to know who purchased that paint,'' Diana continued. Hal said nothing, though Myrtle had come from the back of the store and moved to stand beside him. "We'll subpoena your records if we have to.''

Suddenly Hal's face turned very red. "You don't have to do that,'' he said, turning and going over to put the Closed sign on the front door and pull down the shade. "I know who did it.''

"Hal!'' Myrtle gasped, stunned.

Hal was quiet, for a long moment looking as if he was going to cry. "I did it,'' he said finally, surprising them all. "I just...couldn't take any more of that darn woman's guff. And what she did to Ernie, about his paintings—that was inexcusable.''

"You heard about that?'' Diana queried gently.

Hal nodded, looking angry just talking about it. "The whole town did. She told it like it was some big joke pulled by the lady of the manor on the lowly serf. Then when she wrote that article bad-mouthing them, I don't know—" he shook his head sadly "—something in me snapped. I just knew I had to get her to stop. I came over to the store and I, I don't know, I was so mad I wasn't even thinking straight. Then I went back over there and I wrote all that stuff. By then the boys were long gone, or at least I thought they were. I—I never figured they'd be blamed. How was I to know they would stop by the next morning and pick up those cans?" He swallowed emotionally. Hanging his head, he continued, "And after that, I was too embarrassed to come forward. I just...felt like such a hoodlum. I'd never done anything like that in my life. Do you think it would help if I confessed and offered to make restitution?" he asked Diana.

"Yes, it would help," Diana said. Though she didn't envy him having to face Agnes, who purportedly was still on a rampage.

They shook their heads. And Diana knew instinctively that there was even more to the story than they'd just discovered. This time, she decided firmly, she wouldn't rest until she had the whole truth.

"OF COURSE," Diana explained to Kay Reaves, "that still doesn't explain the snake-in-the-salad-bowl trick, or tell us who might've torn up my flowers, but—"

She stopped abruptly when she looked at her secretary, whose skin was suddenly blotchy with patches of red and white. "What's the matter?"

Silence.

"Do you know something about those incidents?"

Kay turned redder.

"You've got to tell me," Diana insisted. "Please—" Heaven help her. Had she made a mistake, sending those boys away?

Kay gulped. "I never meant... I was just so worried. You know Billy's temper and the way he felt about teenage boys in general after his sister, Jenny, died." Tears welled up in her eyes. Kay blinked them back. Her voice turned hoarse. "I just didn't want him to do anything he'd regret, and after the way they trampled on Agnes's lawn that day..."

She stared at Kay incredulously. "You tore up my flower beds? And put the snake in the salad bowl?"

"I knew you were the only one with the power to get rid of those kids."

"But why the rubber-snake trick?"

Kay shrugged, her expression both helpless and apologetic. "I couldn't think of anything else that wouldn't hurt someone else." The tears she'd been holding back finally spilled over her lashes onto her cheeks. "I'm sorry, Diana. I never meant to cause so much trouble."

But she had.

The only question now was, could the trouble be undone? Diana knew she had to try.

"CARLOS, I KNOW you feel a loyalty to Ernie and Kevin. I know that. But don't you understand? Mike is hurting. He's hurting so much. He feels he let you all down in some fundamental way and he doesn't know what that is."

"Mike didn't do nothin' bad to us, you know that," Carlos said, thrusting his hands in his pockets of his Levi's and walking to the end of the small backyard. The child-welfare agency had placed him and the others each with a set of new foster parents, and although they were nice, it wasn't the same for him as being at Mike's ranch. Diana knew it, and so apparently did Carlos.

"Then please," Diana begged. "Talk to me. Tell me what you were doing at Agnes's that night, climbing that trellis."

"That was my idea," Carlos said finally on a sigh. "I wanted to say goodbye to Miss McCarthy's niece. I know it was a stupid thing to do. I hardly knew her, but...it just seemed like a fun idea."

"But you were running away."

"Well, yeah." Carlos shrugged. "We had to."

"Had to?" Diana repeated, incredulous. "Why?"

Carlos was silent. "We care about Mike. He was good to us and we just wanted to see him happy."

"I don't understand," Diana said, stymied. None of this was making any sense! But it would, soon, she promised herself stalwartly.

Carlos looked at her and shook his head. "Well, you should, because it all had to do with you."

Chapter Fourteen

Diana drove back from Houston, exhausted by everything she had discovered. Knowing she needed some time to absorb what she'd learned before she confronted Mike, she stopped at the drive-through window of the Dairy Queen to get some supper, then headed home.

Carrying her purse and keys in one hand, the red-and-white bag that held her meal in the other, she emerged from her car and started for the front door.

"Junk food for supper?" a low, achingly familiar voice drawled from the other end of the porch.

Her heart pounding, Diana watched in wide-eyed surprise as Mike Harrigan started her way, her eyes following him as he came down the steps in fluid, easy motions. He no longer looked at her as if she had betrayed him, but rather as if he wanted to make amends. Was determined to make amends.

Was that what she wanted, too? Did she want to give him another chance to break her heart? To desert her when the going got rough? Finally regaining her poise, she sailed back coolly with, "As it happens, Mr. Harrigan, I love chili dogs with cheese and onions." He had said he never wanted to see her again! And here he was darkening her doorway!

He held his stomach in comical fashion. "Don't talk like that. You're making me hungry."

Maybe she was a fool, but she was glad to see him. Knowing, however, that he didn't need to know that, Diana pretended undue reserve as she fitted her key in the lock. Then, unable to resist another peek, she sent him an appraising sidelong glance. No doubt about it, Mike looked good, happier than she'd seen him in days, more content with himself and, for once, not angry with her. Relief shimmered through her. Her feminine pride might be telling her to make him suffer, but the rest of her was too happy to see him. She chuckled as his stomach growled. "Relax, Mike, I have enough to share," she said easily, finally deciding that no purpose would be served by continuing to play games. "But I get most of the onion rings."

"Mmm. You do know how to live." He held the door open for her, his arm stretched over her head, then followed her inside.

No sooner had the door shut behind them than he was doing what she'd wished he would for days and taking her in his arms. He clung to her, not loosening his grip. And she knew then from the way he held her that he still loved her and had never stopped, even if for a while he'd been too stubborn to admit it. "Diana, I'm sorry," he murmured sincerely, his own pain evident. "I really am. I've acted like the worst kind of heel the past week."

Her eyes filled with tears at the raw emotion in his voice. Knowing all he'd been through, and the sheer unfairness of it, it was impossible for her to hold his actions against him. "You were hurting. I knew that."

His fingers lightly caressed her cheek. "But that was no reason for me to take it out on you." He held her in his arms ever so gently. "I want you in my life, Diana," he admitted huskily. "I want us to go back to where we were before we left off. I want you to give us another chance.

I love you," he whispered tenderly, his own eyes moist. "I always will. Whatever else happens, I need you in my life."

Tears of happiness welled in her eyes, and for a moment she was too overcome with emotion to speak. "I want that, too," she said quietly. She had been lonely without him, more than she had ever imagined possible.

Then his mouth was on hers, and they were kissing like there was no tomorrow. Later, still wrapped with the glow of their lovemaking, they heated her take-out feast in the microwave and took the repast back to her bed. "So what are your plans for the ranch?" Diana asked, glancing surreptitiously at the clock. It was just after nine, which meant she had about another hour. "You're still going to continue working as a foster parent, aren't you?"

Mike's eyes were serious. "Yes, as much as I love you, Diana, I can't give up my dream." Maybe he had started this in the beginning out of sheer stubbornness, because others—his father especially—said it just couldn't be done. But he knew now he was doing the right thing.

"I know. And I'm glad. I think one of the reasons I love you so much is because you are so committed. You see I think I understand now why you believe in the kids the way you do, why my father had to pursue social work, too."

"Because there's always a chance you can reach someone, you can help."

"And knowing you've made a crucial difference in someone's life is a feeling that just can't be duplicated."

"Right." He looked at her, amazed. "So, my dedication to social causes won't get in the way of us again?"

"No," Diana promised softly, with all her heart. "No, it won't because I won't let it. Which isn't to say we can expect only smooth sailing from here on out, because I know we can't."

"We can handle everything if we stick together," Mike said.

Diana nodded. How well she knew that. Finished with her dinner, she got up impulsively and went to her closet. "What do you say we get dressed and go on out to the ranch tonight?"

"Tonight, why?" He looked at her as if she were crazy.

She smiled mysteriously and lifted her hands in a helpless gesture. "Just a whim. Humor me. Please?"

He took her hand and pressed a light kiss to the back of it. "Anything m'lady pleases."

By ten they were pulling into the drive. Mike did a double take as he saw the Mercedes in the drive. "My parents! What are they doing here?" he asked, confused.

Diana held back an enigmatic smile with great difficulty. "I don't know," she said slowly, "I guess we better go see."

They walked in the door to see Ernie, Carlos and Kevin sitting in the living room, chatting with Mike's parents. Mike looked at his father. "I admit it," Tom, Sr., said, raising a surrendering palm. "I've been pulling some strings again, but this time I didn't do it alone. Diana and the boys, your mother—they all helped and pitched in. We want to make your dream a reality, son. And we want you to know we're all here to help."

For a moment, Mike was too overcome to speak, as one by one the boys came up to give him a welcoming hug.

Mike's parents quietly exited.

"The guys have some explanations for you," Diana said quietly when it was clear someone needed to take charge.

Kevin admitted, "It was my idea to run away, Mike. I wasn't trying to hurt you. I thought I was helping."

"See," Ernie continued, "he heard you and Diana arguing about us, and we knew we were just in the way."

"And even an unromantic fool could see how much the two of you loved each other," Carlos continued.

"So we decided to step out of the way."

"Then later, we saw how many people were looking for us. We saw you, too, driving all around, and we felt bad. So we decided to come back."

"Which is how they ended up on Agnes's front lawn that morning," Diana continued quietly. "They were walking back when they saw what had been done."

"And the rest is history," Mike said.

"We got mad when you believed we were guilty, too," Kevin said.

"So we decided to go with the original plan and split," Carlos continued.

"Only none of us figured on how lonely we'd be," Ernie said. "Or how much we'd miss you and Melanie and Jim and Diana and the ranch. We never meant to make you unhappy."

Ernie's eyes were shimmering with unshed tears, but then, so were literally everyone else's in the room. "We're ready to come back if you'll take us."

"The child-welfare department assumed you'd take them," Diana added. In fact, it had been her urgent phone calls and pleas, along with those of his influential father, that had expedited the process. "Welcome home, guys," Mike said, giving them all a hug.

The boys hugged him back, then went in to the kitchen to help with the celebratory pizzas being made. Mike went to Diana. "You are one special lady, you know that?" he said, pulling her close.

"Yes, I know."

He drew back, to better see her face. "Modest, aren't we?" He still had his arms linked around her waist, holding her as if he planned never to let her go.

"Yes, I'm prone to think in modest terms," she teased back. Then more seriously, wanting him to know how she felt deep inside, Diana added, "I didn't realize until I met you how much I had isolated myself. I now know that I need to reach out to others, to lend a helping hand, every bit as much as I need to protect myself and others from getting hurt."

He paused, realizing finally what she had neglected to take credit for earlier. "It was you who brought this all about, who figured out the boys weren't guilty, wasn't it?"

She nodded, pleased she'd been able to help. "When I calmed down enough to think about it and logically review the evidence, I realized there were several things amiss." Briefly she explained.

Mike glanced in the direction of the kitchen, where merry sounds were spilling forth. "I guess I owe them an apology," he said quietly, shaking his head in disbelief. "I underestimated them, the same way I was underestimated in my youth. Incredible!"

"Well," Diana teased and smiled, "so long as you don't do it again, I think they can forgive you. I know I do!"

Mike grinned back at her saucy tone. "You do, huh?" She nodded, and he continued, more softly, "Enough to marry me?" She stared at him in stunned amazement, knowing he was serious. "I love you, Diana. That will never change," he said.

She linked her arms around him, holding him close. "And I love you."

"So?"

"My answer is yes," she whispered softly, meeting his lips. "Yes to you, yes to love, yes to the boys." She reached up on tiptoe, kissing him soundly. "And we can have as many kids here as the ranch can handle," she promised.

"We'll have counselors on hand, I promise you that."

"I like your promises, Mr. Harrigan," Diana agreed.

"And maybe a baby or two of our own?" His eyes lit up hopefully.

Diana nodded, glad his vision of the future accorded with her own. "And maybe that, too." Finally, she thought joyfully, it seemed all her dreams were coming true.

"Hey, you guys, what's holding you up?" Kevin shouted from the kitchen, his impatient gleeful voice followed by the sound of footsteps.

"Oops," said Ernie audibly sliding to a halt beside him.

"Hey, can't you see they're kissing?" Carlos continued.

Behind them came Tom, Sr.'s, laughing voice. "This, I've got to see."

And Mike's mother, ribbing the boys, "I thought he hated girls..."

Mike and Diana broke apart, laughing. Tom, Sr.'s, eyes gleamed with merriment. "Nothing like being part of one big happy family, is there?" Mrs. Harrigan asked.

Diana and Mike answered in unison as they linked hands and prepared to join the others in the kitchen. "Nothing indeed...."